Best Wishes,

James D. Brewer

NO VIRTUE

Also by James D. Brewer

No Bottom

NO VIRTUE

A Masey Baldridge / Luke Williamson Mystery

JAMES D. BREWER

WALKER AND COMPANY
NEW YORK

All the characters and events portrayed in this work are fictitious. First published in the United States in 1995 by Walker Publishing Company, Inc.

Published simultaneously in Canada by Thomas Allen & Son Canada, Limited, Markham, Ontario

Library of Congress Cataloging-in-Publication Data
Brewer, James D.
No virtue : a Masey Baldridge/Luke Williamson mystery / James D. Brewer.
p   cm.
ISBN 0-8027-3259-3
I. Title.
PS3552.R418N64   1995
813′.54—dc20   94-40125
CIP

Printed in the United States of America
2 4 6 8 10 9 7 5 3 1

To my brother, Vernon,
and my sister, Nelda—
Thanks for believing in me
and being there when I need you.

NO VIRTUE

1

Tuesday, April 1, 1873, Eight A.M.

THE HEAD RHYTHMICALLY bumped against the paddle wheel as the wake from a passing steamboat bobbed the body in the chilly brown water. From the boiler deck of the *Paragon*, ten or fifteen passengers braved a driving rain to watch the deckhands recover the corpse.

"Keep the boat steady!" a crewman shouted, the rain slapping against his oilcloth parka as he reached over the side of a rowboat. "Her arm's caught in the shaft," he shouted to First Mate Jacob Lusk.

Captain Luke Williamson motioned for Lusk, a broad, muscular Negro, to hurry the men along; then he stepped back under the overhang on the lower deck. He removed his hat, shook the water off, and replaced it on his head.

How much longer? Maybe she isn't my passenger. Maybe she floated up from some other boat along the wharf.

Williamson took a long draw on his pipe and leaned his head back against the wall. The schedule was a bust. It was just a matter of how bad a bust. With the rain, and with visibility down to less than a mile, and with the questions the police were sure to ask, he'd be lucky to get out of Memphis by midnight. He watched as the *Capital City* backed away from the wharf nearby and made for the channel, her stacks spitting black smoke that hung low in the saturated air. The song of a roustabout carried over the water. Williamson felt sick.

"Easy there," Lusk said as the deckhands hoisted the dripping corpse onto the deck. As they pulled the woman the final few feet, a metal shard near the paddle wheel snagged her dress, a last indignity that made Captain Williamson flinch. He could tell by looking at Lusk that the news wasn't good, so he stepped out into the rain and stood nearby as a policeman rolled the dead woman onto her back. Raindrops landed on a pale, bloated face, glassy blue eyes dimly staring into nothingness, the mouth slightly open, water trickling out, the neck crooked awkwardly to the right.

"Is she yours?" the policeman asked Williamson.

"I'm afraid so. Her name is Pierce. . . . Miss Cassie Pierce." Williamson glanced up to the second deck and searched among the passengers gathered there. He saw Salina Tyner turn quickly away from the railing and disappear into the ballroom.

"I'll need to talk with you, Captain," the policeman said, offering a quick handshake. "My name's Ben Crawford. I'm with the Memphis police." Leaning over for a closer look at the body, Crawford shook his head. "Don't look like no suicide. Her damned neck's broke." He pointed at the body. "See that purple place under her chin?" Williamson nodded. "Dead giveaway."

The rain slackened and more onlookers gathered on the deck above.

"Can we move her now?"

"Might as well," Crawford said, "but I don't want nobody

messing with the body until I get a chance to look it over closer."

"You men move the body over there out of the rain," Williamson said. Calling over first mate Lusk and his mud clerk in charge of cargo, Steven Tibedeau, he instructed them to keep the passengers away. Then the captain led Crawford into a small room on the lower deck.

Closing the door behind him, the officer turned to Williamson, who, standing six foot one, seemed to dwarf the policeman. "What can you tell me about her, Captain?"

"Well, Miss Pierce came up with us from New Orleans."

"Was she alone?"

"If you're asking me if she came aboard with anyone, the answer is no." The officer looked puzzled. "Mr. Crawford, I guess you'd say Miss Pierce was a regular on our boat. She made the trip from New Orleans to Memphis, or up to St. Louis, five, maybe six times a year."

"So she traveled alone?"

"Not exactly."

"I don't think I understand," Crawford said.

"Look, Mr. Crawford. The *Paragon* handles all kind of people—wealthy, dirt-raking poor, cultured, low-class—everything. Miss Pierce enjoyed the company of many of the more wealthy customers. . . ." Crawford still didn't get it. "The men passengers, Mr. Crawford. The *men*."

"Oh! She was a whore! All right, I understand now."

Williamson glanced across the empty room as though someone might overhear. "I don't like to use that word—"

"Hey, Captain, if you want to run whores on your boat that's your business. Except when they come floatin' up at the wharf. Then it's my business." Crawford nodded confidently. "Well, this shouldn't be too tough. Probably stole money off one of her customers, and he decided to toss her overboard. You got any idea who she was with?"

"I saw her briefly in the company of a couple of different gentlemen, but I couldn't say who they were. Jacob or Steven might know."

"That would be the colored fella—"

"First mate."

"And the other one was—"

"The clerk."

"Right." Crawford nodded. "Anybody else on board know her? I mean, other than her customers?"

"She was friends with Salina Tyner."

"She a whore, too?"

"Miss Tyner is a frequent passenger."

"Is this Tyner still on board?"

"Yes. She's in the ballroom, I believe."

Crawford extended his hand. "I thank you for your time, Captain. We probably won't keep you tied up here too long. We get whores killed down here two, three times a year. Usually it's somewhere on the wharf or down by Front Street. Hardly ever anybody talking. Nobody sees nothing, if you know what I mean." Crawford started out the door, then turned back. "When we do catch somebody on one of these, we don't usually have to look too far."

"How's that?"

"A woman of no virtue gets herself killed," Crawford said, "there's usually a man of less virtue not far away."

Crawford walked down the deck alone, then stopped abruptly. Using his hand to shield his face from the blowing rain, he looked back at Williamson, who was still standing in the doorway. "I suppose I'd better let you show me which cabin she was staying in." Williamson nodded and accompanied him.

SHORTLY AFTER ONE P.M., Salina Tyner sat at a table in the corner near the bar, looking blankly across the near-empty ballroom. Rain was still slapping the porthole behind her as she poured two fingers of whiskey into a shot glass. When she drank, a strand of hair slipped over her eye. She pushed it back brusquely.

"Cassie was always doing that," she said without looking around. "Poor girl, never could keep her hair out of her eyes."

Luke Williamson had been listening to her for almost half an hour, desperately hoping to understand what had happened. Crawford had talked to some crew members and passengers, including Tyner, and was still nosing around the ship; and although Williamson didn't like him, he knew that letting the law work was the only way he'd ever get the *Paragon* cleared to sail for St. Louis.

"They just hauled her out of the river and laid her out on the deck like a piece of driftwood. She was so full of life last night, laughing and talking and carrying on, right here by the bar." Tyner allowed herself a small laugh. "Cassie was teasing some planter into buying her another drink, while the whole time she was working the rest of the room. Nobody could wrap a man around her finger the way Cassie could, except maybe me."

The captain wondered if perhaps Pierce hadn't brought her death on herself. Women like Tyner and Pierce were a necessary evil, one that Williamson and most other riverboat captains tolerated. Two or three Bible-toting packet captains had tried denying passage to such women, and even tried to limit gambling; but they fast found themselves hauling only freight. Paying customers expected amenities on a Mississippi River steamer, and that meant more than just polite cabin stewards and excellent food set on fine china. The *Paragon* had a reputation as one of the most elegant packets, and Williamson looked the other way as long as the women kept their business discreet. But bodies turning up in the river was too much.

"One night on the *J. M. White* we had us this contest,"
Tyner began, "just to see who could get the most offers. For
three hours we worked that room, both of us watching to see
how the other was doing." She poured another drink. "We
looked out for one another."

Williamson was surprised she was telling him all this, for
it was a matter of custom that the prostitutes didn't openly
admit their trade. Prostitutes and riverboat captains played
a silly game of cat and mouse, both knowing what was going
on and yet neither willing to admit it openly. He listened as
Tyner, her dark eyes flashing, described the time a drunk on
the *Princess* started slapping her around in his cabin. He was
a huge man, she explained, and bull strong; if it hadn't been
for Cassie showing up when she did, wielding an accurate washbowl, Tyner wasn't sure what would have happened. "But I
wasn't there for her. When she needed me I wasn't around."

The bartender walked up. "Can I get you or the lady
anything else, Captain?"

"Coffee." He looked across the table. "I think the lady's
had plenty."

Tyner turned to the bartender. "The *lady* will tell you
when she's had enough. Bring me another bottle."

"Bring her coffee," Williamson said.

"A bottle," Tyner said, staring at the captain.

"The lady will have coffee," he said. They eyed each other
for several seconds; then the bartender departed. "I'm sorry
about your friend." Tyner just nodded, her lower lip trembling. "You knew her a long time, didn't you?"

"Seven years," she said softly.

The bartender brought two cups of coffee and placed a
bowl of sugar between them. Tyner watched the captain load
six heaping spoons into his cup.

"You must have one hell of a sweet tooth," she said. "If I
ate like that I'd be as wide as a barge."

Williamson stirred his coffee and took a cautious sip. "You got any idea who might have done this to Miss Pierce?"

"You're gonna start on me too, aren't you?"

"I beg your pardon?"

"I've been through this with that policeman." She shook her head in disgust. "He called Cassie a whore. I couldn't believe it." She tapped on the table. "He sat right here and called her a whore. Wanted to call me one, too. I could tell he did, but I think he knew I'd slap him across his nasty little face."

"So what did you tell him?"

"I told him he'd better find out who did this to her or they might find *his* ass in the river. I told him I didn't have any idea who'd want to hurt Cassie, but God knows as many people as she comes across there's bound to be some bad ones. She's had some close calls, but never nothing she couldn't handle. I remember one time in New Orleans—"

"Were you able to give Crawford anything that would help?"

Tyner took a deep breath and closed her eyes. "Captain, I told that policeman the last time I saw Cassie was about eleven o'clock last night. I came out of the ballroom with a gentleman. We were turning left to go . . . to go for a walk, and I saw Cassie come out of the walkway between the ballroom and the dining room. The light wasn't that good, but I could tell it was Cassie."

"Who was she with?"

"I don't know. I couldn't really see his face."

"So you couldn't tell Crawford what he looked like?"

"I told you, Captain, it was dark out there. If you'd put some decent lamps on deck, a girl could see."

It was times like this that made Williamson wish he ran only freight. Back in November he had lost his friend and business partner, Ed Smythe, when the *Mary Justice* went down. A lunatic with a grudge left over from the war had sunk the *Mary Justice* and nearly succeeded in destroying the *Paragon*. But the captain had survived, and having defeated the rival VanGeer Shipping Line in a race to New Orleans, he had secured for himself the guaranteed business of the St. Louis Merchants' Association. It was just enough to keep Williamson's packet service going, and ever since the ice had cleared in mid-January, he'd been making his runs on time, meeting his payroll, and even paying down on his debt at the bank. But while a contract meant steady business, it also meant keeping a tight schedule; Williamson could not afford to miss the run to St. Louis. The quiet was interrupted when Steven Tibedeau burst into the room.

"Captain!" He ran up to the table, water dripping from his parka. "Captain, you got to come down below."

"What is it, Steven?"

"It's that policeman." Tibedeau shook his head in bewilderment. "He's about to take Jacob."

"Take him where?"

"To jail, Captain! He thinks Jacob killed that woman."

Williamson leaped to his feet, with Tyner close behind. Tibedeau began to apologize as they made their way to the bottom deck. "It's all my fault, Captain. It's all my fault."

"What are you talking about?"

"That policeman, that Crawford man, he was asking me all kinds of questions and I was trying my best to help, I swear I was. . . . Anyway, he wanted to know if I'd seen this woman with anybody, and at first I said no, but then I remembered seeing her talking to Jacob last night."

They made the turn on the passengers' quarterdeck and started down a second flight of stairs.

"When was this?"

"Ten, maybe a quarter after ten last night."

"I don't see what difference—"

Tibedeau stopped in the middle of the stairs and looked over at Williamson, then briefly at Tyner. "That's just it, Captain. I saw Jacob and this woman arguing. I don't know what they were arguing about, but it was something that had the Pierce woman pretty mad." Williamson pushed ahead of Tibedeau and continued down the stairs. "I'm sorry, Captain. I didn't think nothing about it. I never thought . . ." He looked back at Tyner. "I never dreamed that . . ."

When Williamson reached the lower deck, he saw Lusk sitting on a whiskey barrel with Crawford and two men he didn't recognize standing nearby.

"Crawford, what the hell's going on here?"

With his hands extended before him, Crawford stepped between Williamson and Lusk. "Now just hold on, Captain. I think we're about to get to the bottom of this."

Williamson looked at Lusk, who stared back at him in amazement. Two men lifted the first mate's hands behind his head and bound them with rope.

"You men let him go," Williamson said.

"Captain, I'm just doing my job. Seems your colored man here was the one that sent Miss Pierce for a midnight swim."

"That's crazy as hell!" Williamson shouted. He looked at Lusk. "Jacob, what's this all about?"

"Cap'n, I ain't got no idea. These here officers—"

Crawford turned around and pointed at Lusk. "Now you don't need to be doing no talking, boy. You'll get a fair chance to have your say."

Williamson grabbed Crawford by the lapel. "That man is an officer on my boat. You'll let him go and you'll apologize—"

Crawford pulled himself free. "Now listen, Captain, I'm a patient man. But I've got my limit. You wanted me to wrap this thing up as quick as I could, now didn't you?"

"Yes, but—"

"Now I've talked to your crew and about half a dozen of

your passengers and it was just like I said it would be. We didn't have to look far."

Lusk appeared bewildered. "Cap'n, I ain't got no idea—"

"Boy, I told you to shut your mouth!" Crawford said without looking back. "Captain, I got three different people that saw your man here, *Mister* Lusk, shouting it out with Miss Pierce on the upper level of this boat last night about ten o'clock."

Williamson looked first at Lusk, then at Crawford. "So they had a disagreement."

"They weren't exactly arguing over the price of tobacco, Captain. Seems Lusk here owed Miss Pierce for services rendered—"

Salina Tyner stepped close to Crawford. "I don't believe it."

"Now, Miss Tyner—"

"Cassie didn't . . . She wouldn't—"

"Listen here, Crawford," Williamson said, silencing both of them, "I'll vouch for this man myself. He's been with me for eight years. He wouldn't ever harm one of our passengers. Just because someone has a disagreement with one of the crew—"

From another whiskey barrel nearby, Crawford produced a pink-and-blue crocheted bag and held it up before Tyner.

"Miss Tyner, do you recognize this?"

"It's Cassie's. Did you get that from her cabin?"

"No, from Lusk's."

"Captain, I can explain that," Lusk said.

"And you'll get the chance," Crawford said. He motioned for his men to take the first mate away. "But for now, Captain, I'm going to have to arrest Lusk here for the murder of Cassie Pierce."

"Crawford, you're making a mistake!" Williamson shouted, reaching for the policeman.

"Don't grab me again," Crawford said, "else you'll be going with me, too. I ain't never arrested no captain before, but I'm willing to start. From the looks of the crowd gathering, you've got your hands full right here on the boat. I suggest you tend to your passengers and let me tend to the law." Crawford started across the landing stage. "He'll be at the Adams Street jailhouse if you want to see him. Just make sure it's late this evening." Pausing on the wharf, he turned back toward the boat. "And Captain, don't move this boat until I say it's all right. We may need to come back and talk to more of your passengers."

Anger churning inside him, Williamson watched the men lead Jacob Lusk across the landing stage and on to the shore.

"Jacob!" he shouted. "Don't you worry. Don't you worry about a thing." He moved two or three steps up the stairs to keep Lusk in sight. "I'll be coming for you. I'll be coming for you, Jacob!"

2

"I DONE TOLD you for the last time, Mr. Baldridge, the room is rented to someone else."

"But I've been staying here for almost five months," Baldridge protested.

Mrs. O'Reilly, owner of the Crestview Gentlemen's Boardinghouse, shook her finger at him. "And you ain't paid for but two of 'em. I done give you fair warning."

"Come on, Mrs. O'Reilly, I can give you a little something toward the bill." Baldridge began digging through his pockets, but came up with only a few coins.

"Probably some more of your ill-gotten card money," she said. "I ain't about to take the devil's money. No sir, not one dime."

Baldridge started up the steps. "Look, Mrs. O'Reilly, I admit I've been a little short lately—"

"And you've been a lot drunk lately, and I done told you, Mr. Baldridge, I ain't gonna have it." Baldridge halted on the second step as he saw Mrs. O'Reilly's two grown sons descending the stairs with his trunk. Instead of continuing onto the front porch, the men turned and disappeared toward the back of the house.

"That's my trunk! Where are they going with my things?"

"I had 'em packed up. You'll find everything there— when you come up with the back rent you owe me."

"Now, that's not right, Mrs. O'Reilly. You got no call to take my things, to toss me out like this." He started up the steps again, but the woman stepped in front of him. Baldridge halted and looked around her at the two strapping young men who appeared in the doorway, arms folded, strictly business.

"You got the devil in you, Masey Baldridge," Mrs. O'Reilly said. "Out running around till all hours of the night, drinking, carousing." She glanced down at his left leg. "I suspect the Lord give you that bum leg as punishment for the sin you're living in."

"Mrs. O'Reilly, I've told you how I got this leg, and it ain't got nothing to do with the Lord."

The landlady gave him a holier-than-thou look, turned, and walked inside. "Your things will be here for you when you bring me my money." She slammed the door.

"This ain't right, Mrs. O'Reilly!" Baldridge shouted. "You ain't doin' me right." For a few moments he stood on the steps, watching her watch him from a window beside the front door.

"Now you go on, Masey Baldridge, else I'll have the law out here!" she shouted from inside.

"Go get the damned law, I don't care!" Mrs. O'Reilly left the window, so Baldridge shouted even louder. "This place ain't worth the board you're charging anyway! The rooms are too small!" He kicked the step. "You got roaches! This place is falling apart!" He stared at the vacant window. "And you can't cook worth shit!"

Maybe *I'll* get the law, Baldridge thought, limping down

the brick walkway to the edge of the street. But he knew better. The old woman had him and there wasn't much he could say. He had been promising the rent for weeks now, expecting Mr. Ferguson to contact him with work any day. Hadn't he done a good job on the *Mary Justice* case? Hadn't he saved the Mid-South Insurance Company a bundle? What about all the lives he'd saved?

Baldridge leaned against a gas street lamp and slipped his flask from his jacket pocket. He took two quick swigs and gazed down Front Street. At least the rain had stopped. It was bad enough being thrown out, but getting thrown out in the rain . . . A man riding alongside his teenage daughter gave Baldridge a nod as he passed, which Baldridge answered, but the man appeared distressed as his eyes fell upon the flask, so Baldridge hid it inside his jacket.

What's the matter with these damned people? A man can't have a little drink without somebody looking down on him. Baldridge watched as the two continued down the street. *I'll bet he socks it away every chance he gets.*

Glancing back toward the boardinghouse, he shook his head. He was sick and tired of people thinking they were better than him. How could they forget what he'd done? It had made all the papers up and down the river. He still had the *Memphis Appeal*—or rather, Mrs. O'Reilly had it, in his trunk—with the headline "Local Man Saves Riverboat." They were certainly glad enough to see him when he got back from Natchez. The notoriety got his drinks bought through Christmas, with everybody in Memphis wanting to hear the story. But with the coming of the new year, things changed. People forgot. The Mid-South Insurance Company, so grateful for his efforts at the time, had offered no work for three months, and between his back rent at the boardinghouse and the stiff tab he had run up in the taverns along Whiskey Chute, Baldridge was broke. Most days he was proud of his efforts in Natchez, and he figured he could easily do as well again if they'd just toss him another case. But then there were other days, days when he questioned every decision he'd made, days when he blamed himself for the death of poor Asa Turner—days when he wondered if it had been all just blind, dumb luck. With his leg no better, the whiskey seemed more and more important, and the cold, damp winter air had been particularly hard on him.

At first he paid no attention to the carriage pulling up nearby. Then:

"Masey? Masey Baldridge?" someone shouted. When Baldridge walked over, Captain Luke Williamson stepped down and shook his hand.

"It's been a while."

"Damned sure has," Baldridge said. "Last time I saw you was when you let me off at Natchez." Williamson nodded. "Congratulations on beating the *Apollo* to New Orleans."

"Couldn't have done it without you."

"What brings you around here?"

Williamson looked back at the carriage. "Miss Tyner and me . . . You remember Miss Tyner, don't you?"

Baldridge bent slightly and glanced inside the carriage. Salina Tyner waved at him. "Oh yes, I definitely remember Miss Tyner."

"Well, Baldridge, we got a little problem here. Mr. Ferguson at the insurance company said we'd find you down—"

"Ferguson sent you?" Baldridge brightened.

"Well, yes and no." The captain glanced back at Tyner, then spoke to Baldridge. "Is there someplace we could go to talk? How about your place?"

"Oh, well . . . uh, why don't we go to the Eddy instead? It's just a little ways toward the river."

"I know the place."

"Good. Good. We could have a drink and talk."

Williamson glanced at the boardinghouse. "Were you on your way somewhere?"

"Nothing that can't wait," Baldridge said, climbing into the carriage. He took a seat across from Tyner and tipped his hat to her. "Good day. You go by Sally, if I remember right."

"Masey," she quietly replied. Williamson took the seat next to Tyner. Adjusting his stiff leg, Baldridge noticed their worried faces, and figured this was anything but a social call.

"So what seems to be the problem?"

On the way to the Eddy, Williamson told Baldridge about Cassie Pierce's murder and Jacob's arrest. Tyner didn't say much, which, as Baldridge recalled, was unusual for her. She still had that silky black hair and those dark, piercing eyes; but the luster seemed gone, as if someone had blown out a lamp. She kept staring out the window, only occasionally commenting on what Williamson said. The captain, on the other hand, kept fiddling with his long dark-brown mustache, like those worn by many of the riverboat captains Baldridge had encountered along the Mississippi. It became clear from the conversation that the notion of sailing the *Paragon* without his trusted first mate was unsettling.

"We've been together over eight years," Williamson told him at the Eddy. "You get to know a man when you've worked with him that long. Jacob wouldn't do something like this."

"Are you saying he was never involved"—Baldridge glanced at Tyner—"with the women on the boat?"

"Jacob is a man, Baldridge. He's not a saint. But—"

"Not with Cassie," Tyner interrupted. "She was strict about that. She wouldn't be with a colored man. 'Stay within your color,' she always said."

"Maybe that was the problem. Maybe Jacob got turned down."

"Damn it, I told you Jacob wouldn't do nothing—"

"Hold up, there, Captain," Baldridge said, raising his

hands. "I'm just trying to figure what the police are thinking."
He poured Williamson another drink. "I ain't said your man
did it. But you did tell me they found her bag in his cabin."

"Jacob can explain that."

"I'll expect he'll have to," Baldridge offered the bottle to
Tyner, but she refused. "What do you make of this, Sally?"

"I don't know what to believe. I want to believe Jacob had
nothing to do with Cassie's death. All the times I've been on
the *Paragon*, he never gave me—or Cassie, as far as I know—
any reason to think . . . I just don't know."

Luke Williamson leaned over the table. "Baldridge, I
need your help."

"Well, if Mr. Ferguson said he would put me on the case . . ."

"Ferguson didn't say anything."

Baldridge was stunned.

"He won't help," Williamson explained. "Says this isn't
covered by Mid-South Insurance."

"So he's not giving me the case?"

"There is no case, except for what we make of it. Ferguson
basically said tough luck. Can you believe that? As long as
I've been paying that son of a bitch premiums, and when I
need help, he won't give me the time of day. Guess I used up
my goodwill with him over the *Mary Justice*."

"He's an asshole, if you ask me, which you didn't," Tyner
added. "Sat there chomping on that cigar like a cow chewin'
cud. From the minute we went in that office, he had no inten-
tion of helping the captain, and he sure couldn't care less
about helping me."

"But he said you might be free," Williamson said.

"Well"—Baldridge laughed—"I ain't free, but I'm available."

"I don't know that I can pay you what the company would,
but I'd be willing to offer you, say, three dollars a day, plus
meals—that is, as long as we're docked. I'll have to be moving

on to St. Louis as soon as they release the ship. If you were on the ship, I'd of course see to it you had a cabin."

Baldridge rocked back in the chair and studied the two of them. Odd, it seemed, that they would be together, him a respected captain and her a . . . traveler. And yet they had one thing in common that Baldridge recalled from the *Mary Justice* investigation. They spared nothing to get what they wanted, running full throttle all the time, and other people could either jump on board or get out of the way. That they would want his help both surprised and pleased him. But then again, they were desperate. Who else did they know in Memphis? He decided to take the job before they offered it to somebody else.

"I suppose I could find the time to help you out. I'd hate to see anything happen to Mr. Jacob Lusk."

Williamson seemed relieved, then grew intense. "They're likely to move fast, seeing as how Jacob's colored and Miss Pierce was white."

"That fool Crawford thinks he's got it all figured out. Why, he couldn't find his ass in the dark," Tyner said.

Baldridge saw a bit of that spark return to her eyes. "Crawford's the lawman, right?" Tyner nodded. "I reckon we ought to talk to Jacob first."

"Can't. Not till tonight," Williamson said. "We came by there first thing this afternoon, but they wouldn't let us see him. Said to come back tonight."

"Oh." Baldridge scratched his head. "Did the law find anything else on the boat?"

"Just Jacob. From the crew members I talked to, Crawford didn't look too hard. Oh, he interviewed some of the hands, and he talked to Miss Tyner and a couple of the passengers . . ." Williamson frowned. "He searched Jacob's cabin and Cassie Pierce's. I swear, it's like he knew what he wanted before he showed up."

"I'd like to have a look around the boat."

"That shouldn't be hard. She sure isn't going anywhere until they give us the all-clear. They're blowing my schedule right out of the water." Williamson looked down. "Still, without Jacob, and with him in trouble and all, I don't much want to leave."

"But you have to, don't you?" Tyner asked. "What about your schedule?"

"If I don't finish this run, keep my contracts and all, I won't have a boat for Jacob to come back to." He held out his hand, and Baldridge shook it firmly. "That's why I need you. I can't possibly get this cleared up before the police let us sail, and I've got to know somebody's working to get Jacob free. Have we got a deal?"

"Yeah, we got a deal." Standing up, Baldridge looked deliberately at the bottle, then over toward the bartender, reaching all too slowly for his pocket.

"Let me get that," Williamson said. Baldridge offered a mild protest, but gave in quickly. He noticed that Sally Tyner was eyeing him curiously. Williamson started for the door. "I'll get a carriage and we can swing by the boardinghouse and get your things."

"No, that's all right," Baldridge said.

"Don't you want your clothes or your gun or anything?"

"No, not now. I'd just as soon get over and take a look at the ship."

"Suit yourself," Williamson said, holding the door as they walked out.

"Masey's traveling light today," Tyner said with a knowing smile. "Aren't you, Masey?"

3

THEY HADN'T BEEN on the *Paragon* two minutes before Williamson had the pilot sound the ship's whistle in four long blasts. He said he just wanted Jacob to know they were still there. Next, the captain showed Baldridge where they found Pierce's body; then he, Baldridge, and Tyner went to the place Miss Pierce was last seen alive; the hallway between the dining room and the ballroom, on the hurricane deck. Tyner described, as she had to Crawford, seeing Pierce emerge that evening in the company of a man she'd not recognized. Nothing in Pierce's behavior indicated a problem, at least as far as Tyner could tell, so she had just waved and gone on about her business—which at the time was a mildly intoxicated watchmaker from Helena. From the spot where Tyner had last seen her, Pierce's cabin was one deck below, on the port side nearly amidships. Williamson found Mac-Cauley, the steward working that sector of the ship, and had him open the room.

Staterooms lined the ship, some thirty on each side, and each had a door opening to the water side and a door opening to the grand dining room. One key fit both doors. As MacCauley opened the deck-side door, Williamson stepped inside first, followed closely by Baldridge. Tyner squeezed into the cramped room behind them, and MacCauley remained outside. The first thing Baldridge noticed was the heavy odor of perfume, a musky-sweet smell, no doubt compromised by the rainy weather.

"She loved that fragrance," Tyner observed. "Wore it all the time. Said it brought her luck."

Stepping over a skirt that lay crumpled near the bed, Baldridge squeezed past the captain. The bedcovers were pulled off and piled near the foot, the mattress was askew on the springs beneath it. Pierce's belongings seemed to be everywhere, and even the drawer from the washstand was standing on end in the corner.

"Look at this place. That damned Crawford's got no respect for anybody's things." Tyner began picking up the belongings near the door.

"They had to take a look around," Williamson said, recovering a broken mirror from a small dressing table. She jerked it from him.

"Look around?" She held the spidered glass up in front of the captain. "You call this looking around? How'd you like the police to 'look around' your cabin like this?"

"They sure made a helluva mess, all right," Baldridge agreed. He leaned around the captain and called to the steward. "Come here a minute."

MacCauley stuck his head in the door. "Yes, sir?"

"Were you the one that let the law in here?"

"Yes, sir."

"Well, what in the hell did they find in here worth making this kind of a mess?"

MacCauley looked puzzled. "They didn't."

"They didn't remove anything from the room?"

"No, sir." The steward glanced at the captain. "The *police* didn't take nothin' out of here. I watched 'em real close," he added, as if waiting for the captain's approval. "But . . ."

"But what?" Williamson said.

"But the police didn't make this mess, Captain."

Baldridge perked up. "You saying the law didn't search this room?"

"That Crawford fella looked around. He looked real hard," MacCauley said, "but this cabin was already a mess when I let the police in."

"Cassie would never have allowed her place to look like this. She had too much pride," said Tyner.

"You figure the killer did this?" Williamson asked.

Baldridge surveyed the room with renewed interest. "Maybe. Sure looks like somebody was working up a sweat to find something. See there?" He pointed to the washstand. "It's been pulled out from the wall."

"Cassie kept her clothes neat," Tyner added, picking up a crinoline that had landed between the bed and the wall.

"Bed's been moved out and pushed back again," Baldridge said.

Williamson nodded. "Must've been looking for money— probably figured she had a stash."

Baldridge noticed a smile creeping over Tyner's face as she glanced at the twin lanterns mounted on the wall behind Baldridge's head and beside the bed.

"Let me by," she said, pushing her way between them. "I'll bet you they didn't get it. I'm the only one she ever told about her hiding place." Her smile broadened as she took the first lantern from its mount. Removing the glass globe, she began unscrewing the burner from its sea-blue base. When she turned the base upside down, Luke instinctively reached for it, expecting oil to spill onto the floor. Instead, a couple of coins dropped into Sally's hand. She shook the lamp, and eight more fell from its base. The smell of kerosene mixed with perfume. Baldridge peered over her shoulder.

"Well, I'll be damned," he muttered.

"I guess Cassie gets the last laugh," she said, squeezing the coins tightly in both hands. Williamson found a hand towel beside the edge of the bed and handed it to her.

"Kind of messy way to bank, ain't it?" Baldridge said.

Tyner was carefully cleaning each coin, wiping away the light oil that coated them. "A girl does what she has to. A woman by herself learns. You get slapped around once or twice, you learn to fight. You get robbed like me and Cassie did, you learn to hide your money. She never kept money in her purse."

Baldridge scratched his head as he looked about the cabin again. "They sure wanted it mighty bad."

"How much is there?" the captain asked.

"I don't know," Tyner said curtly. "I haven't finished cleaning it yet. But I can tell you that Cassie did all right." She lifted her head confidently. "There's always some planter more than willing to spend his money on a woman—especially if he thinks he's gonna get her to bed."

"Captain, did this Crawford fella tell you he found Pierce's cabin ransacked?"

"No. He said he checked it out, but he didn't mention anything about this."

"Wonder why?" Baldridge continued. "I mean, if Miss Pierce was killed for her money"—he looked around again—"and it's starting to look like she was, then why wouldn't he tell you that?"

" 'Cause he's a fool," Tyner said, still wiping the coins.

Baldridge continued. "If Crawford found her room like this, and he found her purse in Jacob's cabin, he must figure Jacob tore the place up." He stepped over, lifted the other lamp from its support, satisfied himself that it contained only oil, and replaced it. "But even if Jacob killed her and searched the room—"

"He didn't," Williamson interrupted.

"All right, all right, just bear with me for a minute." The captain listened reluctantly. "Even if Jacob searched the room, why would he take Pierce's bag? Sally says the woman never kept money in it. And once he figured out there was no money in it, why would he hold on to it? If he killed her, that is."

"Makes no sense. That's what I've been saying."

"Eighteen dollars," Tyner announced, "and forty . . . No, wait a minute . . ." Her voice trailed off as she wiped the last coin. With the cloth in her right hand, she took the coin in her left and held it toward the open door. "Step back a second," she called to MacCauley, "you're standing in the light."

"Forty what?" Williamson asked.

"I'm not sure." She examined the coin closely. "I thought this was a twenty-dollar gold piece at first." She flipped the coin to view the opposite side. "Well, it says 'Twenty Dollars,' but it's not real."

Williamson leaned closer. "What are you talking about?"

"I mean . . . look right here. Does that say what I think it says?"

Williamson took the coin and read aloud the raised lettering. "C.S.A."

"Let me see that." Baldridge grabbed the coin. It was solid gold, bearing a denomination of twenty dollars and carrying the imprint of the Confederate States of America.

"I never saw a twenty-dollar Confederate coin," Tyner said, "and I handled a lot of coins during the war."

"Ain't no such thing," Baldridge said, continuing his examinations. He pressed his teeth around it, tasting the kerosene residue. "But it sure as hell feels like real gold."

"Gold's gold," Tyner said.

"Not exactly," Williamson said. "Confederate money is not legal tender. Lord knows I've had enough passengers try to pass it off since the war. You can't spend that stuff anywhere."

"Somebody did," Baldridge said. He reached toward his pocket, but stopped short. "Captain, have you got twenty dollars on you?"

Williamson shook his head. "No. Why?"

"I need a coin to compare this one to."

Williamson called to the steward. "MacCauley, go get a twenty-dollar gold piece from Steven Tibedeau."

"Yes, sir," MacCauley replied, disappearing from the doorway.

"Hell, don't send *him* after it," Sally said, but she was too late. Gathering her skirt, she began lifting the hoop along with her undergarments, but stopped abruptly when she caught both men watching. Making a half-turn, she continued until she had retrieved a small purse and carefully fished out a coin. "Here." She handed it to Baldridge. "If all men were as broke as you two, I'd be out of business in a week."

Baldridge compared the two coins. They were the same size, the same thickness, and roughly the same weight. "If it was dark, or if you weren't paying attention . . ."

"You could pass it off," Williamson said.

"But why?" Baldridge said, more to himself than to the others. "Captain, you said yourself this ain't legal tender. But I can't see it being counterfeit, neither. I mean, if somebody made up a bunch of these things, who'd be stupid enough to make something they couldn't spend? If you were going to counterfeit a coin, you'd copy the real thing, wouldn't you?"

"Yeah, but the gold's still gold," Tyner said. "Wouldn't it be worth its weight?"

Baldridge looked at the captain. "Unless . . ."

"Unless they passed it by accident."

"And then they wanted it back," Baldridge said. "A man might tear a room plumb apart to get back something like this."

The captain nodded. "He might."

"So?" Tyner folded her arms. "So . . . are you two saying Cassie got killed over a twenty-dollar coin? But by who?"

Baldridge held up the gold piece. "Find out about this and we may find out who."

After a few more minutes of talking and looking through Pierce's room, Williamson suggested they grab some supper; after that it would be time to visit Jacob. MacCauley had returned with the twenty-dollar coin, but the captain took it from him and charged him to keep his mouth shut about the condition of Pierce's room and what they found there. Baldridge slipped the other two coins into his vest pocket and was following Williamson along the deck when Salina Tyner spoke from right behind him.

"Uh, ain't you forgetting something?"

"What's that?" Baldridge said over his shoulder.

"My twenty dollars," she said, extending her hand. Baldridge stopped abruptly outside the doorway to the dining hall. He pulled the U.S. coin from his pocket and handed it to her. At least his dinner was covered, but he knew he couldn't afford the price of a drink that evening. And he wasn't sure why, but Tyner seemed to take great pleasure in making him give up that gold piece. As he stepped inside the room, he felt the captain slip something in his hand: the coin MacCauley had brought him.

"What's this?"

"Advance payment," Luke said, "I hired you, didn't I? I figure that gets me about a week according to our agreement."

"Much obliged."

Sally slapped him on the back as she passed. "I just bet you are. Let's eat. We got a long night ahead of us."

"SO, WHEN DID you get thrown out?" Salina Tyner asked Baldridge, not looking up from her plate.

"What?"

"I said, 'When did you get thrown out?'"

"I don't know what you're—"

"Sure you do." She raised one eyebrow. "No grown man picks up and leaves his place without his gun and his clothes—that is, if he's got any." She grinned wryly.

"I don't think you know—"

"I know plenty. As I recall, you don't go anywhere without that bowie knife of yours. Seems I remember you even taking it to bed with you. And I ain't seen you spend a penny on anything since we picked you up today, and with the way you pocketed my twenty dollars—"

Baldridge grinned. "You don't miss much, do you?"

Her smile slowly disappeared as she gazed out the porthole. "Apparently I do. I missed what was happening to Cassie."

Sally Tyner was a puzzle. One moment she seemed like ice, the next minute Baldridge could swear she was going to break into tears. That she could see through him was clear— and yet she didn't seem accusatory. Her voice had an "I been there" tone.

Luke Williamson had long since left the table; he'd barely sat down to eat when he was informed by Steven Tibedeau that the Memphis police had cleared the *Paragon* to leave. It was a mixed blessing for Williamson, and Baldridge sensed his struggle. Before he left the dining hall to make arrangements for departure, Williamson reminded Baldridge how important it was to clear Jacob. Sally Tyner agreed to remain in Memphis and help Baldridge. It was help he hadn't requested, but he figured she might come in handy, and he didn't see much he could do to stop her. It would be five days before the *Paragon* returned to Memphis, and Williamson made it clear he expected Baldridge to have Lusk out of jail and ready for duty when he got back.

The crew was completing their preparations, and Tyner

and Baldridge had almost finished their dinner, when Baldridge heard someone address him.

"Excuse me, Mr. Baldridge." The woman's soft voice was barely audible over the conversation in the dining room. As he turned around in his chair, the ship's steward and head cook, Miss Anabel McBree, stood a few feet behind him, near a door that led down the deck to the kitchen. Dressed in the immaculate white all of the dining room staff wore, McBree was a dark-skinned, middle-aged Negro woman whom Baldridge had met during the Natchez incident in the fall. She seemed uncomfortable standing amid the diners.

Tyner kicked him under the table and Baldridge started to rise.

"Don't stand up on my account, Mr. Baldridge." She looked across at Tyner. "Good evenin', ma'am. Are you folks enjoying your supper?"

"Always." Tyner smiled. "You're the real reason I ride this boat, you know."

Anabel smiled broadly. "Oh, now, ma'am, ain't no need carryin' on." She looked at Baldridge. "I hate to bother you, sir, but I wanted to ask about Jacob." Looking around, she moved closer to him and lowered her voice. "There's talk among the crew that once we leave for St. Louis, you're gonna stay behind and get Jacob out of jail. Is that right, Mr. Baldridge?"

Baldridge had returned to his seat. "That's right, Anabel. I'm sure gonna try."

She let out a long, low sigh. "Well, that makes me feel a whole lot better. I remember what you done for us last fall." Anabel looked down. "Mr. Baldridge, I know you know this, but I just got to say it anyway." Her eyes returned to his. "Jacob Lusk didn't do nothin' to hurt that woman. Jacob's the kindest man I know. Why, he wouldn't hurt nobody, 'cept maybe a roustabout that got out of line." Baldridge nodded. "You just got to get him loose. This boat don't run nothing like it should without Jacob. And that ain't takin' nothin' away from Captain Luke. He's the best captain on the river. Ain't no doubt. But Jacob . . . he . . ."

"I think I understand, Anabel," Baldridge said.

"All right, sir. I won't keep you no more from your supper. It's gettin' real close to time to leave, so I reckon you'll have to hurry." She turned to depart, paused a moment, and said, "If you get the chance, tell Jacob I'm . . . that is, we're all thinkin' about him."

"I'll do that, Anabel."

"And, oh yes." She walked quickly out on deck, where a dining room attendant had been waiting, and took a covered dish from him. "If it wouldn't be too much trouble, Mr. Baldridge, could you take this to Jacob when you see him tonight? Lord only knows what they'll feed him."

"Be glad to, Anabel."

4

BEFORE LEAVING THE *Paragon*, Baldridge secured a hurriedly prepared copy of the New Orleans-to-Memphis passenger manifest from Steven Tibedeau; then he and Tyner took a carriage from the wharf to the jail, a two-story brick building on Adams Street. Once inside, they spoke briefly with the jailer and were surprised to discover that Jacob Lusk had already had visitors. They were led down a dimly lit hallway, past a snoring drunk, and around a corner. As they approached Lusk's cell, Baldridge saw three neatly dressed Negro men and a thin, redheaded white man standing outside the bars and talking with Jacob. Lusk saw Baldridge coming.

"Mr. Baldridge!" he called. His expression as he spoke with the other men had been serious, but now it gave way to a broad smile. "Evenin', Miss Tyner." Tyner nodded. Baldridge eyed the men before him. The black men, hats in hand, stood in a neat row, like choir members behind a preacher. "What you folks doin' here?" Lusk asked.

"Workin' on gettin' you out."

"Cap'n sent you, didn't he?" Baldridge nodded. "I knew

he would. Cap'n Luke takes care of folks." After a few seconds of awkward silence, Lusk introduced the redheaded man as Mr. William Jenkins Dodd, and his Negro companions. "Mr. Dodd come to help me, too. Come to see to it I had proper lawyerin'."

Dodd acknowledged Tyner and shook Baldridge's hand.

"Have we had occasion to meet?" Dodd asked him.

"No, we haven't met," Baldridge said as he turned to look down the hallway. "Jailer! Let us in to see this man." He turned back to Dodd. "But I've heard of your horse tradin'."

Dodd gestured with his hat. "These gentlemen and I are here to see to it that Mr. Lusk is treated fairly."

The jailer fumbled with the keys as he opened Lusk's cell.

"And how'd you hear about Jacob being in jail?" Baldridge asked. He stepped inside the cell, followed closely by Tyner. The jailer locked the gate and disappeared down the hall.

"Word travels fast, Mr. Baldridge," Dodd said. "When a man of color is arrested for killing a white woman, it behooves all decent men to sit up and take notice. I'm formerly with the Freedman's Bureau—"

"So I've heard."

"And I've seen how these things can turn out, so I'll have my lawyer, Mr. Quillen, down here first thing tomorrow. Old ways die hard around here, Mr. Baldridge. Men have been lynched for less than—"

"Spoken like a true Republican," Baldridge said. He turned Lusk away from Dodd and the men with him, then looked back over his shoulder. "Now don't misunderstand me, Mr. Dodd. It's real decent of you to send your lawyer down here. I'm sure he'll be a lot of help, seein' as how I ain't had a chance to get one yet. But ain't nobody gonna lynch ol' Jacob, and if you'll excuse Miss Tyner and me, we need to talk to him."

Dodd appeared surprised but did not protest. "Mr. Baldridge, I assure you that we have the same purpose in mind. We of the Republican League will be sure that justice is done." He pointed at Lusk, who looked back at him over his shoulder. "Be assured, Mr. Lusk, you won't be forgotten."

"Thank you, sir," Lusk said.

The black men, each in turn, bade him farewell and started down the hall, but Dodd hung back.

"Pleasure to meet you, Mr. Baldridge. I hope together we can make things right for Jacob." When he got no answer, Dodd followed his colleagues to the outer office.

"You certainly know how to extend every courtesy," Tyner said.

"What you got against that fella, Mr. Baldridge?"

"Politics."

"Politics? Why, I didn't know you was a politickin' man."

"I ain't. That's what I got against him. Let's talk about what happened."

Jacob sat down on the end of the wooden bunk, which was minus a couple of slats and was attached to the wall by a rusty chain at each end. Baldridge joined him, then quickly stood and offered the seat to Tyner.

"I'll stand." She kept looking at Lusk, who averted his eyes.

"I heard the whistle," Lusk said softly. "Cap'n done gone, ain't he?"

"He had to leave for St. Louis."

"Yes sir, I reckon he did at that. I expect he'll be double-stokin' the boilers to make up time." Lusk peered into the dim hallway.

"Jacob, we've got to talk. Tell me what happened last night. I've got to know all of it."

"Mr. Baldridge, I didn't kill that woman." He looked at Tyner. "Lord knows I didn't."

"Well, the Lord ain't talking, so you'd better start," Tyner said. "What were you doing with Cassie's bag?"

"The police is right about that, Miss Tyner. I had her bag in my cabin. But I didn't hurt her. I never touched her." He began rubbing his palms over his legs and rocking nervously. "I got to my cabin about one in the morning, right after I had checked in with Thomas Neely—he's the night pilot. I was sound asleep when the next thing I knew somebody knocked on my door. I thought it was one of the hands needin' something, but when I opened the door nobody was there. I looked down on the deck and there was this woman's bag. I called out if anybody was there, but nobody answered."

"So what did you do then?" Baldridge asked.

"Well sir, I looked inside the bag, but I didn't find no name. And they wasn't no money in it, neither. So I reckoned that with the late hour and all, wouldn't nobody need it till morning. So I laid it on my dresser and I figured I'd give it to Steven Tibedeau first thing in the morning."

"But you didn't," Tyner said. She was leaning back against the bars with her arms folded.

"No, ma'am, I didn't."

"Why not?"

"You see, when we're on the river, I normally gets up about thirty minutes before daylight to check on the crew. But when we're in port, that's my day to rest in. Cap'n knows about it," he added, as if seeking approval. "I woke up about six-thirty with somebody banging on the door. It was one of the hands saying there was a body in the water. I dressed as fast as I could and hurried on deck. I got so busy with gettin' that woman out of the river, I done forgot about the bag. Next thing I knew, the police was asking me questions and had me roundin' up the crew. I never had a chance to get back to my cabin."

"When did the police arrive?"

"They got there fast, Mr. Baldridge. Why, I bet it wasn't even an hour from the time I got out on deck and saw that woman's body in the water, to when that Crawford fella come on board."

"Why didn't you bring the body on board before Crawford got there?"

"Ain't supposed to. If we find somebody drowned like that, cap'n goes straight by the book. He wants the police to know about it right off."

"So who sent for the police?"

"I reckon the cap'n did."

"That's right," Tyner confirmed. "Williamson told me he sent for the police about seven o'clock."

"They sho' *did* got there fast," Jacob said again.

"How's that?"

"That Crawford fella was on the boat by seven-thirty."

Baldridge figured it was a good fifteen minutes from the jail to the wharf, and though Crawford could certainly have made it in that time, he had never known the Memphis police to be so punctual.

"Did you see Cassie Pierce last night before you went to bed?"

"Yes, sir, I seen her. She was with a Mr. Quick that come on board in New Orleans."

"What time was that?"

"Oh, I reckon about seven o'clock. Right after supper."

"What does this Quick fella look like?"

"Kind of scrawny-looking man, maybe five and a half feet tall. He wasn't dressed like no real gentleman."

"What do you mean?"

"Well sir, when you see as many folks as I do, you can just tell. He had him a notion he was a gentleman, though. I've seen him on the *Paragon* before. About a year ago he come up to Memphis."

"From New Orleans?"

"Yes, sir."

Baldridge took the manifest from his coat pocket, opened it, and ran his finger down the list of names. He found Dillard Quick assigned to cabin twenty-three, just down the deck from Cassie Pierce's. He turned to Tyner.

"Did you ever come across this Quick?"

"Nope. Never heard of him. But from the way Jacob described him, he sounds like the man I saw Cassie with last night."

"Jacob, what else do you know about this fella?"

"Not too much, Mr. Baldridge. Like I told you, he come up from New Orleans with us last year, and the year before, too. I remember him because he got real upset that first time. Come to me complaining about his cabin being too small. Wouldn't hush until I moved him to a bigger one. 'Course that trunk he travels with takes up most of the space in his room. And I offered to store it for him every time, but he wouldn't hear of it. He's always come on the boat alone, but once he's aboard, he's generally got a lady nearby."

"And when he was with Miss Pierce," Baldridge said, "did she seem upset?"

"No, sir," Lusk said, scratching his head. "They seemed to be hittin' it off right good."

"Did you tell the police about seeing Quick with Miss Pierce?"

"Yes, sir, I did. But that fella—he didn't pay me no mind. He said"—Lusk glanced warily at Tyner—"he said she was probably with a lot o' men last night, but he couldn't very well hunt them all down."

"That sorry son of a—" Tyner began.

"Jacob," Baldridge interrupted, "Steven Tibedeau told the police he saw you and Miss Pierce arguing last night."

Lusk looked down at the floor and used the toe of his shoe

to pick at a crack in the wood. "Steven don't lie."

"So you did argue with her?" Tyner asked.

"We had some words. Yes, ma'am, we did." Lusk looked first at Tyner, then at Baldridge. "But it wasn't like what you think. And it wasn't like the police is making it out to be." He walked over and grasped the bars, peering out into the hallway. "I wasn't tryin' to bed no white woman, even if the law says she was a . . ."

"A whore? Is that what you were going to say?"

"That's what *they* say, Miss Tyner." He turned and faced her. "But it ain't for me to say. I don't bother with the passengers' business."

"So what were the two of you arguing about?" Baldridge asked.

"It was near 'bout eleven o'clock. I was passing by Miss Pierce's room when she come out the door of her cabin like a wildcat. What times I've seen her, I ain't never seen her that mad before."

"Where was Dillard Quick?"

"I don't know, sir. He wasn't nowhere around."

"What was she mad about?" Baldridge asked.

"She started in on me about the steward. Claimed either him or the chambermaid had been in her room. Said she found it open when she come up from the dining room. I looked in the room but I couldn't tell that anybody had been in there. I asked her was anything missing and she said no. But she kept on about my cabin help until I guess I got my back up, Mr. Baldridge. If they're wrong—the help, that is—they got to deal with me. But I don't hold with nobody bad-mouthin' my help, unless they know for sure they's done something wrong."

"You said nothing was missing from Miss Pierce's room?"

"Not that she could tell. I even asked her did she maybe leave the door open herself, but she wouldn't hear none of that."

Tyner shook her head. "Not Cassie. She was careful about

that. She'd been robbed before. She would never have left her room open."

"Yes'm, I can see that now, what with all that's happened. But at the time—"

"At the time you didn't believe her," Tyner said.

"I know my crew, Miss Tyner. They're good people. They wouldn't— "

"What about a passenger?" Baldridge asked.

"But there wasn't nothing missin', Mr. Baldridge. The lady told me so herself."

Baldridge stood up and walked to the cell door. "All right, Jacob. Here's the plan. The jailer said they'll arraign you tomorrow morning at the courthouse. This Dodd fella says he'll have his lawyer here first thing in the morning to go with you and make sure you get a fair shake. I'll be here if I can, but if I'm not, I'll be back when I've got something—something to get you out of here."

"Yes, sir."

"In the meantime, you keep quiet. Don't talk to the law anymore about any of this. You understand?"

"I understand." Lusk nodded.

Baldridge called for someone to let him and Salina Tyner out. As the jailer made his way back to the cell, Lusk stepped over to Tyner. Her face was stern, her jaw tight as she listened to him.

"Miss Tyner, you got to believe I didn't do nothin' to Miss Pierce. I know you was friends with her, and I'm sorry about what happened." The jailer opened the cell door. "But it wasn't me that hurt her."

Tyner walked out of the cell and down the hall without a word, but Baldridge, stepping outside the cell, lingered momentarily as the jailer secured the door.

"Mr. Baldridge, I got a pretty good idea what you're facing. . . ."

The jailer, walking toward the office, called back to Baldridge. "Are you coming or not?"

"In just a minute," Baldridge said, stepping closer to Lusk. "What are you saying, Jacob?"

"You don't know what it does to me hearin' that whistle blow and not bein' on the boat. The *Paragon*'s just like a woman, Mr. Baldridge. Ain't no two that sound alike. The whistle blew this afternoon about three o'clock, and I knew it was the cap'n callin' to me, sayin' he was still here. Then I heard that long, low moan when he said good-bye tonight. I been runnin' this river all my life, Mr. Baldridge. And me and the cap'n go back a long way. . . ." Lusk stood straight and proud. "And I done pretty good for myself, seein' as I'm the only colored first mate on the river."

"I'd say you did real good, Jacob."

Lusk's face grew stern. "But that won't make a lick of difference if they're convinced I killed that woman. Ain't *no* colored man can kill a white woman and go free, no matter who he is. That's the thing about Cap'n Luke. He looks at me and he don't see no color. He just sees his first mate." Baldridge felt Lusk's eyes searching his own. "And you, Mr. Baldridge. What does you see?"

"A river man, Jacob. A river man."

On their way out of the jail, Baldridge and Tyner ran into Crawford. The name hadn't seemed familiar when Williamson mentioned it earlier, but upon seeing the policeman Baldridge remembered running across him about a year ago. In a moment of extreme inebriation, Baldridge had gotten into a disagreement with a tavern owner on Monroe Street. He had taken his frustration out on one of the proprietor's tables and spent the next two days in jail for it. He recalled seeing Crawford come and go from the building during that time, and though a bad hangover had blurred the memory, he seemed to recall talking with him briefly. Apparently, Crawford's memory was better.

"Well," Crawford said, "looks like you haven't been wrestling any tables lately." He nodded to Tyner. "Evenin'. What brings you two around here?"

"Jacob Lusk," Baldridge replied.

"Oh, our newest guest! You kin to that whore he killed or something?"

"I'm working on Jacob's case for Captain Luke Williamson."

"Case?" Crawford laughed. "What case? That's one guilty nigger sittin' in there."

"I'm not so sure."

"Well, I am." Crawford gave him a condescending glance. "And Williamson hired *you*?"

"That's right."

"It's his money."

Tyner could contain herself no longer. "How come you didn't mention that Miss Pierce's room was torn up when you got to it?"

"What?" Crawford laughed again. "Did Williamson hire you, too?"

"Cassie Pierce's room," she repeated. "Someone was in there before you."

"Now that should be plain enough. Lusk probably tore it up when he killed the woman."

Baldridge thought of showing Crawford the coin, of demanding that he look further into the case, but decided against it. Maybe after he himself found out more. Besides, Crawford would probably expect to hold on to the coin, since it came from Pierce's room.

"What are you doing to locate Dillard Quick—the man Jacob told you he saw with Miss Pierce?" Baldridge asked.

The policeman looked annoyed. "I ain't about to go chasin' after every man that whore slept with. Besides, we got evidence on Lusk. Ain't no need to look nowhere else." He turned to Tyner, obviously trying to change the subject. "Your friend here was higher'n a kite when I saw him about a year ago. Got in some argument about the war as I remember. Tore up a table and a couple chairs." He looked back at Baldridge. "Had something to do with General Forrest, didn't it?"

"I don't remember."

"No, I reckon you don't. But I sure remember you. I'll tell you one thing, Baldridge. You'd have spent a lot longer in jail if it hadn't been for me."

"Just a guardian angel, aren't you?" Tyner said.

"Hey, Confederate soldiers stick together, don't we?" Crawford said, slapping Baldridge on the shoulder. "I was in the Orphan Brigade from the great state of Kentucky, myself. I just saw to it they let a fellow soldier out a little early."

"I suppose I should thank you."

"You can thank me by stayin' out of my business. Let this thing go. You're wasting your time." He turned to Tyner. "And you . . . you ought to be happy we caught that murderin' bastard." He winked at her. "You could be a little more grateful."

"I'd be grateful to know your mama didn't have any more kids," Tyner told him. And she stormed outside.

"You might want to stay away from that whore, Baldridge. Looks like she's trouble."

"I'll be back to see Jacob tomorrow."

"He ain't going nowhere."

5

Wednesday, April 2, 12:15 A.M.

BALDRIDGE AND TYNER began checking the hotels in search of Dillard Quick. The Overton Hotel, their third stop, occupied the northwest corner of Main and Poplar, and though business had been good after the war, the hard times of 1873 were beginning to take their toll. Except for the tiny bell that announced their entry, the lobby was empty and deathly quiet when, shortly after midnight, they stepped in to speak with the desk clerk. From a room adjacent to the registration desk emerged a sleepy little man. He recognized Tyner immediately.

"Salina Tyner? Is that you?"

"Good morning, Thomas."

The clerk came around his desk and took her hand. "Well, don't you look marvelous! I just love that dress. I can't get over what it does for you."

Something about the way the clerk sashayed out to meet her, and something in his voice and the cast of his eye, made Baldridge reasonably certain they *were* just friends. He took a step backward.

"Thomas, I want you to meet a friend of mine, Mr. Masey Baldridge." Thomas extended his hand, which Masey took and shook quickly.

"You know, this is one wonderful lady," Thomas told him. "She's a princess, that's what she is." Baldridge nodded and looked away as Thomas slipped back behind the desk. "Now, did you want a room?"

"No," Baldridge said, "we just need a little information." This guy was beginning to bother him, and he figured the best thing to do was to check for Quick's name on the register and leave.

"Thomas," Tyner began, "we're looking for a man—"

"He might have checked in here yesterday. His name is Dillard Quick. He's from New Orleans."

Thomas began to nod. "Yes, yes, I know Mr. Quick. Well, I don't *know* him–know him, but I did rent him a room. Came in about this time yesterday morning. Anyway, I was surprised. Mr. Quick stays with us on occasion, but he usually gets here at a more reasonable hour."

"When exactly did he check in?" Baldridge asked.

Thomas looked at Tyner, as if wondering whether he should be answering these questions. Tyner nodded. Thomas continued, "Well, it must have been a little after midnight." He pointed toward a small room adjacent to the hotel desk. "I have a cot I sleep on when I'm pulling nights. I remember the bell waking me. Yes, it must have been right around midnight."

"What's the room number?"

"Why are you looking for Mr. Quick?"

"He's an old friend," Baldridge said impatiently. "Just give me the room number."

"He's in 204, but—" Baldridge started for the stairs. "But I don't think he's in." Baldridge stopped on the second step, turned around, and limped back over to the desk.

"It's almost one o'clock in the morning. What do you mean he's not in? Where could he be at this hour?"

"Well, I really wouldn't know," Thomas said, his face reflecting oversensitivity to Baldridge's question.

Tyner leaned across the desk and took the desk clerk's hand. "Thomas, forgive Masey. He's had a long, hard day. And if he's lucky"—she winked—"he'll have a long, hard night. We'll take that room you offered us." Thomas pushed the registration book toward her and turned to get a key.

"I ain't staying here," Baldridge protested. "I just want to find Quick and get out of here."

Tyner looked back at him, the smile she'd mustered for Thomas instantly replaced with a look that could kill. "I'll pay for the damned room," she said under her breath, then turned back to Thomas. Her smile reappeared. "We'd like the room next to Mr. Quick's, if it's available." She began to fill out the guest register. "So, tell me, Thomas. This Mr. Quick. You say he's stayed here before?"

"A couple of times a year. But never more than two days. I don't know what business he's in. He sends us a telegram before he comes, to make sure we've got a place for him, although with business falling off like it has, having room for our guests hasn't been a problem." He leaned in close to Tyner. "There's rumors among some of the hotel employees."

"What kind of rumors?" she asked.

"That maybe the hotel's going under. Everybody's suffering with times like they are. Everybody."

"I want to see that telegram," Baldridge said.

"I beg your pardon?"

"The one Quick sent you about his room. I want to see it. You still have it, don't you?"

"Well, I *might* . . . if you were to ask nicely."

Nicely? Masey thought. *I'll come across that counter and—*

"Masey doesn't mean to be rude," Tyner said. "Do you, Masey?"

"All right," the desk clerk said; after rummaging through some papers in a nearby table, he produced a telegram. Masey took it from him and slipped it inside his jacket pocket, then picked up the room key.

As Baldridge walked across the lobby, Thomas hurried to follow. "The bellman's off tonight, but I could help you with your bags, Mr. Baldridge."

"I can handle it," Baldridge said without looking back. He was about a third of the way up the winding stairs, with Tyner close behind, when Thomas called up to them.

"Funny thing about Mr. Quick."

Both of them stopped.

"What's that?" Tyner asked.

"After checking in so late last night—or early Tuesday morning, I should say—he never went to bed."

"How do you know?" Tyner asked.

"Because I saw him leave again not more than an hour after he arrived. And he didn't come back while I was on duty. The maid told me his bed hadn't been slept in, either." Thomas moved up three or four steps and whispered to Tyner. "She's such a gossip," he said with a smile and a wink.

"I tell you what, Thomas," she said. "When Mr. Quick returns, how about coming up and letting us know?" Thomas nodded. "But don't tell Mr. Quick. We want it to be a surprise."

THE BLOODSTAINS ON the floor of the room bore mute testimony to the Overton Hotel's use as a hospital during the war; as Baldridge sat rocking near the window, he couldn't keep from staring at the dark blotches on the wood near the foot of the bed. He had, no doubt, left such a mark in that farmer's house just north of Selma, Alabama, back in '65. Three days before the war ended, he stopped a Yankee sharpshooter's bullet in his left knee. He remembered hitting the ground, but that was all he remembered until he came to in a feather bed some two miles away. At first he thought he was dreaming—dreaming of being home, of being a boy again and having his mother awaken him. But the image of the surgeon, with his flat, emotionless talk about removing Masey's leg, had quickly brought him to his senses.

"You'll get gangrene," the surgeon warned. "Then there won't be anything we can do for you. The leg must come off." But Baldridge had refused, demanding that they not operate—a demand that might have gone unheeded had not General Nathan Bedford Forrest himself stopped by to check on the wounded. As he gazed out the window over the first-floor awning and into Main Street, Baldridge recalled Forrest's words to the surgeon.

"If he wants to take his chances, you'll damned well let him," the general had said. "Masey's a good soldier. He can stand a lot more than you think."

Taking his silver flask from the windowsill, Baldridge let a drink crawl down his throat. There were times—like tonight—when the pain got so bad that he wished he had let that surgeon cut him. But the whiskey dulled the ache, at least for a while. And though every year it seemed to take a little bit more to tame the pain, Baldridge told himself that was a fair price to pay for remaining whole.

Salina Tyner came in the room with a pitcher of water and poured it into the washbowl. From a drawer she took a washcloth, dampened it, and began cleaning her face. "Why are you staring out the window?" she asked. "You wouldn't recognize Quick if you saw him. I'm not even sure I would. It was dark on deck that night."

"Jacob said he was a skinny man. Dressed well. Wore a derby."

Tyner laughed as she folded the washcloth and placed it neatly on the edge of the bowl. "So you're gonna jump up and go after every skinny man who comes in the door?"

"Well, there hasn't exactly been a parade of people coming into the hotel. The street's dead out there."

"So am I," she said, collapsing across the bed. She rolled onto her stomach and propped her face in her hands. "Why don't we get some sleep. Thomas will let us know when Quick comes in."

"You go ahead. I'm staying up."

"Don't you trust Thomas?" Baldridge raised one eyebrow as he glanced at her. "Oh, Masey. Thomas is all right. He's just a little . . . different."

"He's *different*, all right. But if it's all the same to you, I'll keep watch."

"For skinny men?"

"Maybe."

"All night?"

"If that's what it takes."

"I'll bet Thomas would help you," Tyner said with a wink.

"Why don't you just go to sleep?"

"Nope. If you're stayin' up, I'm stayin' up."

"Suit yourself."

"I usually do."

After an extended yawn, Tyner asked Baldridge why he'd wanted the telegram. He took it from his coat pocket and opened it. After reading it twice, he began to explain to her how every telegram had an origin code—a small series of letters in the upper lefthand corner that told the telegraph operator which station originated the message. He explained how the identification code came into effect during the war, when Confederate cavalry would send false telegraph messages to confuse the Union forces as to their whereabouts. He started telling her about a man he'd heard of named Lightning Ellsworth, who rode with John Hunt Morgan. He'd climb a telegraph pole, tap into the line, and send out lies that had the Yankees running all over the country. His story was interrupted by the sound of Tyner snoring, and for several moments he just watched her. She had a small, straight nose and full, delicious lips, which he recalled tasting once, on board the *Paragon*. But that had been just business. A strange business, he thought, for a woman who looked as good as Sally. Most of the whores he knew were used-up women with a vacant look in their eyes, just going through the motions. Many of them were drunks, pitiful creatures selling themselves to men for liquor money. But Salina was different.

Taking his flask in hand, he swished the contents around and immediately realized there was no way that little bit would last him until daylight. He glanced outside, where the light in a second-story window above the livery across the street brought a smile. He had a pretty good idea where he could get a refill.

Elijah T. Rawls. The old bastard was still up—but then, as Baldridge recalled, the man never seemed to sleep. As hard and loud as Tyner was snoring, Baldridge figured she would be out until daylight, so he tucked his flask into his pocket and slipped quietly out of the room and downstairs to the lobby. He told Thomas where he would be and that he should come and get him rather than wake up Miss Tyner should Quick slip in the back door. Thomas rolled his eyes when he heard Eli Rawls's name.

"You got something against Eli?"

"No, sir."

"Good. I'll be watching out the window of Eli's place."

Elijah T. Rawls, a free Negro since long before the war, was the gate man at Terrell's Livery. For the past thirty years, he had sat on the same stool outside the same door, every day, rain or shine, until he seemed part of the landscape. Most everyone in Memphis knew him, and spoke to him in passing or when quartering a mount. As he crossed the street, Baldridge thought back to the last time he had talked to Rawls. It was during the war, August of '64, and Baldridge was with a company of scouts in advance of General Forrest's raid into Memphis. They had slipped past the Federal pickets and into the heavily fortified city with the intent of capturing Union general Stephen A. Hurlbut. They might have spent hours locating those Federal pickets had it not been for Rawls. The old Negro had made it very plain to the Federals, upon their initial occupation of the city, that he hated Yankees more than any white Southerner ever did. Thus, he took great pleasure in seeing Forrest's men ride into the lobby of the Gayoso Hotel, even though they narrowly missed capturing Hurlbut. Baldridge had occasionally shared a drink with Rawls, and a little over two years ago, during one of those rare instances when he had some extra money, he had bought some of Rawls's homemade wine. But, being horseless, and out of a job most of the time, Baldridge had spent little time this past year around Poplar Street.

Once up to the second floor, Baldridge knocked on the door.

"Who's there?"

In his best whining voice, Baldridge said, "I'm lookin' for General Hurlbut. Somebody done took the general!"

Baldridge heard rustling inside and then the bolt slipping free from the door. The door cracked slightly and a gray-haired Negro peered out.

"Who in the world's out here this time of night?"

"I told you, I'm lookin' for my general."

"Lord above," Rawls said. "Masey Baldridge. Good Lord, man, what you doin' roamin' 'round here in the middle of night?" Rawls opened the door fully.

As Baldridge stepped inside he waved his empty flask. "I seemed to recall you had some mighty fine blackberry wine."

Rawls laughed out loud. "Come on in here, Masey. Lord above, man, I ain't seen you in months." He closed the door. "Man, you had me wonderin' if the Yankees was finally comin' after me."

Baldridge headed straight for the window next to the street and parted the curtains.

"What you lookin' for? You in some kind of trouble, Masey?"

"No, I'm watching for someone."

"Then somebody else's in trouble."

"Maybe."

Rawls took the flask from Baldridge and shook it. "I believe you *is* out." From a cherry cabinet containing a dozen or more different homemade fruit wines, he pulled a bottle of blackberry, placing it on the table along with two glasses.

"You did say blackberry, didn't you? 'Cause I got some fine elderberry and some damson in a real good port."

"Blackberry," Baldridge affirmed.

"How'd you know I was up?"

"Hell, you're always up."

Rawls took a seat and Baldridge adjusted a second chair so he could watch the entrance of the Overton Hotel. Rawls filled his glass. "Where in the world have you been keepin' yourself?" he asked. "And who are you watchin' for? Somebody tryin' to take your woman?"

As he explained why he was watching for Dillard Quick, Baldridge savored Rawls's wine. It went down smooth. He still made the best. Nobody could come close.

"And you're workin' for a Yankee riverboat captain?" Rawls frowned and shook his head.

"It's a job," Baldridge said.

"You must have needed one *real* bad."

"Williamson's all right. A little short-fused sometimes, but . . ."

"At least he keeps moving," Rawls said. "A Northerner that keeps moving on down the river I can tolerate. It's them that stops here and plants roots that I can't stand."

Rawls' gray hair rested like a dusting of snow over his wrinkled ebony forehead. His deep-set eyes were fixed upon Baldridge's.

"Why do you hate Yankees so much?" Baldridge asked. "You've got to admit, most colored don't feel the way you do."

"Most coloreds ain't seen what I seen. Or they don't want to see it." He took a sip of wine. "I been a free man since 1842, when Mr. Walter Rawls give me my papers. I was twenty-four years old when I come into Memphis and found me some work. I worked hard, too. Saved my money. Done right by Mr. Terrell who owns the livery. He done right by me. Give me a place to live."

"So what happened?"

"When the Yankees come into Memphis, they let their soldiers run wild. They robbed us, took our valuables, and they didn't bother to ask if you were a Union man or not. And they sure didn't care what color they took from."

A buggy clopped down Main Street, the only sound disturbing the stillness of the early morning, and though it slowed in front of the hotel, it did not stop. The air coming through the window was cool, though tainted somewhat by the odor of hay and horseshit that drifted up from the livery below.

"What time is it?" Baldridge asked.

"Almost four o'clock. Looks like your man ain't comin'."

"Maybe. Maybe not." While Rawls refilled Baldridge's glass, he sat staring at the old man. "Eli, I expect you see about everybody that comes along here during the day. Think hard on it for me. Dillard Quick is maybe five and a half feet tall. Jacob Lusk says he's scrawny, kind of dark-complex-ioned, and tries to dress real uptown. Probably hauling a trunk around with him."

Rawls shook his head. "I might have seen him, but I see hundreds of people passing by here every day."

"Yes, but who do you remember coming out of the hotel?"

"Masey, a lot of people come in and out of that hotel yesterday. Not as many as usual, I'll grant you that. Business is off. Still, there was lots of folks—"

"Jacob says he wears a little black derby."

"A derby?"

Baldridge thought he saw a sparkle in Eli's eyes.

"Yeah."

"A derby hat?"

"You saw him, didn't you?" Baldridge said.

"Could've been him. Ain't that many folks wear a derby around Memphis." Rawls leaned back in his chair and stared up at the ceiling, rubbing his chin. It crackled as his fingers raked the beard stubble.

Baldridge leaned closer in anticipation, momentarily taking his eyes off the street.

"I don't know, Masey. It might've been the fella you're after, but . . ."

"But what?"

"The fella I saw coming out of the hotel had a trunk all right, and he put it on a wagon and left. But . . ."

"What is it, Eli?"

"The man I saw loaded up and rode off with some boys from William Dodd's ranch."

"Dodd? The Dodd I told you about, from the jail?"

"No, not Dodd himself. His men." Rawls pointed out the window. "You see, Masey, the man I saw—and I ain't sayin' for sure it was this Quick fella, but from what you've said it sure looked like him, derby and all—anyway, this man went off with three of the hands from Dodd's ranch. About two or two-thirty yesterday afternoon."

"How do you know it was Dodd's men?"

"I see almost every horse that comes into town, at least the ones gets put up with Mr. Terrell. I know most folks by their horses. Them boys that come in here yesterday had a paint and a roan pulling a wagon, and I recognized the mounts the other two men were riding. They were all Dodd's horses. Now, I don't know Dodd's men, at least by name, but I'd know their horses in the dark."

"But you think it could've been Dillard Quick that went off with them?"

"I ain't sayin' that for sure, but I *am* saying that Dodd's boys picked up somebody at the Overton Hotel yesterday."

Baldridge turned to watch out the window again. "How well do you know William Jenkins Dodd?"

"Most folks in Memphis has heard of Dodd." Rawls frowned. "Pure carpetbagger. Come down here with the Yankee army and damned if he didn't stay. I remember seeing him around town when he was a captain back during the war. Had something to do with granting paroles to Confederates. Got to be a bigwig in the Freedman's Bureau after the war." Rawls pointed his finger. "He'll run for governor. You watch him."

"Governor? I knew he was a big politician, but—"

"On the Republican ticket."

"You think so?"

"Hell, I *know* so."

Baldridge couldn't resist smiling. When he had a serious point to make, Rawls had a way of looking at you that made you think he was ready to come across the table and cut your throat. "He come by here politickin' with me a few months back. But I stabled his horse and sent him on his way. He didn't know quite what to make of me."

"What do you mean?"

"Well, he come by here with that pretty wife of his and a couple of his men. I guess they come to town to shop. Anyway, I was out front on my stool where I always sit and Dodd started passin' the time of day with me while his men took their horses inside. Oh, he was politickin' heavy." Rawls chuckled. "You should've seen his face when I told him I was a conservative Democrat and that I voted for John Calvin Brown for governor last election." Rawls contorted his face to imitate Dodd. "He says to me, 'Mr. Rawls, it's an *impossibility* for a colored man to be a states' rights Democrat.' "

"I said, 'Impossible, you say?' "

"He said, 'Yes, sir, it is. *Impossible.*' "

"Masey, I looked him square in the eye and I said, 'Well, Mr. Dodd, you'd best send after your preacher.' 'How's that?' he asked me. I said, ' 'Cause you done seen a miracle!' "

He and Baldridge shared a good laugh. Rawls refilled their glasses and his tone grew serious.

"Masey, a man like Dodd is lookin' for niggers. He can control niggers. He can't control me 'cause I ain't no nigger. Ain't never been a nigger."

Baldridge stirred in his seat, and though he glanced occasionally at Rawls, the whole conversation made him uncomfortable.

"You *do* know what a nigger is, don't you, Masey?"

Baldridge just smiled and kept his gaze fixed on the hotel.

"Well, it ain't got nothin' to do with color. A white man can be a nigger." Rawls tapped his finger on the table. "A nigger is anybody that lets another man tell him what to think."

"Is that right?"

"Damned sure enough." Rawls made a sweeping gesture toward the street. "All those boys that just got freed after the war . . . most of 'em are actin' like niggers. They vote the way people like Dodd tell 'em. They listen to the promises of all those scalawags and carpetbaggers. . . . I tell you, it makes me sick to see folks of my color being led around like mules."

During the next few moments, as Baldridge watched the entrance of the hotel, he thought about what Rawls had said. He was one strange man, and though his ideas were different, Rawls was genuine. Baldridge always knew where he stood with Eli, and he had usually known him to be right on most things—which bothered Baldridge, particularly as he thought about what Quick could have been doing with Dodd's men. *If* it was Quick at all. Maybe it wasn't. Maybe it was someone else.

Baldridge leaned his head back against the windowsill. It would be daylight in about an hour and he would return to the room and sit down with Tyner and figure out what to do next. For now he would watch the hotel and talk to Eli. But his eyes grew heavy and the wine had relaxed his body and even assuaged the ever-present dull ache in his leg. He propped the bad leg up in an empty chair on the other side of the table. Rawls was going on about some Kentucky thoroughbred he had cared for last week, but Baldridge gradually drifted away from him. He shook himself to stay awake. He mustn't go to sleep. Quick might return anytime. He had to watch out for Sally, too. He tried to concentrate on Rawls, who was saying something about how he was hoping for a hot, dry summer so the fruit for his wines would have more sugar and less acid . . . but the air was cool, the night was quiet, and it had been a long, hard day; and the low, steady drone of Rawls's rich voice made his eyelids heavy and he slipped further and further away.

6

Wednesday, April 2, nine A.M.

THE ROUSTABOUTS ROLLING flour barrels up the landing stage to the deck of the *W. J. Lewis* stopped in their tracks as Salina Tyner stepped out of the registry shack and strolled across the planks of the wharf boat. In her dark green dress, highlighted with black piping about the shoulders, she seemed to fairly float as she wove her way between the men. Each continued with his barrel after she passed, but not without glancing over his shoulder for another look. The work song, which had suddenly stopped when she appeared, began again with even greater fervor, each man trying to impress her with his voice and movement.

It had been the same with each boat she had visited—three boats in all—for she was the kind of woman who would make a man stop and wish. Right now *she* wished she could find Dillard Quick, particularly after having no luck at the Overton Hotel last night. She shouldn't have fallen asleep, she told herself. Given Masey's affinity for drink, leaving him to watch and listen hadn't been very smart. He had come hobbling up the steps and into the room, liquor-breathed and dull-looking, shortly after seven, and he swore he'd been up the whole time. There had been no sign of Quick. After she washed up, she and Baldridge checked in with Thomas, whose replacement was just arriving. Quick had not returned. It was that simple. And after talking with the daytime desk clerk, they learned that no one had seen Quick at the hotel since two P.M. on Tuesday. The day clerk remembered him departing with his trunk, accompanied by two men. Quick had refused the help of the bellman and insisted instead that his companions carry the trunk. They had loaded it into a wagon out front, and that was the last he had seen of Mr. Quick.

Tyner, figuring Quick had left town, determined to check the wharf boats and the train station, but Baldridge had other ideas. He told her he just had a feeling Quick was still in Memphis—he didn't say why—and he seemed convinced he could turn up a trail; so he set off to see Jacob Lusk and accompany him to the arraignment. They parted, agreeing to meet back at the hotel sometime after noon. Tyner proceeded directly to the wharf.

The passenger clerk working the shack on the *Glencoe*'s wharf boat saw her approaching and came outside to meet her.

"Afternoon, ma'am," he said, tipping his hat. "Would you be looking to book passage on the *Glencoe*? She'll be returning about eleven o'clock Friday morning." Tyner gazed out across the water, a forlorn look coming over her. A tear began to creep down her right cheek.

"Ma'am? Ma'am, are you all right?"

She began to sob softly. "I just can't believe it."

"Believe what, ma'am? What's wrong?"

Tyner wiped her eyes and looked at the clerk. "If it were just me he was leaving, that would be one thing." Her eyes pleaded with him. "But the children . . ."

The clerk pulled up a stool. "Here, ma'am, won't you have a seat?"

Tyner seemed unsteady as she sat. "It's my husband," she said. "I fear he's left us . . . and he's taken all we have."

"Your husband's run off on you?"

"Sir, I'm afraid he has." She wiped her tears and looked up at him. "If only I knew what boat he was on, then I might be able to reach him. The children are crying for him already, and before long . . . Well, it's just all too much to bear. If I only knew where he went, I'm sure I could . . . but it's no use."

"Do you think he took the *Glencoe*?"

She turned away and looked down the wharf. "Perhaps. I don't know. There are so many ships, and I'm only one person. Why, there must be a dozen boats tied up right here. Besides, most of these men won't tell me if he's on their manifest. They say it's 'privileged information.' "

"Well, ma'am, a passenger list is generally regarded as—"

"I understand," Tyner said, pulling herself together. "You have a job to do. I must be strong and accept what is." She arose from the stool, then staggered slightly. The clerk steadied her. "It's just that there are so many boats to check, and I'm—I'm sure no one will help me." Tyner buried her face in her hands. "What will I tell the children?"

"Now, now, ma'am. Won't you just sit back down right here?"

"No, no. I must move along. I must check each and every boat"— she gathered herself and took a deep breath—"or as many as I can, while I last."

"Wait a minute. Just wait a minute." The clerk whistled at a young black boy who had been loitering near the water's edge. "Maybe I can help you. Have a seat right here. What did you say your husband's name was?"

"My husband's name is Dillard Quick."

"Was that Q-U-I-C-K?"

"Yes, sir, that's correct," Tyner said, still wiping the tears.

Stepping inside the shack, the clerk rummaged through some records, then wrote something on a piece of paper; when the young boy arrived, he handed the paper to him, along with a coin, and gave him instructions. The boy dashed out of the shack and headed for the next boat in line along the wharf.

"Ma'am, I'm sorry. Your husband did not take the *Glencoe*. But we have an agreement on the river," the clerk said. "These other clerks along here may not tell *you* who's on a boat, but they'll tell *me*. Now, you just wait here for a little while and we'll see what happens."

"I can't thank you enough."

"It's all right, ma'am. I've got a wife and children of my own."

"They're very lucky," Tyner said, forcing a brave smile.

TOO MANY DIRTY clothes. That's all there was to it. But they would just have to do; there wasn't time to have anything washed. She sprayed some extra perfume on the dress, folded it once, and hung it carefully on the right side of her trunk. It was just after two o'clock and she was starving. Where in the hell was Masey? He said he'd meet her in the room after noon. She walked over and looked out the window. The street below was busy, but the noise of an irate customer shouting at the livery attendant across the street carried as if he were in the room with her.

"Loudmouthed fool," she muttered. What was it about men that made them think they had to get loud to have their say? And the more loud, the more stupid. For several moments she watched the man gesture and stomp around; occasionally she glanced up Main Street for some sign of Baldridge. Surely, he hadn't gone off and gotten drunk.

The knock on the door startled her. "It's open," she called from beside the window. A tired-looking Baldridge stepped inside, tossing his hat onto the bed. "Well, it's about time."

"What?" He appeared to be in too good a humor.

"I said, 'It's about time.' You said you'd be here after noon."

Baldridge walked over and lay across the bed. "It *is* after noon."

"It's in the middle of the afternoon, and I'm starved."

"So why didn't you eat?"

Tyner walked over to the foot of the bed, her hands on her hips. "Because I thought you were going to eat with me. How did you get in here, anyway? I didn't see you come in the front door."

"I didn't. I used the back."

"What is it? They won't let you in the front anymore?"

Baldridge sat up. "No. I just had a bad experience once in a hotel in Natchez." He noticed the half-packed trunk. "Where you going?"

"After Dillard Quick."

Baldridge came to his feet. "You found Quick?"

"Not exactly," she said, placing an extra pair of shoes in the bottom drawer of the trunk. "He's headed back to New Orleans. Left yesterday on the *Atlantic*."

"So why are you—"

"I'm taking the *Susie Silver* for New Orleans at five o'clock." Tyner grabbed a shawl from the bedpost and slung it around her shoulders. "I'm going to eat. You coming?"

In the hotel dining room, Baldridge told her of Jacob's arraignment at the courthouse. Primarily upon the testimony of policeman Crawford, Jacob Lusk had been formally charged with the murder of Cassie Pierce, and a trial date had been set for Thursday, April 10—eight days away. The judge, convinced by Crawford that Lusk was liable to flee and a danger to the community, had denied him bail. In spite of the high-dollar attorney sent by William Jenkins Dodd and his freedmen, nothing Baldridge had hoped to accomplish at the hearing had occurred.

Tyner told the waiter to bring her the blackened catfish, then turned to Baldridge. "So what *did* this lawyer do?"

He didn't answer her, but spoke instead to the waiter. "Just biscuits, please." The waiter departed. "Listen," he began, "either Crawford is just lazy, and he's convinced himself that Jacob did it, or he's hiding something. I asked Crawford again if he'd checked on Dillard Quick, and he said he couldn't find him."

"Maybe he couldn't. I told you, Quick left Memphis yesterday."

"I don't think he even tried." Baldridge leaned toward Tyner and lowered his voice. "I'll tell you something else . . ."

"I smell whiskey."

"Congratulations."

"You've been somewhere drinking while I was waiting on you, haven't you?"

"Just listen to me," Baldridge said, glancing behind himself to see if the waiter was coming. "I think Dodd's involved in this. I can't rightly say how, but—"

"Where did you get that idea?"

Baldridge pulled his chair around the side of the table till he was almost next to Tyner. The whiskey was strong on his breath. "You know that livery stable across the street?"

"Yes." She leaned away from him.

"I stopped by there just before noon."

Tyner's eyes flashed. *"That's* where you've been!"

"I talked to Eli again."

"You mean you got drunk with him again."

"Sally, I ain't drunk. Listen to me." The waiter arrived

and filled Tyner's wineglass. Baldridge covered his glass with his hand.

"Bourbon, please." He waited for the waiter to leave before he continued.

"Bourbon and biscuits," Tyner said with a chuckle. "Now, that's a fine lunch."

"It seems that yesterday afternoon, Quick left the hotel with three men—"

"Who saw him leave?"

"Eli Rawls at the livery."

"And how did he know it was Quick?"

"I described him." Tyner looked doubtful. "Anyway, Eli says that the men took Quick and a trunk he was carrying."

"So?" The waiter brought their food and Baldridge's bourbon. Tyner dismissed him with a smile. "They were probably just taking him to the river to catch the boat. I don't see what difference—"

Baldridge sampled the whiskey, his eyes dancing a little too much for that time of the afternoon. He was already half tight, and Tyner wondered how much more he could stand and still have his tongue work. "Eli says the men work for William Jenkins Dodd." He was looking at her as if that should mean something, as if he'd come to some great truth.

"Now, how does he know that? He was probably half drunk himself."

"Eli knows horses. Sees everybody's horses all the time. When I told him the desk clerk said Quick left about two o'clock yesterday afternoon, he remembered seeing a paint and a roan—Dodd's horses— pulling a wagon up to the hotel. Quick with Dodd's men."

"And he knows Dillard Quick?"

"No, but he described a fella that matched Jacob's description. And he recognized two of Dodd's horses. He's sure about that."

Tyner shook her head as she tasted a piece of the catfish. "So, even if he's right, what's that supposed to mean?"

"What in the world would a man like Dodd have to do with Dillard Quick?"

"Business?" she said after swallowing a bite of peas.

"Maybe." He took another drink. "But what kind of business?"

"Masey, Dodd hired a lawyer for Jacob Lusk."

"I know that."

"You said he's supposed to be some kind of big Republican. All high and mighty with the coloreds. Right?"

"That's right."

"Think about what you're saying. What possible connection could he have with the man who killed Cassie?"

"I don't know. But let's face it—Quick was all we had to go on, to get Jacob free. Now he's gone, and I intend to find out what he's got to do with Dodd."

"Why don't you ask Crawford? He thinks he's got all the answers."

"I did."

"And?"

"You should've seen his face. You'd have thought I told him his breeches were down." Baldridge took a bite of biscuit. "He tried to play it off—"

"Don't talk with your mouth full."

Baldridge ignored this. "But you could tell it bothered him." He washed the bite down with ninety proof. "Wanted to know where I got the idea Quick had anything to do with Dodd."

"What did you tell him?"

"Nothing. I just said I had information that Quick was seen with Dodd's men." Baldridge began to butter another biscuit. "Crawford allowed as how he couldn't very well go and question one of the most prominent businessmen in Memphis just because 'some old nigger thinks he saw something.' "

"Crawford can't do anything," Tyner grumbled.

"Maybe not, but I can. Crawford don't like Dodd, I could tell. And he ain't by himself. Dodd's a carpetbagger, pure and simple. And lot of people around Memphis would love to see him disappear. But Crawford ain't stupid."

"I'm not so sure."

"Dodd's a powerful man. He spent three years with the Freedman's Bureau, and that's what made folks around here so mad. He tried to give away their land to the coloreds after the war. Confiscated damned near two thousand acres and 'redistributed' it."

"And this man thinks he can run for governor?"

"He's a radical. He'd get most of the colored vote, and all the Radical Republicans behind him."

"And your friend Rawls?"

"Eli ain't got no use for him. He says Dodd don't care nothing for men like him and Jacob Lusk. Eli says it's because he thinks for himself." Baldridge finished off the Bourbon. "Anyway, I think Crawford's scared of Dodd—scared about losing his job if he starts really checking into him."

"So what now?"

Baldridge reached for the bottle, but Tyner pulled it away. From the look in his eye, she thought for a second he might come across the table after it.

"If Crawford won't check him out, I will."

Not if you keep drinking like that, she thought. But Baldridge seemed determined, and that was fine with her. Maybe he was right. Either way, she had a boat to catch.

Once they'd eaten, Baldridge escorted Tyner to the wharf and saw to it her trunk was loaded aboard. Before she reached New Orleans, it would be Saturday; she planned to locate Quick, find out what he knew about Cassie's death, and wire Baldridge if she found anything he could use. When Baldridge asked her how she proposed to get Quick talking, she just winked and smiled.

Funny thing about Baldridge, she thought. He didn't fuss over her like other men did, even paying customers. Something in her heart expected him to object to her going off alone in search of Quick, expected him to tell her that a woman had no business doing such things, expected him to demand to go along. She'd heard that kind of thing all her life, and she'd readied herself to respond—to declare that she had been up and down the river for years and didn't need some man to nursemaid after her. But the words she expected never came, and that surprised her somewhat. Not that she wanted to hear them. Not exactly. But Baldridge could have been a little more concerned. A little. He was probably too tipsy to care.

The wharf was shrinking in the distance as the *Susie Silver* headed into the channel; Tyner saw Baldridge wave to her again, and she wondered if he'd be sober when she returned. She waved back. He could have acted worried, at least. She watched until he was out of sight; then, with the breeze picking up, she gathered her shawl about her and started toward her stateroom. It didn't occur to her until she picked up the smell of food being prepared on the deck below: Baldridge had stuck her for lunch, and she'd just paid, like a dummy.

7

Wednesday, April 2, 7:30 P.M.

STANDING ON THE boiler deck, Luke Williamson used his overcoat to shield a piece of pork tenderloin wrapped in bread from the blowing rain. He took a quick bite, then tucked the snack beneath his coat again. The *Paragon* was bucking a headwind that blew rain at the crew hard enough to sting their faces; between the wind and the current, it was slow going to St. Louis. They were passing through a stretch of river known as the Graveyard, between New Madrid and St. Louis. This water had claimed a dozen or more steamboats over the years, and he was taking no chances. An hour ago he had ordered Neely, the night pilot, to sound the whistle signaling for a leadsman to take soundings. A deckhand in a poncho had been working the lead line off the port bow and calling the soundings about every hundred feet; Bart Davis, the acting first mate, watched his every move, nervously pacing the deck. Letting the rope drop till it became slack, the leadsman relied as much on touch as on the uneven light from a rosin torch posted nearby. He felt the piece of flannel woven into the rope pass through his hand at four feet, the piece of leather at six, another piece of cloth at nine, and then, as the rope went slack, he felt a piece of leather split into two thongs. Turning his back to the wind, he cupped his free hand around his mouth and sang out loud and strong.

"Maaaark ta-wain!"

Davis kept watching. Within a couple of minutes, the leadsman had repeated the process.

"And we got quaaaarter less ta-wain!" He sang the phrase's characteristic melody.

"Quaaaarter less ta-wain!" Davis echoed the tune toward the pilothouse. It was always touchy going through the Grave-yard, and Davis was naturally a-twitch, Williamson thought. But on this trip everyone seemed on edge. Luke would have liked to believe it was just the weather—the rain and wind keeping Davis on edge, visibility of no more than a hundred feet making the crew jumpy. All of that keeping Williamson from taking supper at the captain's table in the dining room. But he knew better.

"Got a pile of driftwood workin' past the starboard, Cap'n," Davis called up to him. "Shouldn't be no problem."

Luke caught himself tracking the wood as the *Paragon* passed, and he thought how different it was without Jacob Lusk on board. Davis was a good man, a reliable man; Jacob had trained him well. But, the captain knew, if it had been Jacob warning him about that driftwood, he never would have taken a second look. Still, Davis was trying, and that was all Williamson could ask. With Jacob's arrest, he had been pro-moted from shift leader on days to running the entire crew. Boats the size of the *Paragon* manned two watches, forward and aft, with twenty-five men to a watch, and two separate crews, one for day and one for night. Taking Lusk's place was more responsibility than Davis wanted, and he'd made it clear he was perfectly satisfied running the night crew. But he knew as well as the captain that he was the man to take over for Lusk.

Williamson watched him move among the crew. A tall, well-tanned, muscular man, Davis hailed from southern Illinois and was a lifelong river man like Jacob Lusk. He had been with the *Paragon* three years, signing on after the *Zephyr* went out of business. While he wasn't as bright as Lusk and tended to go a bit easier on the crew, Davis worked just as hard, a fact not lost on the captain. Given the hour, Williamson figured Davis must be wearing down. He was used to the night shift, but not to taking it after having worked all day for two days before. Rain and wind take it out of a man on a night like this; Williamson decided he would personally spell Davis for a few hours and maybe even get some of the younger crew some experience . . . just as soon as they cleared the Graveyard.

Watching Davis and the crew brought to mind a night much like this, only colder—much colder. Just three weeks ago they'd been on the run toward Memphis when an ice storm hit. The freezing rain began about three in the afternoon. The temperature started dropping, and by dark a sheet of ice coated every piece of exposed equipment on the *Paragon*. Williamson had ordered Neely to slow the boat to a crawl; deckhands were slipping and sliding all over the vessel. The captain had already confined the passengers indoors and he was concerned that any minute a crewman might go over.

But as they made their way south that night, a full moon created a frighteningly beautiful scene among the ice-coated trees on the shore. The *Paragon*, save for the hot smokestacks and steadily turning paddle wheel, was coated in a shell of ice; she shone like a crystal palace gliding through a sparkling wonderland. It would have been easy to become mesmerized by the panorama, by the moonlight playing over the ice-cased limbs on the tree-lined bank; it would have been

easy to allow nature to lull first mate and crew into compla-
cency. But Jacob Lusk was not lulled. He had even taken the
precaution that night of tying the leadsman to the deck rail
to keep him from slipping overboard, and he had several men
on sounding duty, switching off every fifteen minutes to keep
the cold water from numbing their hands.

Williamson recalled having just stepped out on the boiler
deck beside Jacob that night, not far from where he now stood,
when an incident occurred that reminded him of his first
mate's value. The leadsman on shift at the moment was a
stout-looking black man named Shaw who had been with the
crew for only two weeks. He was calling the depth readings
up to Jacob, who was passing the word to Neely. Williamson
had been talking to Jacob when suddenly the first mate
squinted and leaned forward over the railing.

"That son of a bitch!" Lusk said, slamming his fist against
the railing. He bolted for the stairs.

"What is it, Jacob?" Williamson called after him.

"Son of a bitch is dry-leadin'!" Lusk rushed down to the
deck with the captain not far behind. But as they approached
the leadsman, Williamson kept back. He knew that Jacob
handled the crew best without his interference. Shaw was
leaning against the hull, nearly curled in a ball to avoid the
cold, and to the casual observer he appeared to be working
the lead line properly. But Lusk grabbed the rope that secured
Shaw to the deck rail and jerked it hard. Shaw flew backward,
hit the icy deck, and slid to a stop near the captain. Nearly falling
himself, Lusk moved toward the startled crewman.

"I seen what you done!" Lusk shouted.

Shaw struggled to get up, but Lusk grabbed the icy rope
and pulled it again, sending the man sprawling on the slick
deck. Lusk grasped him by the throat.

"You was dry-leadin', wasn't you?"

"No, sir," the man gasped.

Lusk squeezed his neck. "Don't lie to me!"

Upon the icy surface, Shaw's efforts to break free of the first mate's grip were futile.

"You was dry-leadin'. I saw you."

"All right! All right!" Shaw managed to utter, still trying to ward off Lusk. "But . . . just once . . . or twice."

The lead weight on the end of the sounding rope told the pilot the river depth. Since the pilot depended upon the leadsman's measure to navigate the channel safely, every call had to be accurate. Sometimes, when the water was extremely cold, a leadsman who didn't want to get his hands wet would feign lowering the rope and retrieving it. He'd simply repeat the last depth call, or make one up. It was a practice that Jacob Lusk never tolerated.

Releasing Shaw's neck, he called to some nearby deckhands, "A couple of you men come here and get ahold of him."

"Wh-what you gonna do?" the frightened Shaw asked.

"I reckon we just don't pay you enough to work on the *Paragon*," Lusk said, as the crewmen took hold of Shaw, "so I figure we'll let you find another boat."

"It was my hands, Mr. Jacob. My hands was freezin'."

"You could've killed everybody on this boat."

"I-I-I didn't mean no harm, Mr. Jacob! I was just cold. You understan' that, don't you?" Shaw's eyes darted wildly around in search of anyone who might sympathize, but he found only angry stares, cold as the night. "See here?" He tried to hold out his hands. "They're mighty near froze."

"Ain't no colder than nobody else's!" a crewman shouted from the starboard side.

"That's right!" others echoed.

The wind was slapping Lusk's poncho and cracking the thin, icy coating around the hood as he spoke to Shaw.

"Every man out here's cold. We're *all* cold. But we do our job. And any man that don't is gone."

"I'm sorry, Mr. Jacob. It—it won't happen next time."

"That's right," Lusk said firmly, looking into the river. " 'Cause there ain't gonna be no next time." He moved to where Luke Williamson stood observing the affair; speaking loud enough for any crewman on the bow to hear him, he addressed the captain: "Cap'n, unless you says otherwise, I'm puttin' him in the river."

Shaw began protesting loudly. "Cap'n, you—you can't let him do that! A man would freeze to death and drown in that water!"

Williamson studied Shaw for several moments. "You risked the lives of the passengers, your fellow crewmen, and *my* ship," he finally said. The crewmen were hanging on his every word.

"I didn't mean nothin' by it, Cap'n. I-I-I was just cold. Like I told you, I was near freezin' my hands off."

Williamson looked at his first mate and nodded, and Lusk led the men holding Shaw down the port side of the *Paragon* toward the stern.

"Cap'n! Cap'n!" Shaw cried out. "No! No! You can't kill a man for this!" The slick deck made moving the struggling hand awkward, but the escort pressed ahead. Meanwhile, the rest of the crew went silently about their duties, though not a one failed to watch the scene unfold. Shaw had been hauled almost halfway down the ship when the captain spoke up.

"Hold up there!" Williamson appeared to deliberate a few moments, then yelled to Neely in the pilothouse. "How far are we from Paw Paw Island?"

"About two miles, sir," Neely replied.

"Very well." Williamson turned and shouted toward the stern: "Mr. Lusk, we'll put him ashore at Paw Paw."

Lusk halted the escort and, standing some fifty feet away, his face illuminated by a rosin torch, put his hands on his hips. He sounded angry.

"Cap'n, I really think we ought—"

"We'll put him ashore, Mr. Lusk. Is that clear?"

"Yes, sir, Cap'n," Lusk grumbled.

In a few minutes the *Paragon* had snugged up to Paw Paw Island. Lusk ordered the landing stage lowered, tossed enough dry cordwood ashore to last through the night, and allowed Shaw barely enough time to step off before retrieving the stage and departing. Williamson was standing at the foot of the twin stairs that led to the second deck when Lusk joined him a few minutes after they were under way.

"It's bad on deck tonight, Cap'n. The men is cold. Cold as an old maid's tit."

"Looks like you're rotating them pretty well."

"Yes, sir. Fifteen minutes out and fifteen minutes by the fire."

Williamson nodded. He offered Lusk some pipe tobacco, but the first mate declined and retrieved a plug from his pocket. Opening his pocket knife one-handed against his thigh, he trimmed a strip and put it in his mouth.

"You sho' had me worried for a second, Cap'n."

"How's that?"

"The way you was takin' yo' time back there. I thought you wasn't never gonna speak up 'bout puttin' Shaw ashore." Lusk shifted his chew to the other cheek. "Why, I thought for a minute you was gonna say toss him."

Williamson grinned. "We had him wondering, didn't we?"

"Had *me* wonderin', too. But the crew sure thinks we was serious." Lusk pointed toward the bow. "Look at 'em."

Williamson nodded. "Everybody's tending to his business real serious-like."

"Always do after we pull that."

"Yeah . . . But next time *I* get to be the one that says throw him in the river."

"You mean I can be the nice guy for once?" Lusk said. "And beg the cap'n to put the man ashore?"

"Sounds fair to me."

They looked at each other, and after a few seconds both laughed heartily. They stood in the freezing rain for several minutes before the captain spoke.

"Jacob, now be honest with me."

"Yes, sir."

"Did you ever do that?"

"Dry-lead? *No, sir!*" Lusk frowned. "Cap'n, you know damned well that's the most dangerous thing a crewman can do, next to messin' with the boiler."

"And in all your years on the river you never ran a dry lead?"

"Never," Lusk said, gazing out over the bow. "Not once." The captain eyed him suspiciously, and Lusk couldn't contain a grin.

"What is it?" Williamson asked.

"Oh, nothin', Cap'n."

"No, it's something. Now what is it?"

"Well, I'll just say this here, Cap'n. While I ain't never run no dry lead, I *have* taken care of the folks I like when I was leadsman."

"What do you mean?"

"Well, Cap'n, first two years I worked for you I was leadsman, remember?"

"I remember well."

"Well, that was back when you was doin' more of the pilotin' . . . you and that Mr. Farns that used to be with us."

"You never cared much for Farns, did you?"

Lusk laughed. "Well, Cap'n, let me just say this. When I was leadsman back then, I always give you mo' water than I did ol' Farns."

The sound of Davis snapping at a half-stepping crewman brought Williamson back to the rainy passage of the Graveyard. The remainder of his pork sandwich was soggy, so he tossed it in the garbage pail near the door. God, he missed Jacob.

8

Thursday, April 3

IT WAS JUST before ten A.M. and Baldridge was quickly
combing his sandy-brown hair. His clothes were wrinkled
and still damp, evidencing every minute of their two days'
wear. Any minute he expected that desk clerk to be knocking
on the door and expecting him to pay for Thursday. Salina
Tyner had covered through last night, and just because she
had gone to New Orleans Baldridge saw no reason to waste a
perfectly good room.

After seeing her off, he ate supper at a restaurant on
Commerce Street and, having spent a few nights in the Memphis jail himself, picked up a meal to take to Jacob. He remained with him almost two hours, going over his story again
and again, looking for some clue that might help his investigation. Later, he stopped by the *Eddy* and asked a couple of
the regulars what they knew about William Jenkins Dodd.
One of them had hired on to build a fence for Dodd about a
year back and said he might have stayed on, but he didn't get
along too well with Dodd's foreman. Another man said he had

traded horses with Dodd right after the war, and that Dodd had done right by him. He thought Dodd seemed like an honest type. This man gave Baldridge directions to Dodd's ranch. After talking and drinking until past two, Baldridge weaved back to the Overton Hotel through a driving rain and, laying his wet clothes over a chair, passed out across the bed.

As he came down the stairs into the lobby that morning, Baldridge could sense the desk clerk staring at him.

"I don't see Miss Tyner this morning," Thomas said, peering toward the top of the stairs.

"Now that's real good, Thomas," Baldridge said, limping over to the desk. "Do you see that good every day?"

Thomas tapped three times on a small sign at the edge of the desk. "Checkout time is twelve sharp, Mr. Baldridge. It clearly says so right here."

"You got any messages for me?"

"No, sir. I don't."

"Well how would you know? You haven't looked in the boxes."

Thomas turned and checked the appropriate box behind the desk. "No, Mr. Baldridge. There are no messages." He wheeled the registration book around toward Baldridge. "Now, will you be staying tonight?"

Baldridge leaned over the desk, his breath forcing Thomas to step back. "I realize that this is going to disappoint the hell out of you, Thomas, my man, but I'm afraid I'll have to be leaving." He dangled the key before him, then let it drop to the desk. Thomas lifted his chin and stood erect, his hands folded in front of him. "But don't you worry, 'cause I'll be checking back with you regularly," Baldridge said with a wink. "You see, any important telegrams for me will most likely come here, and I'd be awfully upset if one did and you didn't hold it for me."

"Very well, Mr. Baldridge."

Tiny spring buds, blown off by the strong wind and heavy rain the night before, carpeted his path as Baldridge made his way to the Crestview Gentlemen's Boardinghouse on Front Street. The sun was out but the wind was chilly, particularly without his heavy coat. He'd been wet and cold for two days and this shit was going to stop right now. Entering the front door, he surprised Mrs. O'Reilly at her sewing table.

"Where's my damned trunk?"

"Now, I done told you, Masey Baldridge," O'Reilly said, pointing a needle at him for emphasis, "when you pay me what you owe me, then we'll talk about—"

Baldridge tossed twelve dollars on the sewing table. "I'm taking my things," he said, walking into the hallway where he'd seen her sons move his trunk.

"This isn't all you owe!" she called after him from the sewing room. "You're short eight dollars."

"It's all you're gettin' for now," he shouted back. Opening a large closet underneath the stairs, he spotted his trunk, dragged it out into the hall, and immediately began to pull some things out and place them in a carpetbag.

"David! Wesley!" Mrs. O'Reilly was shouting from the base of the stairs. "Come quick!" Her sons were huge corn-fed boys; Baldridge had just as soon not run up against them. He strapped his bowie knife on his waist and tucked the Smith & Wesson revolver he'd acquired in Natchez into his belt, as the O'Reilly boys came thundering down the stairs above him. Quickly he closed the carpetbag, leaving a worn-out pair of shoes and a ragged shirt in the trunk, and slipped through the kitchen and out the back door.

"You come back here, Masey Baldridge!" Mrs. O'Reilly shouted, her sons breaking into a full run down the hallway and through the kitchen. Baldridge rounded the corner of the boardinghouse as fast as his bad leg would carry him, but the O'Reilly boys were easily overtaking him. Baldridge stopped short, dropped the carpetbag, and wheeled about. He pulled his blade with his left hand and drew and cocked his revolver in his right. The O'Reilly boys stopped dead, breathing hard and staring wide-eyed.

"You boys don't really want to catch me, now do you?" Baldridge glanced past them to see their mother standing on the front porch. "Tell your boys to back off, Mrs. O'Reilly. I ain't got no quarrel with them."

"You're the devil's own handiwork, Masey Baldridge!" she shouted.

"I don't want to hurt these boys," he called to her. The O'Reilly brothers wasted no time in retreating when, after several agonizing seconds, she finally called them back to the porch. "Now, the way I figure it, my trunk is worth a couple of dollars. And the rest . . . I'll just have to bring the rest to you when I get it."

"Don't you dare set foot back on my property, Masey Baldridge! If you do I'll have the law down here."

He carefully released the hammer on the revolver, returned it and the bowie to his belt, and picked up his carpetbag. "Now that's mighty decent of you to forgive a debt, Mrs. O'Reilly. Mighty decent."

EXCEPT FOR THE Confederate coin, Baldridge had only two or three dollars left out of the money Luke Williamson had advanced him; and though his leg was aching from the long walk back from the boardinghouse, he was determined to talk to a coin dealer and try to see William Dodd before nightfall.

Upon reaching Terrell's Livery, he collapsed onto Eli's stool and began massaging his knee.

"Botherin' you again, huh?" Eli Rawls closed the livery gate behind him.

"I need a horse, Eli."

"Well, let's see. I got a roan in there that's a good ride. She rents for—"

"I'm broke. I need you to loan me a mount."

"Loan you? You want me to *loan* you a horse?"

"Come on, Eli. It's just for a couple of hours."

Rawls shook his head. "Mr. Terrell don't loan no horses, Masey. He'd skin me alive if I was to—"

"I got a lot of places to go today," Baldridge said, still massaging his knee, "and there ain't no way I can walk to 'em."

Rawls eventually gave in and found a horse. He led the animal out of the gate and handed Baldridge the bridle.

Baldridge looked it over. "Good Lord, Eli. That old mare is swaybacked as hell . . ." But from the look on Rawls's face, he figured he better keep quiet. The gate man gave him a used livery ticket just in case somebody should ask to see it, and in return Baldridge slipped him his whiskey flask.

"Don't you be gone no longer than two hours," Rawls warned, checking over his shoulder to make sure the owner hadn't seen him. "I can't cover you no longer than that."

"I appreciate it, Eli."

"Go on and get the hell out of here."

Baldridge mounted, and wheeled the horse about. "Don't you drink all that," he told Rawls. "That's more than two hours' worth of whiskey."

Uncle Melton's Boot Shop, a narrow storefront on the southeast corner of Second Street and Monroe, was one of the better boot stores in the city. Baldridge closed the door behind him and breathed in the smells of leather and pipe tobacco. A rather bulky man sat hunched over a worktable next to the window.

"Be with you in just a minute," he said, his dark bushy eyebrows scrunched up as he punched a series of holes in what was becoming a boot sole. Baldridge waited patiently for several moments until the man looked up. He peered first, almost instinctively, at his customer's boots, then into his face.

"What can I help you with?"

Baldridge walked over and offered his hand. "I'm Masey Baldridge."

The man quickly wiped his hand on a rag in his lap, then stood up awkwardly, his large belly barely clearing the worktable. He shook Baldridge's hand vigorously.

"Name's Dave Melton." He glanced again at Baldridge's feet. "Looking to replace those old boots, are you?" He moved away from his workbench and retrieved an adjustable foot mold from a nearby table. "Probably about a nine and a half, I'd guess. Have a seat there, Mr. Baldridge, and let me measure you."

"I'm not here about boots."

Melton, surprised, stopped short of squatting down, in a position Baldridge wasn't entirely sure he'd be able to rise from. "Oh. Well, uh . . . all right."

"I'm here about coins."

Melton's eyes lit up. "Coins!" He tossed the foot mold back on the table. "Well, why didn't you say so? I'm always ready to talk coins." He walked over to a counter on the other side of the room. "Boots may be my business, but coins . . . coins are my love. My wife says they're my mistress. But I say they're better than a woman. You can take 'em out when you want to and you can put 'em up when you're tired of 'em." He laughed at his own joke. "Can't do that with a woman, can you, Mr. Baldridge?"

Baldridge smiled. "Depends on how much you pay for her."

Melton's belly shook when he laughed; his face was aglow, like that of a child anticipating a new toy. "Got something you want to trade?"

Baldridge stepped up to the counter, from behind which Melton had retrieved a glass case full of coins. "Not exactly. I hear tell you know more about coins than anybody in Memphis. A friend of mine said you know about every coin ever minted in the United States. Is that true?"

"Well, I don't know about *every* coin, but I know more than most traders." His anxious eyes followed Baldridge's hand into his pocket. "What you got?"

Baldridge handed him the coin recovered from Pierce's room and watched as Melton used a magnifying glass to study it, all the while taking loud fat-man breaths through his mouth. In a few seconds, he raised his head slowly from the magnifying glass, his expression one of bewilderment.

"Where did you get this?"

"From a friend. Recently deceased. What can you tell me about it?"

Melton's eyes returned to the coin and again he peered through the magnifying glass. He was breathing faster now as he turned the coin from side to side.

"Well, sir, either somebody's playing a bad joke on you, or . . ."

"Or what?"

"I've heard tell of such a coin as this, but I've never seen one. Don't know anybody that has." He rubbed it gently between his fingers.

"What's it worth?" Baldridge asked.

"Huh!" Melton exclaimed. "That would be hard to say. If it's one of a kind, that is, if it's a proof . . ."

"I never saw a coin like this the whole time I was in the army."

"Confederate, I'll bet."

"Seventh Tennessee Cavalry."

Melton nodded with approval. "Confederacy didn't make a coin like this . . . at least not officially. Mr. Baldridge, the

South only struck two coins in any quantity during the war. About thirteen thousand twenty-dollar gold pieces that looked just like the U.S. coin—made from the U.S. dies—and about two million half-dollars. But the thing is, all those were identical to the U.S. coins."

"How's that?"

"When the Confederacy took over the U.S. mint in New Orleans at the beginning of the war, they struck the coins I mentioned from regular U.S. dies. They were struck by the Confederate government, but they just looked like regular United States money."

"But this is a *Confederate* coin."

"Damned sure is," Melton agreed. "Problem is, there isn't supposed to be no Confederate twenty-dollar gold piece."

"So where did it come from?"

Melton pulled a tiny bottle from beneath the counter. "Mind if I check something? It won't hurt the coin none, I promise you."

"All right."

From the bottle, Melton drew a small amount of a clear solution into a piece of glass tubing and, observing carefully through the magnifying glass, he deposited a tiny bead of the solution on the edge of the coin. After a few moments, he looked up at Baldridge. "Well, sir, that's the real thing, all right. It's real gold. If I had to guess, I'd say .900 fine gold, same as in the U.S. twenty-dollar gold piece." He held it up to the window's light again, then put it on a scale near the edge of the counter. "Same weight, too. This coin would probably be nine-tenths of an ounce of pure, twenty-four-karat gold, alloyed with a tiny bit of copper if it's the same as the U.S. coin." The rotund man lay the coin on the counter and stepped back, scratching his head. "I guess Ol' Man Truett was right."

"Who's he?"

"Oh, he was a coin collector, used to live in Little Rock. I corresponded with him for years. He died about two years ago. I bought a bunch of his coins from his widow. He used to claim the Confederacy minted such a coin, but nobody believed him. Me least of all. I'm a hard man to convince, Mr. Baldridge. I take my coining serious-like."

"This Truett," Baldridge asked, "he knew a lot about Confederate money?"

Melton nodded. "Taught me everything I know about it. But still, I never believed him on the twenty-dollar gold piece 'cause he could never produce one to prove it. I teased him about it, yet he swore up and down—"

"So the coin is real?"

"Yes, as far as I can tell. Look right here." Holding the magnifying glass over the coin, Melton began to explain its markings. Baldridge was amused at the agility of his short, pudgy fingers. "See this here? That would be the Goddess of Liberty seated. She's holding a staff that supports the Liberty cap. Her left arm's resting on a shield." He rotated the coin slightly. "And that looks like the Constitution she's got her left hand on." Melton went on to point out the flag of the Confederacy, surrounded by figures of sugarcane, cotton, a sugar hogshead, and a bale of tobacco. The back of the coin revealed an endless chain of fifteen links, eleven of which contained the name of a Confederate state.

"These stars," Melton said, pointing out the tiny details, "may have something to do with the border states, like Missouri or Kentucky. I can't say for sure." Melton was enjoying his speculation about the coin's design, but Baldridge needed more.

"Where do you reckon this coin came from, Mr. Melton?"

"That's hard to say. Ol' Truett thought such coins were minted in New Orleans. He wrote Dr. B. F. Taylor several times over the years—Taylor was the chief coiner at the New

Orleans mint before the war—asking him about Confederate coins. Taylor answered a couple of his letters, but he never said anything about a coin like this. But then Truett never heard from him again." Melton laid the piece of gold on the table, but couldn't seem to leave it be and picked it up again. "As to whether or not there are others, or where you'd find them—there *was* a rumor."

"A rumor about what?"

"Well, I can't say there's any truth to it, but ol' Truett sure as hell believed it."

"Believed what?" Baldridge asked, becoming increasingly impatient with Melton.

"Truett heard a rumor that several thousand high-denomination coins—and he never said what denomination—were held in the Confederate treasury in Richmond and were never circulated. I always teased Truett about that, saying how it was easy to claim you knew about coins you never had to produce. I always figured he was just trying to show he knew more than I did. But he swore up and down—"

Baldridge was confused. "Any such coins would have been found when the Federals confiscated the Confederate treasury after the war, wouldn't they?"

Melton laughed out loud. "Mr. Baldridge, I don't know what you were doing when the war ended, but—"

"I was in a hospital," Baldridge said solemnly, "for six damned months."

"Oh." Melton looked down at Baldridge's leg. "I didn't mean no insult by that. I was just trying to say that those were confusing days. Real confusing. Why, the contents of the Confederate treasury never *have* been completely accounted for. Believe me, I know. Tried to get my hands on some of the Mexican silver Jeff Davis hauled out of Richmond when him and the cabinet ran south."

"Mexican silver?"

Melton waved his hand. "That's a whole 'nother story. Mr. Baldridge, the U.S. government never did come up with all the money that ol' Jeff Davis and his cabinet took out of Richmond."

"But Davis was imprisoned."

"Yeah, they caught him, all right, but over a quarter of a million dollars in gold and silver coins never has been accounted for. Even figuring some of the Federal officers made off with part of the money, and maybe even some of our boys, that still leaves a lot floating around out there."

"Are you saying this coin was part of that?"

"I don't know, sir. Personally, I doubt it. But Truett sure thought so. Then again, I didn't believe ol' Truett was right about the coin, and right here it is."

"So this coin is worth a lot of money? And if there's a lot more of them—"

"Not *face* value. Face value it ain't worth a dime. It's Confederate. To a collector, if it's one of a kind, it'd be worth a lot. But if there's a thousand of them somewhere, then the value is mainly in the gold content. Remember, I told you, it's probably nine-tenths of an ounce of fine gold, so it would be worth whatever gold is getting on a given day." Melton raised one finger. "Unless the government caught you."

"What do you mean?"

"Confederate specie—coin—is contraband, Mr. Baldridge, and all Confederate gold or silver is supposed to be the property of the United States government. That's why I'd have a hard time dealing in such coins even if I could find them. If the government found out about—"

"But if the coins were smelted into gold bars, nobody would know."

Melton frowned and stepped back from the counter. "Don't even say that! Why, melting down a beautiful coin like that would be a crime! In more ways than one. It hurts just to think about it." He looked intently at Baldridge. "I'll tell you what I'd do if I was you, Mr. Baldridge."

"What's that?"

"Well, if I wanted to know whether this actually came from the Confederate treasury, I'd ask the one man who would know."

"The treasurer of the Confederacy?"

"No. He's dead."

"Who?"

"The man I'm talking about lives right here in Memphis." Baldridge looked puzzled. "Jefferson Davis. If anybody would know what the Confederate treasury contained, it'd be the former president. I tried to see him once myself, right after he came back from Europe. I wanted to ask him about that Mexican silver. But I never could get to see him. That was over a year ago. Who knows? He might talk to you."

From Uncle Melton's, Baldridge rode to the Mid-South Insurance Company to see Ferguson. As president of Mid-South, Ferguson had some business dealings with Davis, who had come to Memphis over a year earlier to take the presidency of the Carolina Life Insurance Company. He was also a personal friend of the former president. Once Baldridge had prevailed upon Ferguson to try to get Baldridge an appointment for the next day, he proceeded to the telegraph office. There he used his next-to-last dollar to wire Luke Williamson in St. Louis. It was almost one o'clock; the smell of lunch being prepared in a room above the telegraph office made his stomach growl. He had eaten no breakfast, and by the time the agent sent his message and received the confirmation, Baldridge was starving.

"Smells mighty good," he remarked, casually gesturing toward the ceiling. The clerk looked up at him, nodded, and returned to his work. "That wouldn't be turnip greens somebody's cookin' up there, would it?"

"Yes, I believe it is," the clerk said, still attentive to his paperwork.

"I do love a good bowl of turnip greens," Baldridge said. "With some pan-fried cornbread." He paused to let his words sink in. "You can't hardly beat that." He waited a few more seconds. "Ain't hardly no use even eatin' greens without cornbread. Don't you think?"

The clerk ceased writing and looked up at him. "Will there be anything else, sir?"

"No, I reckon not."

Leaving the building, Baldridge felt the dollar in the bottom of his pocket. He should have passed on those drinks last night. What kind of fool doesn't save enough money to eat on? Reaching for his flask to quiet his empty stomach, he remembered leaving it with Rawls. "The least that fella could've done was offer me a bowl of them greens," he mumbled to himself as he mounted.

9

Thursday, April 3, three P.M.

"DAVIS, GET THAT man off his ass," Williamson shouted from the door of the pilothouse. The *Paragon* had been at the St. Louis wharf for almost an hour, and barely a third of the cargo had been loaded ashore. "Steven!" he shouted below. "Steven!"

Steven Tibedeau came trotting up the stairs toward the texas. "You call me, Captain?"

Williamson pointed at the landing stage. "Go down there and help Davis."

"Help him do what, Captain?"

"Help him get the cargo unloaded, what do you think?"

Tibedeau glanced toward the bow then looked back at Williamson. "Captain, Davis don't like it when—"

"I don't give a damn what Davis likes." Williamson pulled his watch from his vest pocket and held it up to Tibedeau. "It's taken him over an hour just to secure the cotton in the foredeck. Jacob would have finished and been taking on the next load by now."

"Captain, Davis ain't Jacob."

Williamson slowly returned his watch to his pocket. "Has anybody checked with Anabel about the food? Jacob always sends some crewman with one of her cooks to pick up what they need for the return to New Orleans."

"I—I don't think Davis has got to it yet," Tibedeau said.

"Hasn't got to it yet? That should be going on while he's supervising the loading."

"I'm sure he'll take care of it just as soon as he gets the deck— "

"That's too late. Hell, it's liable to be dark before they're through loading. Anabel shouldn't have to work in the dark, and God knows she doesn't want to wait until tomorrow morning." Williamson thought for several moments. "All right. Forget the cargo. Let Davis do that. You go see Anabel and find out what she needs. Then see to it she and her cooks get enough help to get it on board."

"What about the cargo?"

"I'll talk to Davis."

"Captain, Davis is a good man. He doesn't mean to be—"

Williamson nodded. "I know, I know."

Tibedeau looked worried. "Captain, what's gonna happen to Jacob? I mean, we're gonna get him back, aren't we?"

"He better be out of jail when we get back to Memphis," Williamson said. "I hired Masey Baldridge to see to it he was freed."

Tibedeau nodded. "I believe Mr. Baldridge will do right by us. He'll get this straightened out."

There was a brief silence. Williamson wished it were that simple. But he kept seeing that look of satisfaction on Crawford's face as he led Jacob away. And Jacob looked as if he'd been betrayed. But what else could Williamson have done? If he had interfered they would have jailed him too. Then who would have seen to Jacob? No, he'd done the right thing—the only thing he could. Hiring Baldridge and continuing with the run made sense, and yet . . . Sure, Baldridge had come through at Natchez. He'd saved his boat and the lives of his passengers, even when Luke had doubts. But the ex-Reb's fondness for spirits worried him. Would he really go after Pierce's killer, or just take the money and get drunk? Maybe having Salina Tyner there would help. Maybe not. Either way, the captain figured he had to trust Baldridge. He had no choice.

Tibedeau said something the captain didn't hear.

"I beg your pardon?"

"Captain, I asked you if you were still going ashore. I got you that horse you wanted."

"Yes, I am. I'm going to the telegraph office. Maybe there's some word from Baldridge."

Tibedeau pointed to a small shack some two hundred feet from the river, along the cobblestone wharf. "See where those rousters are rolling those barrels?" Williamson nodded. "I rented you a sorrel over there. Told the fella you'd need it for two or three hours, just like you said."

"Thanks, Steven." A nervous little man who never seemed to sit still, Tibedeau was, next to Jacob Lusk, the most important crew member on the *Paragon*. He kept the passengers happy and insulated the captain from all but the most important matters. Williamson gripped Tibedeau's arm and squeezed. "You're in charge while I'm ashore."

"Yes, sir." As Williamson descended the stairs, Tibedeau called to him, "Anything special you want me to tell Anabel to make for supper?"

"Anything but chicken," Williamson called back.

As he rode for the telegraph office, Williamson couldn't keep from thinking about Jacob sitting in that jail in Memphis. He'd dealt with local lawmen like Crawford before—two-bit yokels out to make a name for themselves. There was the time one had tried to charge him a landing fee at New Madrid. The man had waited until the *Paragon* docked and was taking on cargo before he presented himself as if he were P. T. Barnum, surrounded by his so-called deputies. Most of them looked like hired drifters—filthy, hard-looking men the very sight of whom had unsettled the passengers. Jacob had been busy with a busted flour barrel near the stern, while the sheriff and his men surprised Steven Tibedeau with their demands. Before Williamson confronted them, they had succeeded in terrorizing Tibedeau, brandishing weapons and threatening to hold the boat in New Madrid until they were paid. One of the deckhands brought word to Williamson, who, removing his Henry rifle from the pilothouse, met the sheriff halfway across the landing stage. After exchanging some heated words, during which Williamson told him what he could do with his landing fee, the sheriff reached for his revolver. Before he could clear his holster, the captain had caught him in the nuts with the butt of his rifle, sending him headlong into the river. Two or three of the men backing the sheriff drew their guns, and probably would have shot Williamson had not a shotgun just then discharged from the deck of the *Paragon*. Its pellets sprinkled the water in front of the sheriff's men.

"I got another barrel if any of you men needs me to show you!" Jacob Lusk shouted. "And this time I'll aim a mite higher." To back him up, Jacob had produced several more deck hands armed and ready. Hastily, the sheriff's men reconsidered their loyalty and disbanded, leaving the sheriff to wade unassisted back to the shore, cussing and threatening all the way. Williamson related the incident to other riverboat captains, and it took only three weeks of having no boats stop in New Madrid before the local people decided they needed a new sheriff and could live without a landing fee. The captain wasn't sure how long he could live without Jacob.

APRIL 3, 1873
MEMPHIS, TENNESSEE
CAPTAIN LUTHER WILLIAMSON
COIN IS THE REAL THING STOP HOW
MANY MADE NOT CERTAIN STOP
LOCATION OF OTHERS UNKNOWN STOP
OWNER UNKNOWN STOP WILL SEE
PRESIDENT JEFFERSON DAVIS TOMORROW
STOP TYNER GONE TO NEW ORLEANS FOR
INFORMATION STOP JACOB LUSK WELL
AND SENDS HIS BEST STOP
MASEY BALDRIDGE

"Jeff Davis?" Williamson read the telegram a second time. "Why in the hell is he seeing Jeff Davis?" he said aloud.

"I beg your pardon, Captain?" the telegraph agent said.

"What? Oh, nothing. Nothing." Williamson tossed the man a tip and stepped out on the wooden sidewalk. Maybe Baldridge thought Davis could help free Jacob. He would certainly be a man of influence, Williamson thought. But why was Salina Tyner going to New Orleans? William had specifically asked her to keep an eye on Baldridge. How could she take off like that? She had seemed so determined to find her friend's killer. After reading the message a third time, Williamson did not like the sound of it. Too many "not certain"s and "unknown"s. He had expected—somewhat foolishly, he admitted to himself—that Jacob might already be free. That Baldridge could have uncovered something to clear him, or get him out on bail at least. As it was, he wasn't sure *what* Baldridge was doing, and Salina had left town altogether. Williamson folded the message and put it away. It was time to get some help. Some real help. Somebody he didn't have to keep an eye on and wonder about.

"HAVE HIM STEP inside," the well-dressed gentleman told his clerk. Captain Williamson, hat in hand, stood nearby. The gentleman shook Williamson's hand as he entered the office on the second floor of the courthouse. "I'm Rolf Pittman. What can I do for you?"

"I understand you're the U.S. marshal around here."

"I'm one of them," he said. "Have a seat, Captain, uh—"

"Luke Williamson. I'm captain of the *Paragon*."

Pittman nodded and took his place behind the desk. "Oh, yes. I read about you in the papers. That was some run you made to New Orleans last fall."

"Thank you. I'm here about one of my crewmen."

"You got trouble down at the wharf?"

"Not exactly. At least, not at this wharf." Pittman looked confused. "Marshal, my first mate, Mr. Jacob Lusk, is in jail in Memphis for murder. A murder he didn't commit."

"Is that right?"

"I've come to ask you to help me get him out."

"Well, why don't you talk to the law in Memphis?"

"They're the problem. A policeman named Crawford made the arrest, and he's convinced Jacob killed a woman on my boat."

"Captain, if a Memphis policeman has grounds to arrest your man, it's none of my affair."

"But he doesn't. He has no real evidence." Williamson explained the details of Jacob's arrest to Pittman, who sat listening patiently. Then the marshal stood and walked over to a wall map.

"So what do you want from me?"

"I want you to come to Memphis with me. We leave tomorrow afternoon at two o'clock."

"Now, Captain Williamson—"

"You'd come as my guest. No cost to you or the government."

"Captain, even if you're right—even if your man's innocent—I've got no jurisdiction over a murder in Memphis, Tennessee." He pointed at the map, his finger tapping the spot marked "Memphis." "What you're describing is strictly a local crime. The U.S. government's got no stake in the murder of a woman at the Memphis wharf."

"But, Marshal—"

Pittman shook his head. "Things are touchy right now in the South, Captain. You should know that, since you travel through all the time. Military governors have just recently been replaced in a lot of Southern towns, and those people aren't likely to take too kindly to a U.S. marshal showing up over the murder of a whore. That's certainly not a federal crime, and even if I had jurisdiction—which I don't—"

"Maybe you do," Williamson said. He described the Confederate coin and showed Pittman Baldridge's telegram.

Pittman listened intently and then carefully studied the message. "This is certainly interesting, but I'm afraid I still don't see how it involves me."

"Passing Confederate money is a federal offense, isn't it?"

"Well, yes—"

"Masey Baldridge believes that twenty-dollar gold piece is real. There could be more of them. Thousands more." Williamson got up and walked over to Pittman. "Baldridge believes that the man who killed Miss Pierce was looking for that coin. And if there are other such coins, I'd say there's a good chance that whoever killed Cassie Pierce knows where the rest are."

"Nobody could circulate such coins," Pittman said. "They'd be spotted immediately."

"But if they did—if they could somehow pass them off—that would amount to counterfeiting, wouldn't it? And that's in your jurisdiction, right?"

Pittman shook his head. "Technically, yes. But I don't

know, Captain. You've only got one of these coins. I mean, you don't even know for sure that others exist."

"No, I don't. But what if they do? What if somebody is down in Memphis trafficking in Confederate gold? And killing people to do it?"

Pittman handed the telegram back, a spark of interest in his eyes. "You may have stumbled upon something, Captain."

"I didn't stumble on anything. Cassie Pierce did, and she paid for it with her life. I just don't want to see my first mate lose his, too."

Pittman turned to study the map again; after almost a full minute of silence, Williamson had just about concluded he was getting nowhere. Then Pittman turned around and addressed him in a slow, cautious tone. "Captain Williamson, you've got a reputation in St. Louis as a straight talker. No bullshit. If most anyone else had come in here with such a story, I would have sent them home. Let me see that message again." Williamson waited patiently as the marshal studied it. "You say you've seen one of these coins yourself?"

"Saw it with my own two eyes."

"And when do you leave for Memphis?"

"Two o'clock tomorrow."

"Well, I suppose I could do with a few days out of St. Louis, but I'll tell you right now, Captain, I wouldn't be going to look into this murder. It'd be strictly to find out about the coin. I can't interfere with the Memphis police." Williamson broke into a smile. "And just three days. No more. I can't justify being out of the St. Louis office longer than that."

Williamson shook his hand. "I'll have a stateroom ready for you." He took the telegram back from the marshal and started out the door. Pittman stopped him. "This man Masey Baldridge—experienced investigator, is he?"

Williamson turned and smiled as he slipped on his hat. "Better wait until you get to the boat. I'll tell you all about him."

10

Thursday, April 3, three P.M.

T H E H O M E O F William Jenkins Dodd lay about two and a half miles south of Market Square and some two miles inland from the river. Baldridge noticed first the long, straight, white fencing that separated Dodd's land from that around him. It was well maintained, far superior to any around it, and Baldridge figured it must have cost thousands. And tucked away inside the neat, squared-off pastures stood a dwelling that Baldridge thought out of place amid the modest houses in the area. Framed on both sides by large hickory trees, it was an imposing, three-story brick affair, with long, narrow, arched windows and detailed woodwork about the eaves. Dominating the fields around it, drawing all attention to itself, it reminded Baldridge of the European castles he had read about as a child.

As he approached the house he could see three men watching him from a large white barn some seventy-five yards away. One of them mounted and rode toward him. To the left of the steps and below the front porch, a woman knelt amid freshly turned soil. She glanced over her shoulder as Baldridge reined up, her gloved hands covered with dirt.

"Good afternoon, ma'am," Baldridge said, removing his hat.

"Good afternoon," she replied, wiping her brow with the clean edge of her glove.

"Would I be at the house of Mr. William Dodd?"

"Yes, you would. I'm Mrs. Dodd. Are you here about a horse?"

Baldridge saw that the rider from the barn was closing on them. "Not exactly, Mrs. Dodd."

"A railroad matter?"

"No, ma'am, but I do need to speak with your husband privately, if you don't mind."

She looked toward the barn. "Well, William is over—"

"Anything wrong here, Mrs. Dodd?" the rider called out as he stopped near them. He kept his gaze fixed on Baldridge.

"No, Grady. Nothing's wrong." She gestured with a garden spade. "This gentleman—"

"Masey Baldridge, ma'am."

"Mr. Baldridge needs to see William."

"What about?" Grady said. Baldridge noticed that Mrs. Dodd seemed a bit annoyed.

"Well, Grady, that would be between Mr. Baldridge and my husband, now wouldn't it?" The man eyed Baldridge hard.

"That's a mighty fine-looking rifle," Baldridge said, admiring the new Winchester Grady carried in a sleeve on his saddle. "I'd hate to be on the receiving end of that." He smiled. "Have much occasion to use it?"

Grady was silent, but Mrs. Dodd spoke from the porch. "We have a problem with foxes, and an occasional wolf spooking the horses at night. Grady takes care of anything that threatens the farm—don't you, Grady?"

"I'll get Mr. Dodd." Grady returned to the barn.

"Cilla! Oh, Cilla!" Mrs. Dodd called, removing her

gloves. From around the corner of the house, a Negro woman appeared. "Would you take this and I'll be back to finish in a bit." She turned to Baldridge. "Won't you come up and have a seat on the porch, Mr. Baldridge? It'll take William a few minutes to get here. It always does."

"I'm sorry to interrupt your work," he said as he dismounted. Cilla laid the gloves and spade aside and took charge of his horse.

"Oh, that's all right. I was just getting a start on a flower garden. Flowers just add so much to a house, don't you think, Mr. Baldridge?" He nodded and took a seat in a rocking chair. Mrs. Dodd offered him a drink, which he had already accepted before she informed him she only had water or tea. "My husband is a temperance man, Mr. Baldridge. We don't have spirits in our home."

Mrs. Dodd disappeared momentarily to freshen up and a house servant appeared with a glass of water. Baldridge drank half of it, but something was definitely missing.

Mrs. Dodd returned from inside. "As I said, there's no telling how long William will be. He has so much to manage." The servant brought a cup of tea, and Mrs. Dodd took the chair next to Baldridge. "I suppose I should be more involved, but frankly, I'm just not much interested in business. And William prefers it that way. I leave most of the details to him. Do you think I'm terrible to be that way?"

"No, ma'am."

She took a sip of tea. "Now what did you say you wanted to see William about?"

Baldridge placed his half-empty water glass on the porch railing. His stomach began growling again, so he stood and walked over to the porch steps a few feet away. "Mrs. Dodd, I'm investigating a murder."

"A murder? Oh, my goodness," she said, her hand going to her mouth. "Around here?"

"No, ma'am. In Memphis. About two days ago."

"Oh, yes, I believe I do recall William saying something—something about a Negro deckhand."

"First mate. Aboard the *Paragon*."

"Of course. Isn't William helping with the defense or something?"

"Something."

"William does so much for the freedmen. They owe him a debt, I tell you. A real debt."

Baldridge figured Dodd planned to collect on that debt in the '74 election.

"I just wanted to ask your husband if he knows a man named Dillard Quick."

"My husband knows a great many people, through his horse business and the railroad he's trying to build, Mr. Baldridge, though I am personally acquainted with very few of them. Did you know William is planning to hire over two hundred Negroes to build his railroad? Two hundred! As soon as the bond issue is complete, that is. That should offer the poor souls some hope, what with times being as hard as they are."

William Jenkins Dodd came riding up, accompanied by the ranch hand Grady. Dodd quickly dismounted, his companion remaining on horseback.

"William, this is Mr. Baldridge," said Mrs. Dodd.

"We've met," Dodd said, shaking Baldridge's hand.

"He's not here on business. It's about that rather unfortunate matter in Memphis."

"So, how did the arraignment go?" Dodd asked, then called over to the Negro woman. "Cilla, would you bring me a drink of water, please? Do you need more, Mr. Baldridge?"

"No, I'm just fine." Baldridge studied Dodd for a moment before answering his question about the arraignment. The man's face was strictly business, and it looked as if some time had passed since a smile had crossed it. He had a thin nose, small ears, and thick red sideburns that extended below his hat.

"I figured you'd heard."

"No, I confess I've been rather tied up the last couple of days." He took a cup of water from Cilla and thanked her.

"The trial is set for Thursday of next week."

"I see." Dodd nodded slowly as he drank. "Terrible situation. But I'm sure my man Quillen will represent Mr. Lusk as well as possible."

"It was kind of you to make your attorney available."

Mrs. Dodd smiled and took his arm. "William is a generous man."

"Mr. Baldridge, I've spent the years since the war trying to make things better for the Negro. When I heard about the incident at the wharf, it only seemed reasonable—"

"Mr. Dodd, do you know a man named Dillard Quick?"

"Never heard of him," Dodd said, though he was clearly surprised by the question.

"You have no business dealings with him?"

Dodd gazed off into the distance. "Quick," he repeated. "Not that I immediately recall. Of course, I come across a lot of people, Mr. Baldridge. Why, in raising the bond issue alone I'm sure I've met hundreds of people."

"This man arrived in Memphis on Tuesday aboard the *Paragon*. He was on the boat when Miss Pierce was killed."

"Pierce? That would be the woman of no virtue."

"That's right. Quick was the man last seen with her. I know he checked into the Overton Hotel the night she was killed."

"And you suspect this Quick had something to do with her death?"

"Yes, I do."

"You'll pardon me if I don't follow you, sir, but even if he did, what does that have to do with me? It sounds like a matter for the police."

"I have information that Dillard Quick was seen the next day in the company of some of your men."

"*My* men?"

"Yes, sir."

"That's absurd."

"They picked him up at the hotel Wednesday afternoon—"

"Impossible," Dodd said, his expression never altering. "Grady, did we have anyone in Memphis on Wednesday?"

"No, sir. Ain't been nobody in town since Saturday," he said.

"And you, sir?" Baldridge said.

"Me?"

"Yes, sir."

"I was in town on Sunday."

Mrs. Dodd interrupted. "My husband and I attend the Grove Methodist Church in town. Sunday night we were at a temperance meeting there. Besides, William would have nothing to do with the likes of the people you're describing. William is a virtuous man." She stepped over and took his hand, looking up at him admiringly. "You may just be talking to the next governor of the great state of Tennessee."

Baldridge managed a smile. "I heard you may be running."

"Well"—Dodd's laugh seemed forced—"it's still a bit early. There's so much to do with the ranch and getting the railroad started." A few moments of awkward silence passed. "Is there anything else I can do for you, Mr. Baldridge? I'm rather busy."

"And you're sure you've never heard of Dillard Quick?"

"Mr. Dodd's done answered you once, mister."

Baldridge cut his eyes at Grady. "I don't believe I was talking to you."

"Now, now, Grady. Mr. Baldridge doesn't mean anything by that, I'm sure. He's just trying to help that unfortunate Negro boatman. You want the same thing the rest of us want, don't you, Mr. Baldridge? To see justice done?" Baldridge didn't answer him. "Cilla, bring the gentleman's mount." Dodd continued, with a strained smile: "Now, I'm glad to help your friend Mr. Lusk with my attorney, but I'm not in the habit of answering to people who are not in a position of authority. I've told you that I don't know this Quick fellow, and I certainly have no knowledge of some woman's demise at the Memphis wharf, other than to say it is a tragic affair. Now, if you'd be so kind as to leave, I'll get back to my work, and my wife can get back to her garden."

Baldridge nodded slowly, then limped down the steps and took the reins from Cilla. Grady watched him closely as he mounted.

"I'm sorry to bother you, Mr. Dodd. I'm sure the man who said he saw your boys in town was mistaken. He does tend toward the bottle a bit."

"Just out of curiosity, who was it claimed he saw my men in town?"

Baldridge looked first at Dodd, then at Grady, whose stare had never left Baldridge. "Don't recall the fella's name," he said. "He was probably too drunk to know what he saw."

"I realize you want to help Mr. Lusk," Dodd said, "but I must ask you not to pay too much attention to the raving of a drunk. Intoxicating spirits will do strange things to a man."

"How true." Baldridge nodded. "Wicked stuff, liquor is."

"Wicked indeed," Dodd said, mounting his own horse. "Would you like Grady to escort you back to the road?"

"No, thanks, I can find my way." Baldridge tipped his hat. "Pleasure meeting you, ma'am."

"Do let me know if there's anything further I can do for your friend," Dodd said. "My lawyer remains at your service."

IT WAS ALMOST dark when Baldridge rode up to the livery, and Rawls was waiting for him.

"You told me two hours!" the stable man said in an angry whisper, taking the reins from Baldridge. He motioned with his head toward the office. "Mr. Terrell done asked me twice about this mare."

"What did you tell him?"

"Never you mind what I told him," Rawls said, leading the animal into the livery and undoing her girth. "Here I try to help you out and you go off and—"

"I had a lot to do."

Rawls lifted the saddle and placed it on a nearby railing, then took the blanket and shook it out. "That's all you got to say? You 'had a lot to do'?"

"I couldn't get back any faster."

From his pocket Rawls took Baldridge's silver flask and tossed it to him. Baldridge smiled, opened it, and lifted it for a drink. Nothing came out.

"It's empty."

Wielding an angry currycomb that unsettled the mare, Rawls mocked him. "*I* had a lot to drink."

"But you drank it *all*."

"I couldn't drink no slower."

Nothing was said for several moments, until Baldridge started up the stairs to Rawls's room.

"Where you going?"

"I'm starvin'," Baldridge said. "Figure I'll fix us some supper."

Rawls stopped his brush, and his eyes followed the sound of Baldridge's feet up the stairs and across the floor above him.

"You ain't at the stove!" he shouted. "And stay out of my wine!"

11

Friday morning, April 4

THE FORMER PRESIDENT of the Confederacy appeared to live well, yet not in the splendor Baldridge had imagined. The house at 129 Court Street, while not opulent, was better than anything Baldridge had ever lived in, or likely ever would. The entry hall where he stood was adequately decorated, its floral wallpaper the backdrop for a German-made hall tree. Baldridge checked his appearance in the mirror near where the maid had hung his jacket. His collar was folded under, so he pulled it out; looking in the foot mirror, he noticed mud on his right boot, so he rubbed it off on his trouser leg. The maid had seemed annoyed when he insisted on keeping his hat, but eventually she went upstairs to find Mr. Davis. He could see into the sitting room, which boasted only two modest chairs and a small secretary near the window. It was not what he had envisioned as the home of a president.

The maid returned and addressed him in a crisp English accent. "Mr. Davis will be with you in a moment." Her hands were clasped neatly in front of her. "He *was* resting," she added, as if Baldridge should be sorry for keeping his appointment, "but he indicates he will be right down." She gestured toward the sitting room. "Would you care to take a seat, Mr. Baldridge?"

Baldridge, hat in hand, started into the room.

"Your hat, sir?" the maid said. "Are you absolutely certain I may not take it for you?"

Her unnerving stare convinced Baldridge that he was seriously breaching etiquette; he reluctantly surrendered the hat, then stood near the fire and turned his bad leg toward the heat. Even though the rain had stopped, the dampness lingered, and it always made his knee stiff. As he warmed himself, he noticed on the mantel before him a wooden object carved and painted to resemble a bale of cotton. He made sure the maid was gone, and carefully took the object in hand. The inscription near the bottom indicated it was a gift from the Liverpool Cotton Cooperative. That Davis and dozens of Confederate generals and cabinet officers had spent the past few years in Europe was no secret. But men like Masey Baldridge had remained. The denial of his constitutional rights; the suspicious attitude of the occupying Federal troops; and his position as fair game for armed, militant Negroes with whom he had no quarrel had taken their toll on Baldridge, as they had on most of the veterans he knew. The war had cost him his health—and his occupation: With his leg still carrying a Minié ball, he couldn't stand for long periods and so he could never return to blacksmithing. Reconstruction was proving to be almost as bad as the war; he had struggled through one half-assed job after another. And for him and thousands of other rank-and-file troopers, there had been no European aristocracy to fawn over them and help them lick their wounds. Baldridge figured the Liverpool Cotton Exchange wouldn't have had the time of day for a *real* soldier.

"Mr. Baldridge?"

The voice startled him, and he momentarily fumbled the piece, scarcely recovering before it tumbled into the fire. In the doorway, Baldridge finally saw the man who had seemed larger than life during the war.

"Good morning, President Davis," Baldridge managed to say, replacing the carving on the mantel and moving to meet his host. He noticed the dark, deep-set eyes observing his limp. Davis's gaze immediately returned to meet his own. The ex-president extended his hand. "Welcome to my home, Mr. Baldridge." He was a full six inches taller than his visitor.

"It's an honor, Mr. President."

A cautious smile overcame what looked to Baldridge like chronic weariness in Davis's face. "Thank you, but it's just Jefferson Davis now. Won't you have a seat?"

As the tall Mississippian sat down, Baldridge thought how unlike his wartime images he appeared. While the straight, dignified nose and broad forehead seemed the same, much of the hair about Davis's temples was gray, and his face was sorrowfully serene.

"I appreciate your agreeing to see me, Mr. Davis."

Davis nodded slowly. "Always willing to see a soldier. Mr. Ferguson at Mid-South Insurance, though a competitor with my Carolina Life, has been a friend of mine for years." He again glanced at Baldridge's leg. "Ferguson said you were wounded?"

"Yankee sharpshooter, three days before the war ended."

"Fate can certainly be cruel, can it not, Mr. Baldridge?" Davis's face saddened even more. "As you may know, I recently lost my beloved son, Billie."

"Yes, sir. Back in October. I heard about that. I'm very sorry."

Davis pointed upstairs. "Varina—Mrs. Davis, that is— would have come down to meet you herself, but she's not well

today. It's the grief over Billie. It comes and goes, you know."
The maid entered the room. "Can I offer you something, sir?"

"No, sir, I believe not . . . unless, of course, you might have a touch of brandy."

Davis smiled. "I think we can do that. Eugenia, if you will . . ."

"Yes, Mr. President." The maid glanced at the clock on the mantel, then offered Baldridge a condescending look before departing.

Davis appeared slightly embarrassed. "She insists upon calling me that. Now, exactly what is it I can do for you? Colonel Ferguson told me you had some questions."

Baldridge tried to relax. He shouldn't be uneasy; after all, Davis was just another man now. Yet the breath of the past lingered. The very fact that he would never have gotten an appointment without Ferguson's intervention was enough to make Baldridge nervous, and now he sat before Jefferson Davis, a man who led a nation in rebellion, the man who had been his commander-in-chief for four years. Baldridge swallowed hard and set himself to the task.

"Mr. Davis, I need to ask you about the Confederate treasury. When you and your cabinet left Richmond in April 1865, you carried a lot of money. Is that true?"

"We removed the treasury, that's correct."

"I understand there were a number of gold coins in that treasury," Baldridge said, taking the brandy from the maid.

Davis nodded. "The remaining wealth of a great nation, Mr. Baldridge. Gold, silver, even the valuable jewelry many of the ladies of the Confederacy so nobly donated when finances became strained."

"How much was it all worth?"

"Well," Davis said with a laugh, "not as much as some of these malicious writers would have you believe. Certainly not ten million dollars, as one lunatic claimed. Mr. Baldridge,

I've read some libelous stories over the past three years—stories that accuse my cabinet and I—even my family—of stealing money from the Confederacy."

"You should speak out against them, sir."

"Every time I speak out in public, I'm misquoted; thus I now decline such invitations." Davis swept his hand before him. "Look around you, Mr. Baldridge. Do I look like a man who has profited from ill-gotten wealth?" He stared into the fire for a moment, then back at Baldridge. "The fact is that were it not for the presidency of Carolina Life Insurance, I would be broke. I pay one hundred dollars a month in rent here. The rooms are small and the plan is cranky. And the drainage in the backyard is dreadful. I'm convinced it has contributed to Varina's illness." Davis's face grew stern. "I do trust you're not here to perpetuate the lies."

"Mr. Davis, I ain't no writer. Mr. Ferguson might've told you, I'm investigatin' a murder."

Leaning back in his chair, Davis folded his arms. "Very well, continue."

"I'm trying to find out about a coin I came across a few days ago. It may very well be a key piece of information in a murder—a murder a friend of mine has been accused of."

"I see. And how can I help?"

Baldridge fished the gold coin from his pocket and handed it to Davis, who, appearing quite surprised, studied it for several moments.

"I didn't think the Confederacy minted a twenty-dollar gold piece," Baldridge said, "but I'm told this coin is real."

"It's real, all right," Davis said, deep in thought. He looked at Baldridge. "No wonder you asked about the treasury."

"Sir, were coins like that in the Confederate treasury?"

"They were indeed, Mr. Baldridge, and that's the *only* place they could be found." Holding the coin up to see it better, the visibly bewildered Davis continued, "Where on earth did you get this?"

"From the personal effects of a woman who was killed on the steamboat *Paragon* a few days ago."

"Yes. I recall having read something about it in the paper. One of the crew was arrested, was he not?"

"Yes, sir. But he's innocent," Baldridge assured him. "What more can you tell me about that coin?"

"I approved this to be minted in New Orleans in 1861. I specifically recall this type of coin because I saw the proofs. We had planned to issue them, but later Mr. John Reagan— he was secretary of the treasury by then—suggested we keep the coins in the treasury. Being a soldier yourself, Mr. Baldridge, I'm sure you recall how fast paper money was inflating."

"Yes, sir."

"The secretary and I felt the government would be best served by withholding these coins from circulation."

"For their value in gold?" Baldridge suggested.

"Exactly."

"So what happened to them?"

Davis seemed hesitant. "That is rather difficult to say, but I, too, should like to know the answer." Davis stood and stepped near the fire. "As you know, Mr. Baldridge, I was captured near Irwinsville, Georgia, on May 10, 1865."

"Yes, sir."

"And those vicious lies about me being dressed in women's clothes to avoid capture are precisely that," he said, pointing at Baldridge. "They're lies!" Baldridge nodded, but Davis continued to stress the point. "It was early morning. When the Federals approached I simply grabbed whatever happened to be nearby to protect myself from the cold. One of the items happened to be a shawl. There was no intent to disguise myself—"

"Sir, I understand," Baldridge said. "But about the gold . . ."

"Yes, . . . well, the contents of the treasury, at least what remained after paying the troops who accompanied our retreat, were divided among several trusted officers the moment it appeared we might be captured."

"And these particular coins?"

Again Davis inspected the coin. "It was a difficult time, Mr. Baldridge, as I suspect you can appreciate. My goal at that moment was to get as much of the treasury west, across the Mississippi River, as possible. I held out hope that I might yet escape the Federals who were now all around us, and perhaps I could make my way south and west to meet up with our forces in the Department of the Trans-Mississippi. They had not yet surrendered. I so hoped to continue the fight . . . to not abandon the cause. . . ."

"So are you saying you don't know who had charge of the twenty-dollar coins?"

"There were many details that I could not personally attend to," Davis said. "However, I do know which officer had charge of this particular load of specie, as I had occasion to see it loaded in the wagon just prior to splitting up."

"Who would that be?"

"Paymaster Semple. James Semple of the Navy. A trusted officer."

"What became of him?"

"That, sir, I cannot say. I presume him to be dead. He never returned home after the war. His widow wrote to me in prison to ask the details of those last days, obviously in hopes of locating him. But the Federals would not allow me to answer her letters. As I'm sure you're aware, this government committed the abomination of imprisoning me without trial. But you do understand why they couldn't try me, don't you, sir?" Baldridge didn't. In fact, he really didn't care: He'd sacrificed enough for the cause. But he figured Davis was

going to tell him anyway. "Because the legitimacy of seces-
sion would have gone before the courts, and they knew the
right of the states would be upheld in any fair rendering of
the Constitution. Instead, I was *pardoned.* Wasn't that con-
venient for our government? I doubt seriously, sir, that I shall
ever have my citizenship restored."

"And Mrs. Semple? Her husband?"

"It was not until my release that I could contact Mrs.
Semple in Virginia. That would have been June 1867. I told her
of last seeing Paymaster Semple and two escort riders heading
south toward the Florida line. Semple's plan was to outdistance
the pursuers, then turn west through the panhandle and northwest across Alabama and Mississippi. He would find a safe
crossing of the Mississippi and . . . I guess he never made it.
There has been no word of Paymaster Semple to this day, and
though I've inquired, I have never known what became of him."

"And that is the last you saw of these coins?"

"Until you handed me this one just now." Davis returned
the coin.

"How many were there?"

"How many were minted? Oh, I would estimate in excess
of twelve thousand."

"That would be a lot of money in gold."

"It certainly would. But as to who might have the coins,"
Davis mused, "anybody might have waylaid Semple and his
escort. They had hundreds of miles to travel. Perhaps the
Federals. It wouldn't be the first time some Federal officer
enriched himself with Southern property."

"And yet none of these coins have appeared until now."

"That *is* rather curious," Davis conceded.

"Is it possible that Semple might have just gone off somewhere, taken a new name, maybe—"

"Not James Semple. Never. He was an honorable man
who loved his wife and his children."

"And those who rode with him?"

"The escort?"

"Yes, sir."

"Just soldiers. Some of Breckinridge's men. I knew neither of them."

"General Breckinridge, of Kentucky?"

"Correct."

Both men sat quietly for a moment.

"This entire business both intrigues and disturbs me," Davis said. "I should very much like to know more."

"So would I," Baldridge said, rising to his feet. "This coin is really all I've got to go on. If I can't figure out where it leads, a good man is liable to die for a murder he didn't commit."

"That would, indeed, be a tragedy."

"Do you suppose General Breckinridge would remember what escort he assigned? Or know what became of them?"

"I's highly doubtful, Mr. Baldridge. As I said, that was a difficult time. And, as you may know, John Breckinridge has only been back in the country a couple of years. He fled to Cuba and then to Europe."

Perhaps it shouldn't have, but something about that steamed Baldridge. He started to say something, then held his tongue. What good would sharp words do?

"Still, I'd be glad to contact General Breckinridge on your behalf," Davis added. "That is, if you think it would help. I could ask him about his escort. Of course, it would take a few days, I'm sure. Perhaps longer."

Baldridge considered the offer. He would probably run out of time before he got an answer, but it couldn't hurt to try, so he agreed.

Davis nodded slowly. "Paymaster Semple was a good man. His widow deserves to know whatever we can find out." He escorted Baldridge to the door, where the maid was waiting with his hat. "And as you may know," Davis continued, "a number of my wartime colleagues are urging me to write a book, to chronicle our struggle. Thus, any facts you might uncover would be of particular interest to me—in the interest of accuracy, you understand."

"I'll keep you informed, sir."

"And where might I reach you should anything come of my contact with General Breckinridge?" Davis asked, as Baldridge stepped on to the porch.

That was a good question. He couldn't go back to the boardinghouse and he was too broke to stay at the Overton.

"Terrell's Livery," Baldridge said.

Davis lifted one eyebrow. "The *livery*?"

"Yes," Baldridge said. "I keep a number of my horses there . . . when I'm not traveling abroad."

From the look in Davis's eyes, it was clear that he got the point, but he smiled anyway. "Good luck to you, Mr. Baldridge."

"And to you . . . Mr. President."

From Davis's home on Court Street, Baldridge went to the jail to check on Jacob Lusk. He spent about an hour with the mate, then went to the police stables about a hundred yards away. The officer working the jail desk had said he'd find Crawford there.

The policeman was forking hay over the railing into the third stall. He noted Baldridge's approach, but kept working.

"Jacob Lusk didn't kill Cassie Pierce," Baldridge said flatly.

Crawford's rhythm with the pitchfork never faltered. "Yeah, and I'm Robert E. Lee."

"The man that killed Pierce was after this," Baldridge said, holding up the coin. Crawford's pitchfork halted in mid-air, the hay on the end raining to his feet. He rested the fork in front of him, handle end on the stable floor. For a moment he just stared at the coin; then he inverted his pitchfork and took another load. "What the hell's that supposed to be?" he said casually, tossing the hay over the rail.

"Just what it says it is: a Confederate twenty-dollar gold piece."

"I never heard of no—"

"Neither did I. But it's real."

Crawford leaned over the railing and spread the hay. "So what if it is? What's that got to do with anything?"

"I just got through talking to Jefferson Davis," Baldridge said, bringing a sharp glance from Crawford.

"*President* Davis?"

"Yes. He told me this coin was part of the Confederate treasury he took south out of Richmond in 1865."

Laying the pitchfork against a post, Crawford put his foot on the lower rail of the stall and took a scarf from his pocket. Wiping his brow, he said, "Well, that's just great. But that hasn't got a thing to do with your colored man in there."

"I think it does."

"And how's that?"

"Whoever killed Cassie Pierce was looking for this coin."

"And how do you know that?"

"I found it in her things."

"Couldn't have. I searched that room myself. There wasn't no gold coin in there."

"You missed it."

"I *couldn't* have missed it," Crawford said angrily, pointing his finger at Baldridge. "You understand me? I *couldn't* have missed it. I turned that place upside down." He began to calm down. His tone changed. "Now, what, exactly, are you trying to say?"

Baldridge glanced past him at the horse now chewing his way into the fresh hay. Something about Crawford bothered him. It had from the first time he saw the man.

"I believe Dillard Quick killed Miss Pierce for this coin, and—"

"Oh, here we go again with this Dillard Quick. Your boat boy's been hollerin' about Quick for two days now. You even got William Dodd's lawyer talking about this Quick fella." Crawford stepped closer to him. "You wanna know what I think? I think there ain't nobody named Quick. Your nigger just made him up."

"He's on the *Paragon*'s manifest," Baldridge protested.

"What if he is?" Crawford retorted. "There's nothing to tie Quick to that dead whore."

"You said you thought Quick didn't exist."

"Well . . . I'm sayin', if there *is* such a fella," Crawford added quickly, "ain't nobody been able to produce him."

"We're lookin'."

"Well, you just keep on lookin' all you want. Fact is, we found the whore's purse in your boy's cabin."

"Lusk," Baldridge snapped. "The man's name is Jacob Lusk."

"And we got witnesses that saw him arguing with the woman that night. You're wasting your time and Dodd's lawyer's time. Lusk did it. It's clear to me and it'll be clear to the jury." Crawford retrieved the pitchfork and took up another load of hay.

"How well do you know William Dodd?" Baldridge asked.

"Are you going to start that shit again? I told you—"

"Did you check into him? What do you really know about Dodd?"

"I know he's a nigger-lovin' Republican," Crawford replied, punctuating the last word by tossing the hay hard against the far wall. He picked up more hay. "Like I told you before, Dodd's a powerful man. Some say he'll win the governorship next go-round. If I was you, I'd be glad he lent me his lawyer, 'cause he ain't a man you want to cross." Crawford again lowered the pitchfork. "I can't figure you, anyway, Baldridge."

"How's that?"

"Why do you give a shit about this nigger? I mean, I know that Captain Williamson is paying you, and I can halfway understand that—but . . . Hell, man, you wore the gray same as me."

"What's that supposed to mean?"

Crawford looked at Baldridge as if he thought he was stupid.

"Let me lay it out for you. You're messing in business that ain't yours. I know you want your money. Hell, we all want that. So nose around a little bit, ask a few questions, collect your money, and don't worry about this darkie. I guarantee you we got the killer, and he's sittin' right over there in a damned cell where he belongs." Crawford grinned and rubbed his fist in his hand. "And in the next day or so, I've got a feeling he's gonna confess to the whole thing."

"You better leave Jacob be. And just because I was a soldier don't make me an animal."

"Watch your mouth."

"No, you watch it!" He saw Crawford's grip tighten on the pitchfork. "I don't know whether you're lazy, or stupid, or both. But I'm gonna find out who killed Pierce, and I'm gonna make you admit it." He was getting nowhere, just wasting valuable time. He turned and started out of the stable.

"Now, you be careful!" Crawford called to him. "And I'd watch where I showed that gold piece. That thing looks like it might be valuable."

THREE BLOCKS FROM the jail, Baldridge ducked into a saloon for a drink. He could afford only one shot, which he nursed along as he removed the coin from his pocket and studied it again. Lady Liberty stared back at him, her hair hanging in a band over her right shoulder, showing that look of Southern defiance he had seen so often in the days before the war. Proud women like her sent their bold, cocky men by the thousands off to meet the Northern hordes. "The war will be over in months," they said. "Hurry, or you'll miss the fun." But Baldridge recalled how that look had changed over the years. He saw the change in the eyes of his fellow troopers in Forrest's cavalry, and in the faces of the widows and mothers in hundreds of towns and villages across the south. The confidence of '61 and '62 became determination in '63, then desperation as the war dragged on through '64, and finally turned to resignation in '65. Yet on this coin, Lady Liberty was unchanged, unconquered, as she held the battle flag before her and clutched the Constitution so lovingly in her hand. The one, captured and torn; the other trampled and ignored. So much pain. So much sorrow. And yet . . . Baldridge knew the struggle imbued her with a sweetness the protected would never taste.

Baldridge finished his drink, declined a second, and left the saloon still clutching the coin in his left hand. He liked the feel of it between his fingers—its newness, its shine. En route to the livery he stepped off the walkway and slipped between a horse and a buckboard tied up near a gentleman's clothing store next door to the saloon. Almost a third of the way across the broad street, he noticed the four-horse team and wagon approaching from his left, but he paid little attention. His mind was on the case now, and he was more determined than ever to find out what Quick was doing with Dodd's men. Perhaps Rawls could help. He had spoken, Tuesday night, of having some colored friends who knew a number of the Yankees who hung around Memphis after the war. Maybe they could shed some light on Dodd.

Baldridge was in the middle of the street now, deep in thought; and what made him look up, he wasn't sure. But when he glanced to his left, the wagon and team he had seen seconds before was charging toward him at a full gallop. It bore down upon him—ten feet—five feet—and he could see the terror in the eyes of the lead pair. Or was it his own fright looking back at him? He tried to run, but the street was still soft from the preceding days' rain, and the mud seemed to lock his boots in a death grip. Still the wagon came, with no sign of stopping or veering, its driver unseen behind the charging team. He freed his right foot. The rushing animals closed on him. He freed his left foot—always slow to move because of his wound—and dove forward. A hoof clipped his ankle and stung it as the team and wagon swept past. Rolling in an awkward forward somersault, Baldridge was swept by his own momentum into another wagon that was approaching from the opposite direction. The first wagon continued full speed down Main Street, but the driver of the second pulled up some fifty feet away and stood up, reins in hand, calling back to Baldridge.

"Are you all right?"

Two men from the far side of the street ran toward Baldridge, one calling to the driver, "Did you hit him?"

"I don't think so," the driver replied. "But that crazy fool in that other wagon like to have trampled him plumb to death." The driver dismounted and hurried toward Baldridge. As the three of them approached, Baldridge crawled around on his hands and knees, mud covering his stomach, his right shoulder, his back, and the right side of his neck and face. One of the men from the street picked up his hat, partially crushed in the tumble, and attempted to re-shape it. As the driver and the other citizen reached out to help him up, Baldridge push them away.

"Get back!" he shouted, continuing to crawl around in

circles. "Stay the hell away from here!" The man holding Baldridge's hat looked at the driver.

"You reckon he's dazed?"

"Must be," the driver said. "But I sure thought I missed him."

"Better get him a doctor," the other citizen said, again attempting to help Baldridge up. Baldridge pushed him back, almost sending the Samaritan into mud.

"I don't need no goddamned doctor!" Baldridge shouted. "I just need you to stay the hell out of the way." The three men looked at each other in bewilderment. "Just don't come walkin' over here!"

It had to be right here, Baldridge thought. It couldn't have gone far. He shouldn't have had it in his hand. It should have been in his pocket. No, better still, he should put it up somewhere. There had been no need to haul it around anymore. He had found out what he needed to know. That's what he would do. He'd hide it. Put it in a safe place . . . if he could just *find it.*

"Mister, don't you want us to get you some help?" the driver said. A small crowd was now gathering to watch this man crawl about in the Main Street mire, occasionally leaning down, face only inches from the mud, to stare into the ooze.

"Look at him," one of the gawkers said, "he's touched in the head."

"Acts drunk, don't he?" another added.

"He come out of that saloon over there," a woman put in. "Probably drunk. Probably stumbled into that wagon." She indignantly folded her arms.

"I think he's lookin' for something," said the man holding Baldridge's hat.

"What could a man lose that would make him root around like a hog?"

Baldridge continued crawling about, moving slowly one

moment, then desperately the next, until finally—a glint of light, a reflection. He became very still, extending his hand slowly into the mud.

"What's he got?" the driver asked.

"Beats me."

Baldridge delicately retrieved what must have looked to the onlookers like a clump of mud. He slowly stood up. Traffic had begun to pass nearby again as the group stood at the edge of the street. Gently Baldridge pushed away the mud until he saw the Lady staring back at him; then he smiled broadly and walked to the edge of the street.

"What did you find, fella?"

"A coin," Baldridge said quietly.

Several of the men laughed.

"All that for a coin?" the woman asked. She shook her head. "Must have been some coin."

"Uh, mister . . . here's your hat."

Baldridge took it. "Thanks."

"Are you sure you're all right?" the driver asked.

Baldridge tucked the coin in his pocket. "I am now."

On the sidewalk, he brushed the remainder of the mud from his hat and glanced south where the wild wagon team disappeared. His ankle was throbbing. *Got to quit daydreaming.* Yet, as he stared down the street, he thought it rather strange how fast that wagon came upon him. It hadn't seemed to be going fast at all when he first noticed it. *Probably the whiskey.*

"BOY, YOU BEEN wallowin' with the hogs?" Rawls asked, letting Baldridge inside.

"Feels like it."

"No, no, no!" Rawls said, rushing across the room ahead of him. "Don't you be sittin' on my good chair! Let me get you a wet rag. Better yet, come on over here to the washbowl."

"Eli, I got something I want you to keep for me," Baldridge said, "and I need you to ask around about William Dodd."

Rawls frowned as he handed Baldridge a towel. "Is there anything else I can get for you, Massa?"

"Well, I could use some lunch."

12

Friday, April 4, 6:30 P.M.

THE *SUSIE SILVER* made good time to New Orleans, arriving about an hour before dark. Salina Tyner passed through the endless rows of tarpaulin-covered goods waiting to be shipped north, and took a carriage through the narrow streets of the Vieux Carré, or Old Square, beneath the overhanging balconies and past the courtyards of the French Quarter. After paying the driver to wait outside, she entered the building at 640 Royal Street, at the corner of St. Peter, and made her way to the third floor. At the end of a dark hallway that smelled of must and burned grease, she knocked on the door. There was no reply. Inside she could hear someone moaning softly. She allowed herself a slight smile, then knocked again.

"Go away," a man called from inside. This time Tyner balled her fist and hammered the door so it shook.

"I tell you go away!" the man shouted in a French accent. "Nobody home!"

She listened again, and this time heard a woman whispering. "Come on, Armand. Open up," Tyner called. Down the hall another door opened and a tiny, gray-haired woman peered out into the hall. When she knocked again, the old woman cursed her in French. Tyner stuck out her tongue, then called again, "Armand, I need to talk to you."

"Come back later," he yelled from inside.

"No, Armand. Now. I need to talk to you right now."

Finally, the door opened and Armand DeFuentes's head emerged. She pushed the door open and entered, sending DeFuentes grabbing at his pants with one hand and trying to hold the door shut with the other.

"For the love of God, Sally, can't you see I have company!"

Sitting up in his bed, wearing only a sheet pulled up over her and a look of terror, was a young, light-skinned, dark-haired Creole woman. Tyner walked over to the dresser and fed the wick of a dimly burning lamp. She looked at the woman.

"And whose wife are you?"

The woman's eyes widened and she looked at DeFuentes. "Armand!"

He waved off Tyner. "She's guessing."

Tyner picked up the woman's dress and tossed it to her.

"But a pretty good guess, right, honey?"

DeFuentes looked first at the woman, then at the open door, and threw his hands up in resignation.

"Why you do this to me, Sally?"

"Because I like you so much, Armand." Tyner strolled across the room, through the open French doors, and out on to the balcony. She leaned over the wrought-iron railing, surveyed the darkening street below, and called back into the room. "You'd better hurry up, honey, I think I see him coming." The woman slipped her dress on. Half-buttoning it and holding the front loosely against her breasts, she ran for the door. DeFuentes reached for her, but she tossed him a nasty look and avoided him as she left the room.

"Tomorrow, my darling!" he called to her as she rushed down the hall, still trying to finish dressing. DeFuentes closed the door, turned around slowly, and glared at Salina, his jaw set, dark eyes fixed, his mustached upper lip curled slightly. "That you would do this to me I cannot believe."

" 'Tomorrow, my darling,' " she mocked, looking forlorn.

"What do you want with me?"

"Well, it ain't what she was getting," Tyner assured him. "Don't tell me. Let me guess. She's somebody's quadroon. Right?"

"You offend me."

"Oh, for heaven's sake, Armand. Take it easy."

"'Take it easy'? You say for me to take it easy?" He moved closer to her. "You come to my room, run off a beautiful woman from my very arms—"

"She wasn't *that* pretty."

"Sally, you make me so angry—"

Placing her arms around him, she hugged him tightly and kissed him gently on each cheek. He let out a long, slow breath. "Of course, if you came to see Armand for—"

"Don't get your hopes up," Tyner said, quickly breaking the embrace. "I'm here for your help."

Over the next half-hour, Tyner told him about Cassie Pierce and of her search for the killer. She figured if anyone could help her locate Dillard Quick, DeFuentes was the man. A reporter for *L'Abeille*, New Orleans's French-language newspaper, DeFuentes had for over a decade covered the seamier side of the city as well as the wharf and river news. Outside of his appetite for women, nothing was more important to DeFuentes than news—hard news, and the more embarrassing to New Orleans's finest, the better. He probably knew more people in New Orleans than anyone, and had a gift for locating and nailing the latest gossip.

"What you tell me of Cassie is hard to believe," he said. "I liked Cassie. We had some good times together."

"Then help me find Quick."

DeFuentes stepped over to the balcony. It was fully dark now, yet the narrow street below was still busy and the glow of street lamps betrayed the comings and goings of the neighborhood.

"This man, this Dillard Quick—the name is familiar to me."

"Think about it, Armand. Think carefully. I'm almost certain he hangs around the gambling houses near the river. Jacob Lusk said that on the *Paragon* he was free with his money. Said he liked to play the bigshot. He's a scrawny-looking fella. Got a narrow nose and beady eyes. Jacob said he looked like a little weasel."

DeFuentes turned from the window, his eyes showing a glimmer of recognition. "Like the weasel, you say?"

"That's what Jacob called him."

"And his name is Dillard Quick." DeFuentes began nodding slowly. "Like the weasel . . . like the little creature . . ."

"Come on, Armand. Come on," Tyner said, grasping his arm. "I've seen that look before. You know him, don't you?"

"What you say about the weasel . . ."

"Yes?"

"There is a man—"

"Yes, yes." Tyner was moving her hands as if to pull the information from him.

"About six months ago I covered a fight down near the St. Charles Hotel. It was just a short item for the paper, not more than a hundred words—"

"What about it?"

"Actually, it wasn't much of a fight. This man get his ass whooped some kind of good. I came along just when it ended. The man was as you describe, and I think—I am not sure, but I *think* his name was Quick." DeFuentes walked over to a nearby desk and began rummaging through the drawer.

"What are you doing?"

"I may have that story," he said, lifting the lamp from the table and holding it over the open drawer.

Tyner looked over his shoulder at a disheveled pile of yellowing newspaper clippings jammed in the drawer.

"How could you find anything in there?"

"Well, *pardon*," he said, "but I didn't exactly know you would be coming."

"Do you keep everything you write?"

"Most of it." After several minutes of pawing through the stack of clippings, DeFuentes looked up at Tyner. "I'm sorry. I can't seem to find it. It was just a small piece, anyway. I doubt it would help you."

"Look again. Maybe you missed it."

"Sally—"

"Armand. Please. For Cassie's sake."

"Very well," he said, and again he started through the stack. At last, he noticed a tiny clipping lodged against the inside of the drawer. Retrieving it, he read it over quickly and, with a big smile, handed it over to her.

"*Voilà!*"

Tyner took the clipping and held it close to the light, then immediately handed it back. "Would you read it for me, please?"

DeFuentes smiled. "You know, you really should keep up your French."

"Just read it, Armand."

The metropolitan police arrived at LeBlanc Alley in time to break up a fistfight between two local men Wednesday night. The disturbance occurred shortly after eleven PM when a Mr. Swain ex-

changed words in Edward's Tavern with a Mr.
Quick. Having disagreed over the result of a hand
of cards, Mr. Quick is thought to have drawn a gun
on Mr. Swain, at which time Mr. Swain took the
weapon away. When Quick attempted to leave,
Swain followed him into the alley and a fight re-
sulted. Constable M. E. Frayley immediately took
both men to the city jail, where a doctor treated
Mr. Quick.

"This is all there is?"

"Sally, what did you expect? I told you, it was just a fight.
There are dozens of fights in that part of town every week. It
is fortunate I happened to cover this one."

"Would you recognize Quick if you saw him?"

"Perhaps. He was beaten badly that night," DeFuentes
said. Then he laughed. "But even so, he did look a bit like a
weasel. A badly beaten weasel, but a weasel nonetheless."

"How do we get to Edward's Tavern?"

" 'We?' "

"Put your pants on, Armand."

"But Sally—"

"And hurry up. I might even buy you a drink."

The Friday night crowd at the tavern was loud and the
place was full. A portly woman with a flat voice tried to sing
from a makeshift stage in the corner of the room, but no one
paid attention. Her song and the piano accompaniment got
lost somewhere in the crowd's raucousness. DeFuentes led
Tyner past the bar and into a room where he introduced her
to Damon Edwards, the owner. Tyner sensed that Edwards
was apprehensive about DeFuentes, perhaps afraid that more
bad press would hurt his business. Once she assured him that
neither of them was there to cover a story, Edwards took time
to talk.

Yes, he knew Dillard Quick. Quick had been a regular here for years—at least, up until the incident with Mr. Swain. Perhaps fearing he would run into Swain again, Quick hadn't been seen in the place since the fight. Edwards described Quick as a odd fellow, a small, quiet man, always restrained at the beginning of the evening; but after a few drinks, and once the poker game started heating up, it was as if he took on a different personality.

"Quick came here for five, maybe six years," Edwards said. "He'd drink a little, play a little poker, but I never had no trouble out of him. Then about two years ago he seemed to change. Started dressing real nice, started courting the ladies. We got a kick out of watching him, because he was kind of an ugly fella, and the women wouldn't have much to do with him before—"

"Before what?" Tyner asked.

"Before he had money."

She looked at him curiously.

"Ol' Dillard Quick had some money," said Edwards. "Last couple of years, anyway. And he lost a bunch of it right here. Didn't seem to bother him, though. He never lacked a stake for a high-rollin' poker game. We all used to tease him, 'cause of where he works and all."

"Where does he work?"

"Why, don't you know? Quick works, or at least he used to—I guess he still does—at the United States mint."

"The mint?"

Edwards laughed. "Yeah, we used to tease him about making his own money. It'd get him mad as hell"—he winked—"but that's why we did it. 'Course, ain't no way he could have been stealin'. A cousin of mine works at the mint and he says they got that place watched closer than a bluejay's nest."

"Dillard Quick works at the U.S. mint? You're sure?"

"Well, when he was coming here he did. I don't know about now. Like I said, it's been six or seven months since I've seen him."

"Do you have any idea where he lives?" Tyner asked.

Edwards shook his head. "No, but I hear tell he's taken to playing cards down at a place off Canal Street. I think a man named Freeman runs it."

"Saloon de Bayou," DeFuentes said.

"That's it."

"It's a rough place," DeFuentes said, looking directly at Tyner. "I wouldn't recommend—"

She stood up and extended her hand. "Mr. Edwards, thank you for your help."

"My pleasure, ma'am. You're welcome here anytime. Especially without ol' DeFuentes."

"I'll remember that in my next column," DeFuentes said.

The stupid things that men would bet on never ceased to amaze Salina Tyner. Almost everyone inside the Saloon de Bayou was crowded four and five deep around a table where two miserable-looking fellows were well into a wager as to which one could eat the most crawfish. Tyner and DeFuentes elbowed their way in close enough to see the table piled with a strange mixture of slimy, discarded crustacean parts, and side bets in both coin and currency.

"How can anybody eat those filthy things?"

"It's easy, Sally. You just suck on the head till the insides come out." She quickly moved back away from the crowd. DeFuentes followed. "What's the matter, Sally? You don't like the crawfish?" She was pale and he was enjoying it. "I'm sure I could convince them to share. I bet you haven't had dinner yet, have you?"

"Shut up, Armand. Just shut up."

DeFuentes laughed as Tyner swallowed hard and took several deep breaths. When a young Negro from a nearby restaurant pushed past them bearing a tray piled high with a fresh supply of crawfish for the contestants, he called her attention to them.

"I'll bet these are for you."

"Oh, God, that smell!" she said, pulling away.

Tyner eventually steadied herself and turned back to De-Fuentes. "Armand, look around. Look the place over good. See if Quick's here. I've got to get some air."

The crowd around the table applauded the arrival of the delivery boy, and on the far side of the room a Cajun fiddler and his accompanist, on banjo, broke into a lively tune. The place grew more raucous as the contestants started on the fresh plate, while DeFuentes picked his way through the spectators, eventually circling the table. He went halfway up a flight of stairs near the door for a better look. A smoky haze blanketed the saloon, and DeFuentes could see no one resembling Dillard Quick. Pushing open the saloon doors, he walked to the edge of the porch where Tyner stood.

"Sally, I'm sorry, but it's so crowded in there—"

He was stopped short by Tyner's discreet nod in the direction of two men who stood some fifteen feet away by a hitching post. One of them had just dismounted and was tying his horse as he spoke.

"What the hell's goin' on in there?"

"It's another damned belly-buster," the other man said.

Tyner whispered, "The one on the left. Is that him? I could swear that man called him Dillard when he rode up."

The dark night was penetrated only by the light emanating from the front door and windows of the saloon. As the two men stepped up on the porch and started in the door, their faces caught the glow from inside. The taller man entered first. The man who followed was short and rather skinny; even in the poor light, he had a nervous look about him. Once the two were inside, Tyner turned to DeFuentes.

"Well?"

DeFuentes scratched his head. "It could have been."

"*Could have* been?"

"I-i-it might be him."

Tyner peered inside to make sure she didn't lose track of the man. "Come on, Armand!"

"What do you want from me, Sally?" DeFuentes's Creole blood was beginning to rush. "It's been six months. The man I saw back then was beaten like a dog. I guess it could be him. I mean, it looked like him. Hell, Sally, you bang on my door—you spoil an evening with a beautiful woman—you drag me down here—"

She pushed him aside. "I'll find out my own damned self."

"What are you going to do?"

"Look, Armand. Just wait here. Come inside in about fifteen minutes. If this man is Dillard Quick, I'll wave, and you can leave. If it's not him, I'll go with you."

"You want me to leave you here—in this place—alone?"

"I do my best work alone, Armand. You know that." DeFuentes looked distressed. "Don't worry about me." She put her hands on his shoulders. "Actually, I'm rather flattered. Don't worry, I know where to find you if I need you."

"Sally—"

She started into the saloon, calling back over her shoulder. "And if I don't see you again, stay away from that woman. If her husband finds out, he'll kill you."

Inside, Tyner found the two men sitting at a table in the far corner. She passed by once to see if they would notice, and the small, wiry man's eyes tracked her like a predator's. Offering him a brief glance, she looked quickly away as if embarrassed that he had caught her looking, and pretended to be absorbed in the action at the center table. Her stomach churned as the stench of the crawfish, liquor, and cigars flooded her nostrils. For several moments she thought surely she would vomit. But that would ruin everything. She would not allow it. She would be strong. She would endure . . . for Cassie's sake. Again she swallowed hard; then, before turning around, she tugged slightly on the front of her dress to expose a bit more cleavage. When she started in the direction of the two men, she noticed the weasel's eyes upon her again. *God, he's ugly.* It seemed to take forever to cross those few feet, but the whole time she studied the man's face. She tried to recall that night on the *Paragon*, and sought desperately to evoke the face of the man she had seen with Cassie. She pictured them, two dark shadows moving along the deck from the dining room, but even as she approached the table, the man's face remained that of a stranger. In that moment, it occurred to her for the first time that he might recognize *her*. All this time she'd been wondering if she would know him. If she could identify him. But what if he remembered seeing her on the *Paragon*? What if she'd casually spoken to him and he recalled the conversation? Why hadn't she thought of that before? Instantly, she wanted to cover her face or turn away, but she was almost upon them now. She was committed. She had to gamble.

Once beside the table, she stood looking at the man, as if in deep thought.

"What can we do for you, honey?" the taller one asked.

She pointed at the other man. "I'm almost sure I know you."

The little man adjusted his jacket and grinned at his companion. "Well, maybe you do. Or maybe you'd like to get to know me."

"The mint," she said assuredly.

"I beg your pardon?" the skinny man said, his smile disappearing. His voice had a harsh, nasal quality to it, in sharp contrast to the softer accent of most New Orleans residents Tyner had known.

"That's where I know you. You work at the mint, don't you?"

The man nodded his head. "Yes, but I don't—"

"I see you going to work all the time," Tyner said, forcing a smile. "I'm usually out that time of day myself. I help my brother on his walk every day. He's crippled, you know." His expression hadn't changed, so she pressed on. "Anyway, I see you going to work and I always tell him, 'Richard,' I say, 'there goes that handsome money man.' That's what I call you, the money man." Her hand went to her mouth. "Oh, I've forgotten my manners." She extended her hand. "My name is Salina Tyner."

The man stood and took her hand, his sharp expression giving way to a narrow smile. "I'm Dillard Quick."

The other man also stood. "Name's Shellman, but every-body here calls me Shelley."

"We was about to try to get up a poker game," Quick said, "if they ever quit all this foolishness. We've got an extra chair if you want to play."

"Oh, I'm afraid I'm not very good," Tyner said, giving Quick a look designed to melt his belt, "at *poker*. But if Mr. Quick here is willing to help me . . . I'll bet we could have a lot of fun."

SLIPPING OUT OF bed without waking Dillard Quick took Tyner almost ten minutes, for he stirred every time she produced a squeak. But once she was up, she set about her plan. Thank God she'd gotten him too drunk to do anything when they got back to his house last night. It was one thing to do it for money, but this ugly little bastard wouldn't have been worth it at any price. She stood watching him sleep for a moment. A tiny stream of drool crept from the corner of his mouth and dampened his pillow. Jacob Lusk was right. He did look like a weasel.

Day was just breaking, with enough light coming in for Tyner to find her way through the house. It was a small place, only three rooms, but well furnished. She had lain in bed awake since three, waiting for enough daylight to search the place before Quick awoke. While searching the bedroom, she kept thinking about how Quick had looked at her. For the better part of the evening she'd feared he would suddenly turn to her and say, "Didn't I see you on the *Paragon*?" And that would be that. But the question never came, though he had clearly been suspicious when she first sat down. Saying she had seen him at the New Orleans mint had been stupid, for it only seemed to put him on the defensive. It had taken three hours, nearly a hundred hands of cards, and a river of whiskey to get Quick talking, and even then he didn't say much. Eventually his friend Shelley passed out on the table, and Tyner might have, too, had she not dumped several full shotglasses on the floor when Quick wasn't looking. Scrawny as he was, he could sure drink; but the more he had, the better-looking he thought he was, and that was just what Tyner was hoping for. She played him like a fiddle, and though he could barely walk when they left the Saloon de Bayou, he was able to remember where he lived. Tying his horse's lead to the back of a cab, she and the driver stuffed Quick inside. They drove northwest about a mile, past a dirty, shallow lake called Gormley's Basin, to a modest dwelling on the edge of a swamp.

Tyner had gone through the drawers, looked under the bed, and searched Quick's wardrobe. There was nothing in the bedroom except two or three old letters, his shaving mug, and a couple of tintypes. She moved into the kitchen but found nothing of use there. The only room left was a sitting room, modestly furnished with a desk, a straight chair, a rocking chair, and a table holding a lamp. The desk contained several old payroll stubs from the mint, a can of tobacco, a drawer with pen and inkwell, and a second drawer—locked. She checked the desk again for the key but found none. Returning to the bedroom, she saw Quick snoring hard, and again searched his bureau. She was about to retrieve a knife from the kitchen to open that locked drawer when her eyes fell on Quick's pants, tossed in a pile in the corner. A quick check of his pockets found some change, a shiny new twenty-dollar gold piece, and two keys. Back in the sitting room, Tyner used one of the keys to open the drawer, which was stacked full of papers, mostly letters. On her hands and knees she went through them, glancing quickly at the body of each and looking to see who they were from. She had been through fourteen or fifteen when she came upon a series of telegrams. Pulling the rocking chair to a spot near the window—a place from where she could keep an eye on Quick in the next room—Tyner sat down with the telegram.

```
FEBRUARY 12, 1873
MEMPHIS, TENNESSEE
MR. DILLARD QUICK
PREPARE FOR SHIPMENT OF GOODS STOP
NEED 1,000 ITEMS DELIVERED IN GOOD
CONDITION BY MID-APRIL STOP WIRE
WITH DETAILS OF ARRIVAL TIME STOP
TRANSFER OF GOODS AT SAME LOCATION
STOP
                           G. R. TEETER
```

She found three other communications, going back to 1869, each sent from Memphis to Quick by a G. R. Teeter, all much the same in tone. Unless Dillard Quick was wealthy enough to be speculating in the mercantile business, they made no sense. But she remembered Thomas at the Overton Hotel saying that he came to Memphis a couple of times each year.

She saw Quick beginning to stir, so she jumped up and went over to the doorway. He was starting to wake up, and still she had no answers. She had to keep him under control until she found out what he'd been doing with Cassie that night. She had to keep him restrained, but a quick check of all three rooms produced nothing she could use. He was moving his legs slowly, gradually coming out of sleep, and Tyner began to panic. She considered leaving. Maybe he wouldn't remember bringing her home. Maybe she would have another chance tonight. No, that was nonsense. She had to deal with Quick now. To have come this far, to have gotten this close, and not get the truth was unacceptable.

Then she saw it: Near the top of the bedroom window, dipping along the curtain top like a valance, was a dark blue decorative rope. There might be enough of it, but she would have to act fast. Taking a straight chair, a butcher knife, and an iron skillet from the kitchen, she placed the skillet on the bureau, then hurriedly climbed up and cut the rope loose from across the double window. It was about five feet long and almost a half-inch thick, plenty strong for what she needed. Moving to the head of the bed, Tyner cut a foot-long section of the rope. She needed to secure his hands and feet, but to move them any distance would risk bringing Quick around. His right hand was thrown over his head and lay a few inches from the iron railing at the head of the bed. Slowly and gently she slipped the rope's end under Quick's arm and tied it at his wrist; then, moving ever so gently, she eased his hand close enough to secure the other end of the rope to the head-rail. Quick let out a low groan, and Tyner froze. But after a few seconds he was snoring lightly again. Since his other hand was tucked under him, she had no chance of securing it, so she moved to his left ankle, which was closest to the footrail. Cutting a second piece of rope long enough to reach from his ankle to the railing, she repeated the process and secured it.

She had just completed the knot when Quick's body jerked. He mumbled something and Tyner stepped back. His eyes were open but he had not yet seen her. Pulling his left hand from beneath him, he felt the bed where she had been.

"Salina?" he mumbled. Lifting his head slightly, he called her again. As his dull eyes turned toward her, she laid the knife on the bureau and picked up the skillet, hiding it behind her back. Blinking and squinting, he finally saw her. When he tried to arise, he found himself unable to move; he glanced at his right hand in disbelief, and then looked down at his left leg. He looked at Tyner.

"What is this?"

"Good morning, Mr. Quick," she said with a smile.

He tugged on the rope with his hand, and when it wouldn't budge, he reached up to untie it with his left.

"Don't you touch that," she said, offering a soft smile.

"The hell I won't!" He was waking up fast now and groping for the knot. "I don't know what kind of crazy game you're playin'—"

Tyner moved to the bedside. "The question, Mr. Quick, is what game *you're* playing," she said, delivering a backhanded blow with the skillet that caught Quick in the cheek and sent his free hand grabbing his head.

"Ohhhhhhh!" he yelled.

When his eyes rolled back in his head, Tyner knew he was addled, and she knew she must work fast. Moving to the other side of the bed, she placed the remaining rope around his left wrist, tied it, and pulled his hand toward the other corner of the headrail. He was tugging against her, but his effort was weak and she easily overcame him, eventually securing his other hand. He now lay before her spread-eagled, dazed, moaning, blood trickling from his right nostril. Only his right leg was free. But in a moment he gathered himself enough to renew his struggle.

"You're a crazy woman," he mumbled, "that's what you are." Though he battled the ropes for almost a full minute, he had no success, and a pleased Salina Tyner just stood and watched him.

"What's wrong, Quick? The sex too rough for you?"

Quick was furious. He lifted his free right leg and tried to kick Tyner, but she pulled back.

"Oh, still got some fight in us, have we?"

She swung the skillet and caught him in the side of his right knee.

"Jesus! God!"

"So, you're a religious man, are you, Quick?" He lay there moaning and then began to cry.

"Don't you move that leg again, or I'll have to remind you to behave."

His voice cracking, he lifted his head. "Why . . . why are you doing this to me?"

She sat on the bed next to him. "Let's just say I was a friend of Cassie Pierce."

His cheek was red and swelling now. He rolled his eyes in her direction. "Who's that?"

Tyner stared at him for a moment. "You don't even know, do you? You didn't even bother to know her name."

"Whose name? What are you talking about?"

"I'm talking about my friend. The one you murdered."

"You're crazy," Quick moaned. "I didn't murder no-body—"

"You were with her that night on the *Paragon*."

A glimmer of recognition shown in Quick's watery eyes. "That's where I've seen you . . ."

"Why did you do it? Was it over that silly coin? She would have given it to you, you know. Cassie would have done anything for anybody."

"I didn't kill no girl."

"What is it about that Confederate coin that's so important to you, Quick? What made it worth Cassie's life?"

"Woman . . . I tell you, I didn't kill that girl."

Tyner put her elbow on his hurt right knee and leaned back. "Well, I think you did."

"Oh! Please!" Quick began thrashing again. "I swear to God! Please! I swear I didn't hurt her!"

"Did she hurt like this when you did it?" Tyner asked, maintaining the pressure on his knee.

"It wasn't me! Please! It wasn't me!"

"Then who was it?"

Quick began sobbing. "Dodd had it done."

"Who?"

"Dodd. A man named Dodd."

"William Jenkins Dodd?" He didn't answer. "William Jenkins Dodd of Memphis?" Still he didn't answer. She lifted the skillet.

"Yes! Yes, for God's sake! Please don't—"

"What's your connection to Dodd?"

"I do some work for him."

Tyner propped her foot on the bed rail and leaned on her knee, her arms crossed. She was still holding the skillet. "What kind of work?" Quick lay on his back, moaning. "Quick, it's Saturday morning." She strolled over and peered out the window, the brightness of the morning sun adding to Quick's misery as it flashed across his face. "And it looks to me like you live in the middle of nowhere." She tapped her fingernail on the back of the skillet. "And we've got all day to be together. Isn't that what you told me you wanted last night? A chance to spend the whole day with me?"

"Listen . . . I can pay you, you know. I've got money. Please don't do this."

"Then talk, goddamn it!" Quick began crying again. "And stop sniveling. What do you do for Dodd?"

"I make coins."

"Confederate coins? Counterfeit?"

"No," Quick said. "The real thing."

"At the U.S. mint?"

"Yes."

"But how? I thought they controlled—"

"Dodd gives me the gold—twenty-dollar Confederate coins." Dodd swallowed hard. "Do you think I could have some water?"

"After you tell me about the gold."

"I carry one or two into the mint in my pocket every day, then I melt them down and I press them into U.S. coins at the end of my shift. Never enough to arouse suspicion."

"So the mint is never missing any gold," she said.

Quick nodded. "Because I bring in and take out the same gold. I just change it from a Confederate coin to a U.S. coin."

"And then you carry Dodd's 'thousand items' back to Memphis."

Quick glanced toward the sitting room. "How did you know—"

"Who's G. R. Teeter?"

Quick shook his head, then noticed Tyner rotating the skillet in her hands. "Works for Dodd. He meets me when I come to Memphis. Teeter don't even know there's money in the trunk. Mr. Dodd's real careful about that. Only him and me and one other person know about the gold."

"Who's the other person?"

"I don't know. I've never met him. Just somebody Dodd knows." After a few moments of silence, Quick looked up at Tyner. "Are you going to turn me over to the police?" he said, much like a child who has been caught sneaking cookies. " 'Cause I've got some coins. Some Confederate coins. You could melt them down and sell them for the gold. I'll give some to you if you'll just let me go. I can't go to no jail. I couldn't stand it. I can't take being in tight places. I just—"

"Would you really pay me to keep quiet?"

"Yes. Yes, I swear I would," Quick said. His eyes brightened at the notion that she might free him.

"Where's the coins?"

"Cut me loose and I'll get 'em for you."

"Where's the coins?"

"Ain't you gonna cut me loose?"

"After I see the money."

With his head he motioned toward his pants. "There's two keys in my pants. One of them goes to a trunk I've got hid under the kitchen floor. It's got the coins I just brought back from Memphis—the ones I'm supposed to change for Dodd. You can have them. You can have all of them if you'll just let me go."

Tyner retrieved the keys she'd left on the desk and went to the kitchen. Just as Quick had said, she found a trunk hidden under some loose planks in the floor. Her mouth dropped when she lifted the lid and looked inside. The chest fairly sparkled with rows and rows of neatly stacked, tightly secured, C.S.A. coins, all just like the one she had found in Cassie's room. She figured there must have been at least a thousand of them. Little wonder Jacob said that Quick wouldn't let the trunk out of his sight. She grabbed a handful and returned to the bedroom.

"Take 'em," Quick said, his eyes betraying his fright. "Take all you want."

"And get myself killed like Cassie did?" She tossed one of them at him. "That *is* why you killed her, isn't it? To get back your precious coin?"

"I told you, I didn't kill her," Quick whined. Over the next several minutes, he explained how he had gone with Cassie to her stateroom that night, a few hours before the *Paragon* arrived in Memphis. He had paid her for sex and left. Later, he went ashore and checked into the Overton Hotel. He was to meet Dodd the next day to exchange his trunk, full of freshly minted U.S. gold pieces, for another batch of Confederate coins to bring back with him to New Orleans. When he realized he had inadvertently given one of the C.S.A. coins to Pierce, Quick said, he panicked. Returning to the *Paragon*, he found Pierce away from her room, so he forced his way inside. But a search of the room turned nothing up. Then he rode out to Dodd's farm in the middle of the night.

"When I told him about it, he was furious. I was never to be seen at his farm. He made me return to the wharf with Teeter and show him the room where I'd been with this woman."

"Cassie Pierce. Her name was Miss Cassie Pierce," Tyner said. "What happened next?"

"I can't really say for sure. Teeter met some other man down by the water."

"Who?"

"I don't know. It was too dark and I was too far away to tell. They went on the boat and come back about a half-hour later. Must have been three or four in the morning."

"And?"

"They never found that coin." Quick drew back as if expecting to be struck. "I—I reckon they killed that woman."

"They did. They strangled her, Quick. Strangled her! Do you know what that feels like?"

"No! No, I don't."

"And how do you suppose Jacob Lusk ended up with Cassie's bag?"

"They wanted to be sure the police went after somebody on the boat." Quick looked away from Tyner.

"Why Jacob?"

"I had mentioned to Teeter I'd seen him arguing with that woman— "

She drew back with the skillet. "Cassie Pierce!"

Quick flinched. "With *Cassie Pierce* that night. I guess they figured he'd be as good as any. You know, bein' colored and all."

Tyner looked at him as if she felt like killing him herself. "You're one pathetic excuse for a man, you know that, Quick? You would have been better off if Dodd *had* killed you."

"What are you gonna do?" he asked as Tyner left the room. "What are you gonna do?"

JUST BEFORE FIVE o'clock that Saturday afternoon, Armand DeFuentes stood at the landing stage leading to the *Susie Silver*, where, according to a message he had received an hour earlier, he was to meet Salina Tyner. The ship had already blown its departure signal once, and still there was no sign of her. He continued to watch up and down the wharf until she finally came dashing down the landing stage from the boat behind him.

DeFuentes took her hands. "Are you all right?"

"I'm better than all right, Armand." She smiled.

"Last night, when you signaled for me to leave, I almost didn't. Then, later, I wished I had stayed. I worried about you—"

"I told you I could take care of myself."

"And this Quick fella? Was he the one?"

Tyner nodded. "One of them."

The *Susie Silver* sounded her final departure whistle.

"There were others involved?"

"Yes, Armand, but I don't have time to explain it all right now. The boat is about to leave. Did you bring it?"

"Yes, but—"

"Good! Give it to me."

From a leather pouch, DeFuentes produced a small, stoppered glass bottle. Tyner reached over to a nearby cotton bale and pulled off a handful of fibers.

"Armand, I need you to do one more thing for me." She handed him a sheet of paper. "Send this telegram to Mr. Masey Baldridge in care of the Overton Hotel in Memphis."

The mud clerk from the *Susie Silver* called from the deck. "Miss Tyner! Ma'am, we've got that trunk stored for you in your room like you wanted."

"Thank you," she called back to him without turning around.

"And ma'am, we'll be leaving in just a minute, so I'll have to ask you to come on board."

Tyner leaned over and kissed DeFuentes hard on the mouth. "I couldn't have done it without you, Armand."

"Done what? Sally, you tell me nothing!"

"I've got to go, Armand. Just send the telegram." She turned and hurried up the landing stage. "I'll tell you all about it the next time I'm in New Orleans."

"And when will that be?" he shouted after her.

She stepped on board as the roustabouts began retrieving the landing stage. "Soon, Armand. Soon. And thanks again." She waved at him and couldn't help feeling a little sad at saying good-bye. At another time, in another place, she might have thanked him properly.

13

Sunday, April 6, one P.M.
Aboard the Paragon, Memphis wharf

"WHAT YOU GOT against a federal marshal helping out?"

"The same thing I had against that posse of seventy-five thousand that Lincoln sent down here in '61," Baldridge said.

"So you want to fight the war again?"

"No, that's over and done with. I'm just amazed that you Yankees could fight us for four years and still not know what the war was about."

"Don't tell me what the war was about—"

"It was about Southerners settling their own affairs," Baldridge shouted over him, "without Yankees sticking their nose in our business!"

"I'm not arguing with you," Williamson said. "You've been drinking again. I can smell it on your breath."

"I don't consider partaking of a little wine with a good friend on the Sabbath morning—"

"Wine, hell! You're drunker'n a fiddler. Just like I suspected you'd be when I got back to town."

"For your information, we had communion this morning . . . several times," Baldridge said—gaze wavering, balance uncertain.

"All I know is that my best crewman is rotting in a Memphis jail— a jail I hired you to get him out of—and he'll likely hang if I don't do something. Because you sure as hell aren't doing anything." Williamson grabbed Baldridge's sleeve. "Look at you! You can barely stand up."

Baldridge wobbled slightly as he raised his finger to make a point. "I'll have you know, Captain, that I have come across some very important information—"

"The only thing you've come across is a bottle."

Baldridge continued as if Williamson had said nothing. "And I believe that my infum—" A hiccup overcame him. "My information will—"

Williamson was boiling. He wanted to grab Baldridge and toss him over the railing, but he was afraid that despite his condition the drunk might just know something that could help.

"Baldridge, I don't care who or what it takes, but I'm getting Jacob free if I have to shoot my way in and haul him out."

"Now, that sure makes a helluva lot of sense, Williamson. Things like this take time."

"Time, my ass!" Williamson turned and looked over the railing into the water.

"Why it is . . ." Baldridge said, pecking the captain's shoulder with his finger. "Tell me why it is that you people think the answer to every problem is to bring either the federal soldiers or lawmen down here? Let the local people handle this thing. We've got our own ways of dealing—"

"Yeah," Williamson said, "I've heard about your *local*

ways of taking care of things, and they usually involve somebody taking a night ride with a bedsheet on his head."

"Oh, you've *heard*, have you?" Baldridge's face was reddening, but his tongue wasn't growing thicker—in fact, he
now seemed almost sober. "You Yankees believe everything
you hear, don't you? You probably think I'm a member of the Ku
Klux, don't you? You think every Southern man is a night rider!"

"All I know is—"

"I don't hold with what the Ku Klux does. Not now, anyway. Back right after the war, there was lots of meanness done
on both sides." Baldridge stepped closer to the captain; the
smell of fruit wine was nearly overwhelming. "But don't go
gettin' self-righteous with me, talking about night riders and
Ku Klux, all the while you're saying you'll shoot your way
into the jail and haul Jacob Lusk out."

"Baldridge, this is not about the Klan."

"You're damned right it ain't. It's about getting your man
out of jail. And I'm doing my best to get him free."

"Well, that isn't good enough."

"The last thing I need is a federal marshal sticking his
nose in things."

"Well, you got one whether you like it not," Williamson
said, as Pittman came onto the deck. He held out his hand
as he approached Baldridge.

"I'm Marshal Pittman," he said, offering a smile. "You
must be— "

"Kiss my ass," Baldridge muttered. He pushed past the
marshal and clumped unsteadily down the stairs.

"As soon as I secure the boat," Williamson shouted to
Baldridge, "we're going to the jail to see Jacob. Meet us
there!"

Upon reaching the lower deck, Baldridge suddenly
stopped and yelled up to Williamson. "Do you know what
today is?"

"It's Sunday." Williamson turned to Pittman. "Son of a bitch is so drunk, I'm surprised he even *knows* what day it is."

"It's the sixth of April," Baldridge shouted, drawing attention from the roustabouts nearby. "What were you doing eleven years ago?"

"Hell, I don't know," Williamson said, giving Pittman a "just tolerate him" look. "What were *you* doing?"

"Dodging your goddamned Yankee gunboat shells at Shiloh," Baldridge shouted. "You lobbed them shells without knowing who you were shootin' at . . . or what you were hittin'. You didn't give a damn, did you?" Williamson did not answer. "I had friends that died there. Friends of mine." Baldridge continued across the landing stage, stumbling once but catching himself on the rope railing. "Never came home."

"The jail," Williamson called to him. "Meet us at the jail. We still need to talk." Baldridge acknowledged him with a wave and continued along the wharf.

Luke Williamson tried to contain his anger. How stupid could he have been? Only a fool would have hired a drunk like Baldridge. He should have gotten somebody else. *Anybody* else. Now the fellow had stormed off without telling him anything.

"I don't think your man Baldridge cared much for me," Pittman said.

"Hell, he doesn't care about anything but his liquor."

"That's the man you told me about? The one that saved your boat down in Natchez?"

Williamson nodded. "Incredible, ain't it? Why in the world I thought he could help Jacob . . ."

"Well, he did help you once before."

"That was different." Williamson shook his head. "I even left Salina Tyner to keep an eye on him. I guess I should have left somebody to keep an eye on *her*. All the while Jacob is sitting down there getting closer and closer to the gallows."

JUST HOW CLOSE Jacob was to the gallows Williamson didn't discover until he and Pittman arrived at the jail, shortly before three o'clock. The deputy in the office seemed reluctant to let him see the prisoner, but the presence of Marshal Pittman was enough to convince him.

Lusk lay on his bunk, face toward the wall, and the captain thought initially that he was sleeping. "Wake up! Wake up!" Williamson called, rattling the cell door. "Got to get this boat loaded." Lusk stirred slowly. "Can't have you used to sleeping in," Williamson added.

Lusk lifted his upper body from the bunk and turned to face Williamson. Instantly the captain gripped the bars. He couldn't believe what he saw. His right cheek swollen and his eye nearly shut, Lusk looked like a bare-knuckle brawler bested in a dockside fight. He flinched as he sat up on the edge of the bunk, his left hand going to the right side of his rib cage.

"What the hell happened?" Williamson demanded, jerking at the cell door as if it should open.

Lusk just shook his head. "Cap'n," he whispered, looking at Williamson through his open left eye, "they wouldn't believe me when—when I told 'em I didn't kill that woman."

"Jailer!" Williamson screamed. "Goddamn it!" He bolted down the hall and through the door to the office. The jailer, wide-eyed and anticipating trouble, reached for the gun that hung in a holster near the front door. The weapon had just cleared the leather when Williamson grabbed the man by the collar and shoulder and slammed his face into the wall.

"You goddamned son of a bitch!" Williamson drew the jailer close and again slammed him into the wall, this time hard enough to send a bulletin board full of wanted posters crashing to the floor. Then Williamson snatched away the revolver, cocked it, and spun the man around to face him, poking the end of the barrel under his nose. The captain's eyes were wild, as the jailer, bleeding from the mouth, stared down the length of the weapon.

"I ought to splatter you all over this wall," Williamson growled.

The commotion had alerted the other deputy on duty, who had been attending to a prisoner in the hallway opposite Lusk's cell. When he came through the door into the office and saw Williamson scuffling with his colleague, he reached for his weapon, and probably would have used it had not Marshal Pittman appeared simultaneously through the other door. Pittman drew first, giving the other deputy a look that froze him in place.

"Which one of you bastards beat my man Jacob?"

The deputy from across the room called to Williamson. "You —you got no call to be pullin' no gun on an officer of the law."

Williamson glanced over at him. "I'm not talking to you . . . *yet*." Out of the corner of his eye he saw Marshal Pittman with his weapon drawn. It surprised him. "About time you came on board."

"It's not what you think, Captain. I don't want to see anybody get killed here."

"You got no right givin' no orders in Memphis," the deputy told Pittman.

Pittman just shook his head. "Listen, you stupid bastard. The captain over there is about this close"—he held up two fingers—"to killing your deputy. And probably you, too. And considering what you did to his man back there, I can't say I'd much blame him."

The man in Williamson's grip shook his head slowly. "I—I—I didn't beat nobody. I just come on shift about two hours ago. I swear it."

"Then who did?" Williamson said.

"You ain't got to tell him nothin'," the other deputy said. "And this here marshal ain't got no authority—"

Pittman cocked his weapon. The deputy got quiet.

"Crawford did, I reckon," the jailer said. "He was questioning the prisoner."

"Questioning, my ass!" Williamson said.

The front door opened and in stepped Anabel McBree. She stopped in the middle of the doorway at the sight before her. "Captain Luke— "

"Anabel, come on through here," Williamson said, motioning with his head. "Grab those keys beside the door and go down that hall and see about Jacob. He's been beaten."

The *Paragon*'s cook looked confused, but she hurried past the group and toward Lusk's cell.

"Come on, Captain," Pittman said, "settle down. Let him go. This won't accomplish anything." He looked at the other deputy. "And you, have a seat at that desk over there. There doesn't need to be any more trouble." The deputy took a seat and Williamson released the jailer, but without returning his weapon. "Now, let's just all calm down here," Pittman urged.

Williamson returned to Lusk's cell while Pittman stood in the doorway, where he could keep an eye on the deputies and still be able to hear most of what was being said in the cell. Anabel had secured a water bowl and a washcloth from the office and was cleaning Lusk's face as the first mate described Baldridge's efforts and Tyner's trip to New Orleans to search for Dillard Quick. As he listened to Lusk, Williamson began to wonder if he'd been too hard on Baldridge. It was beginning to sound as if the man had made some headway after all, though Lusk was able to offer nothing more than Baldridge's suspicion of Quick and some question about a man named Dodd.

"We just need something to show the court," Williamson said, pacing inside Jacob's cell. "All this may be true, but we've got no evidence."

"That's what Mr. Baldridge says he's gonna get, Cap'n. I believe him, too."

Williamson looked out through the bars. "Where in the hell is he? I told him to meet us here." He turned to Lusk. "Has he heard anything from Salina Tyner?"

"No, sir. Not a word as of last night. He brought me my supper again. Mr. Baldridge been takin' real good care of me, Cap'n."

Williamson looked around the cell, then back at Lusk. "Yeah? Where the hell was he when they beat you? Tell me that."

"I don't know, Cap'n."

"Probably drunk somewhere." He turned to Pittman, who was still watching the deputies. "Well? You heard what he said. What can *you* do?"

Pittman stroked his chin whiskers. "Captain, it's like I told you in St. Louis. I can't do anything without some kind of evidence. Hell, I've already done more than I should have. I had hoped your man Baldridge would have found something. Just keep one thing in mind." He raised one finger. "I'm not down here about the murder. I'm down here about this Confederate money. And unless you can show some kind of link between the two, these lawmen here in Memphis don't have to give me the time of day."

"Cap'n, you ain't gonna let 'em beat him again, are you?" Anabel asked. "I believe he may have a broke rib."

"I ought to just take him out of here right now," Williamson said.

"You can't do that," Pittman said.

"The hell I can't!" Williamson picked up the keys. "The cell door's open. We can walk him right out of here."

"I know what I'm talking about, Captain." Pittman adjusted his position and leaned against the other side of the door facing. "If you bust him out of here, you'll end up in jail *with* him. And what will that get you? Lusk will look guilty as hell and you'll be off the river."

"Cap'n, I'll be all right," Lusk said, forcing a smile for Anabel. "Don't do nothin' to get yourself in no trouble."

"He's right," said Pittman. "Besides"—he holstered his revolver—"I'm sworn to uphold the law, remember? I won't be part of a jailbreak."

Williamson studied Pittman standing in the doorway, then considered the revolver in his own hand. How could he leave Jacob where Crawford could get to him again? Even if the policeman didn't beat him, there was always the chance Jacob would be found guilty, and they'd hang him for sure. Williamson saw Pittman eyeing him suspiciously as he slowly drew the hammer back on the revolver. There might not be another chance to free Jacob, and breaking him out now would keep him from the hangman's noose. But it would turn Lusk and himself into fugitives. Someone would always be hunting them, if not for the sake of justice then for the reward that would surely be offered. The more Williamson thought about it, the more he realized that to free Lusk at gunpoint was no option at all. Never again would either man be able to return to the river, and that, for Jacob Lusk, would be worse than dying. Pittman was right. He had to prove Jacob was innocent, and he had to do it fast.

Williamson uncocked the pistol and lowered it to his side. He sent Anabel back to the *Paragon* to get a couple of men to stay with Jacob. Once they appeared, about an hour later, Williamson gave the keys back to the deputies, with a stern warning of what he would do if anyone so much as touched Jacob Lusk again. Baldridge still hadn't shown up, and a furious Williamson decided to go looking for him. He and

Pittman took Jacob's suggestion and went first to the Overton Hotel.

"Mr. Baldridge hasn't stayed here in several days," Thomas told them. "He has come by to check for messages once or twice since then. He's really quite a brute, you know. Quite a nuisance indeed."

"Are there any messages now?"

The clerk appeared defensive. "Well, Captain, even if there were I'm not sure I could let you have them."

"Look, mister." Williamson pointed to Pittman. "You see that badge?"

"Yes, sir."

"That man is a U.S. marshal. If you won't give Baldridge's messages to me, you damned well better give 'em to him."

"I'm afraid you're too late. Somebody's already picked up the only telegram Mr. Baldridge's received."

"Who? When?"

"A gentleman came in about an hour ago and said that Mr. Baldridge sent him to pick up his messages."

"And you just *gave* them to him?" Williamson said.

"Captain," Thomas said, tilting his head back indignantly, "Mr. Baldridge is no longer a guest at this hotel. He hasn't been since Wednesday. I only kept his silly telegram out of courtesy. And, as strange as he is, I don't think it the least bit odd that he would send someone here on his behalf." Thomas appeared confident as he looked closely at Pittman's badge. "I warned Sally Tyner about that Mr. Baldridge. What kind of trouble is he in with the law, anyway?"

"The man who picked up the telegram," Williamson said, "what did he look like?"

"Kind of a thin man. Dark hair. Not particularly good-looking," Thomas observed.

"His name?"

"I don't know. I've never seen him before."

"Do you remember what was in the telegram?"

"Captain," Thomas replied, "I'm not in the habit of reading telegrams addressed to residents of the hotel."

"But I'll bet you read Baldridge's, didn't you?"

Thomas folded his arms and looked away from Williamson, his jaw set tight.

"You *did*, didn't you."

"Come on, mister," Pittman said. "If you know something that will help us . . ."

"It was sealed and I didn't open it. But I did peek around the edge of the fold," Thomas admitted sheepishly. "I don't know exactly what it said, but it was from New Orleans. I think Salina Tyner sent it."

"And that's all you know?" Pittman said.

"I told you I didn't open it."

"Listen, if Baldridge shows up, tell him to wait here until we get back," Williamson ordered. "We're going to check a few more saloons over on Whiskey Chute. I'll check back with you first thing in the morning."

Thomas seemed perturbed. He did not answer.

"You *can* do that? I mean, it's not too much trouble, is it?"

"Yes, Captain."

"Yes, you'll tell him, or yes, it's too much trouble?"

"I'll speak to Mr. Baldridge if he should come in."

Williamson's cold stare was enough, he hoped, to keep the desk clerk's head out of his ass—at least until morning.

14

Sunday afternoon

IT WAS AN insult, that's what it was. Pure and simple.
After all he'd gone through to find Cassie Pierce's killer,
Williamson showed up with this meddling St. Louis marshal
to take over *his* case. He ought to walk into that jailhouse and
throw Williamson's twenty dollars back at him and tell him
he was through. Find somebody else. And he might do it
yet—except he'd just spent the last dollar on a bottle of whiskey.

"What time is it?" he shouted to the bartender in Pete
Flanagan's, one of his favorite drinking establishments along
Whiskey Chute.

"Almost four o'clock," the bartender replied.

He ought to go on to the jail. Williamson and his marshal
friend would be waiting, and he figured the captain was still
mad from their earlier encounter on the boat. Baldridge didn't
remember much of what he had said, but it probably didn't
matter now. Williamson was probably pacing the floor. And
that marshal. Who the hell did he think he was?

One more drink before he had to face them. He would quit the case, and with the money Williamson advanced him for a week's work, he figured to call it even. They didn't need him anymore. If only he hadn't come to think so much of Jacob Lusk, it would be easy to tell Williamson he was quitting. But the time he'd spent talking to the first mate had convinced him, beyond any evidence he might uncover, that Lusk was innocent. He had found in Lusk a rare thing—a truly decent man. And for all her gruff manner, he suspected Salina Tyner thought the same, else she wouldn't have dashed off in search of Dillard Quick. But for all his effort, it had come down to one fact. He had failed. Sure, he had traced the coin, and he was convinced that Dodd was involved with Quick somehow, but he had no hard evidence and he was no closer to freeing Jacob than he had been when the *Paragon* sailed for St. Louis last Tuesday. How could he blame Williamson? Hell, he would have fired himself.

Baldridge was pouring another drink when Crawford pulled up a chair to his table.

"Mind if I join you?" he asked without waiting for a reply.

Baldridge looked around at the near-empty bar. "I reckon not. The place could use the business."

Crawford took the bottle Baldridge shoved at him. "Baldridge, me and you need to talk."

"I've been trying to talk to you for a week."

"I been busy." Crawford poured himself a drink. "But I've been thinking about what you said. About William Dodd."

Baldridge perked up. "Did you check on Dodd like I said?"

"I've been asking a few questions."

"And?"

"Well, maybe this Dodd ain't quite the upstanding citizen everybody thinks he is."

"And Dillard Quick? Did you connect him to Quick?"

"Well, not exactly." Crawford removed his hat. "I need to know more. I need you to tell me exactly how much you know about Dodd."

"It's like I been trying to say: The night Cassie Pierce was murdered, Dillard Quick was the last person seen with her."

"I know all that. You've been harping about this Dillard Quick for a week now. But Quick ain't nowhere to be found."

"That's because he's gone back to New Orleans."

"New Orleans?"

"That's right. Sally Tyner went down there to see if she could find him."

"Did she?"

"I haven't heard a word from her. I expected a telegram any day, but so far there's been nothing."

"What do you have to connect Quick to Dodd?"

"Quick was seen with Dodd's men the day after Pierce was killed."

"You already told me that. But you never told me how you found out."

Baldridge wanted to tell him about Eli Rawls, but given Crawford's attitude toward coloreds, that might be enough to make him stop looking. He wouldn't risk it. Not if Crawford was finally starting to do some serious investigating.

"The man that told me is reliable. What matters is that Dodd lied to me. He said he wasn't in Memphis that day, and neither were any of his men." Baldridge tapped the table as if to hold Crawford's attention. "Don't you see what I'm saying? The man lied. A man that's got nothing to hide don't lie."

"You're holding back on me, Baldridge. You know more than you're saying."

Baldridge stared into the whiskey before him.

"Dodd's got no motive to kill a prostitute. Hell, the man

was nowhere near the boat that night. Now, if you're saying one of his men killed that whore, then maybe there's something to it. But a man like Dodd . . . it just don't make no sense. He loves the coloreds. Hell, he even let Lusk use his lawyer."

"Maybe that was just to cover himself—to make us look somewhere else."

"What did you ever do with that coin you said you found in Pierce's room?"

"I hid it."

"Where?"

"Well, if I told you it wouldn't be hid, would it?"

"Come on, Baldridge. You've been dogging me for days about this case, hollering about your nigger friend being innocent, and bringing up Dodd. How do you expect me to help if you won't tell me what you know?"

The alcohol was tightening its grip on Baldridge. He leaned over the table and spoke in a whisper.

"I'll tell you this much." He looked around as if confiding a secret. "That coin was the real thing. Honest to God. And whoever killed Cassie Pierce was trying to get it back. There's probably thousands more like it . . . somewhere."

Crawford refilled Baldridge's glass. "What else do you know about this gold?"

Baldridge's eyes were blurry and his head was spinning, so he leaned back in the chair and stared at the chandelier overhead. "You tell me something, Crawford."

"What's that?"

"How come you locked on to Jacob Lusk like a bird dog from the very start of this case? You ain't been willing to listen to nobody or to look for anybody else."

"Because I got evidence on Jacob Lusk."

Baldridge continued to stare at the chandelier. "Evidence, bull."

"More than you've got. You can't find this Quick fella, you won't produce this coin you've been carrying on about. . . . Hell, I'm wasting my time even listening to you."

"You ain't gonna have to worry about listening to me much longer." Baldridge lowered his gaze. "Captain Williamson's done brought him a U.S. marshal down here to take the case."

"What are you talking about?"

"They come in here this afternoon on the *Paragon*. I met 'em at the wharf. Williamson made a big deal how this marshal was going to get Jacob free."

Crawford appeared stunned by the news. "Are you sure about that?"

"I met him on the boat. Him and Williamson are probably at the jail right now checking on Jacob Lusk." Crawford, hand trembling, poured another drink and took it down in one shot. "Something wrong, Crawford? You afraid of a little competition?"

"I'm surprised that a Southern man like you would stand for that. I thought you told me Williamson hired you to work this case."

"I *ain't* gonna stand for it," Baldridge said. "Soon as I get to the jail I'm tellin' 'em what I know, and that'll be the end of it. I ain't working with no Yankee marshal."

Crawford forced a smile. "Can't say I blame you for that."

"Listen, I got to go on over to the jail. Are you headin' that way?"

"No, as a matter of fact, I'm not. Not right now. You say you're gonna talk to Williamson and this marshal this evening?"

"Soon as I can walk over there. Unless, of course, you're offering me a ride?"

"Can't do that. I've got to take care of some other business. But I'll be along later." Crawford stood up to leave.

"Are you really gonna check into Dodd, or were you just shootin' the shit?" Baldridge asked.

"I'll be watching out for Dodd," Crawford said. "You can be sure of that."

WHEN BALDRIDGE LEFT Pete Flanagan's it was raining again—one of those cold, blowing, chill-you-to-the-bone rains that should be long gone by April. The wind seemed to slice right through his coat as he pulled it close around him and lifted his collar up beneath his hat. He was sick of this weather and ready for the clear sky, the sweet fragrance of dogwood and cherry trees, and the pleasant evenings that were Memphis in the springtime. Instead, he pulled his hat low over his eyes and faced the rain, the cold, and the dark as he trudged up Main Street.

The squish of a damp sock in his left boot reminded him of the crack in the edge of his sole—the crack Uncle Melton had no doubt observed when he asked if he was shopping for a new pair. A damned shame, Baldridge thought. A man couldn't even buy a new pair of boots when he needed it. It hadn't always been that way. Back before the war he would never have let his boots get into this shape. Back before the war he would have had a decent coat instead of a torn, thin piece of trash that allowed even the most modest of breezes to pass through. Back before the war he had money, and a job, and . . . a life. Back before the war he could walk like a man instead of limping like a lame, old goat.

But this was after the war.

He clumped along Main Street, the alcohol spinning through his system, teasing his eyesight, his balance, his mind. A couple of drops of cold rain slipped past his hat and over his collar and crept down his neck. He shivered and holed up around a corner out of the wind. Leaning against the wall not far from a gas street lamp, he pulled his flask from his pocket and took a sip. Yes, the pain was back. Or did it ever really go away? Just more of the same. Too damned broke to own a horse, and too damned lame to walk. He took another swig. Through the thick night air, made to glow by the yellow light of the street lamp, he saw his reflection in a window across the alley. At first he was startled. That couldn't be him. Some street bum had slipped up behind him. He looked left, then right. But he was alone—alone with the figure staring blankly back at him from the window. Who was it? Who was this pitiful creature slumped against that building? It couldn't be Masey Baldridge. No, Masey was a blacksmith, and a damned good one. He had a house out on East Monroe, and two fine horses, and a shop. Why, he was a farrier, too. One of the best around. Folks brought him their horses to treat from all over Shelby County, sometimes further.

Leaving the shelter of the building eaves, Baldridge walked slowly across the street, watching his reflection as the rain began pelting him. Look how he moved! Like some kind of circus freak, or an old man kicked too many times by his mules. He had been kicked all right, he figured. Kicked by life, or fate, or God, or something. He moved within a few inches of the window, the lamplight behind him dancing off the glass. Who was this man? His hand shook as he took another drink, still staring in disbelief. He knew no one who looked like that. The man he knew carried himself tall and proud. He had a profession, a trade, dignity. The man in the window had nothing.

There in the rain and the cold and the near-magical light from the wind-tossed street lamp, it all came back to him as clear as if it were yesterday. He could see it right there in the window. A proud man standing tall alongside his fellow troopers—standing before their mounts, awaiting inspection in his high-collared butternut jacket. His carbine at port, his cartridge box at the ready, he waited for the general. All spit and polish, his brass at a high shine, he stood in that line of troopers, ready for a fight. General Forrest would pass, and his nod of approval would make Masey's blood rush faster than anything but the command of "Mount. By column of fours, march." They would be off on one those great raids that terrorized the Yankees. They owned the countryside as they cut through the night, and somehow the rain and the cold never seemed to hurt the way they did now. He could see Morton's artillery slugging through the mud, and ol' Tyree Bell driving that herd of hogs and cattle out of Jackson that cold December night. He could see the general directing the crossing of the Hatchie at Estanaula—that rickety old ferry, loaded to the waterline and struggling against the current amid the torchlight from the bank. The Federals were closing in from every direction, the breath of death or capture heavy in the air, and yet . . . there had been no fear—only belief in the general, and his buddies, and himself. In the reflection he saw himself riding in pursuit as they whipped the Yankees at Brice's Cross Roads and in a dozen lesser skirmishes. But then the image changed, and that awful moment outside of Selma played out before him. When the patrol left that morning he knew something was wrong. He just felt it, that sick feeling you get when you sense you're flying in the face of fate. Foolishness, one of his friends had called it. Veteran's affliction. The war was over for all intents and purposes, and he and the others knew it. They were just going through the motions now, protecting their supplies and holding their position until . . . until the end. Even a wizard like General Forrest could find no way out of this. There were too few men left, too little ammunition, and far too many Federals. He was in the advance, with Sheppard and Eads alongside. They would simply scout forward and locate the enemy picket line, then return. There was to be no fighting. He remembered how the air felt that morning, how crisp and cool, the smell of honeysuckle floating about the narrow country lane they rode along.

Then came the pain, a sharp, biting sensation like someone stabbing him in his left knee. The pain traveled up his leg and traversed the left side of his body, and he felt himself driven backward and to the right, his carbine rising from its sling, striking him in the left ear as he tumbled from his mount. He hit the ground on his right side, bouncing several inches off the hard clay before settling back. His horse spooked and dashed away and he could hear the others returning fire, shouting to him and cussing the Yankees. Reaching down, he touched his knee and felt warm blood soaking his trouser leg, and in a moment of terror he realized he had fulfilled the dread of earlier that morning. He tried to rise, but fell back to the ground. Then blackness. Then nothing.

Nothing. That was what the man in the window had, all right. Nothing. No job. No home. No land. No Rachael. Baldridge turned from the window and watched the gas street lamp above him. The wind and rain were whipping the flame, which was protected by only a thin glass globe. How cruelly nature toyed with it, pushing it this way and that, having the power at any moment to mercifully snuff it out, yet preferring, apparently, to watch it wiggle and dance and battle to survive. He wished he had died that day in Selma. Just more rotten luck. Or was it? Maybe God just wanted to watch him dance. Funny—no, more cruel than funny—making a cripple dance.

Church bells from a few blocks away echoed through the wet night. He remembered it was Sunday. Almost a week had passed, and still Jacob Lusk sat in jail. He, Masey Baldridge, had accomplished nothing. And it was so late in the evening that he was sure Williamson would fire him now. He should have been at the jail hours ago. What the hell—Williamson had his marshal. Let them figure it out. But he was haunted by the vision of an innocent man walking to the gallows, while Dillard Quick and William Dodd were free. Ah, there was nothing he could do. Or was there? Through the whiskey cloud he tried to remember the name of the church Dodd said he attended last Sunday night. Green . . . No, Grove. That was it. He knew the place. It was on Jefferson Street. Maybe Quick was out of reach, but Baldridge wasn't about to let Dodd get away with this. He would find him and confront him.

After a couple of wrong turns up dead-end alleys, Baldridge found his way to Jefferson Street. Three blocks east of Main, he heard singing emanating from the white wood-frame Grove Methodist Church. To the accompaniment of a slightly out-of-tune piano, the congregation's singing filled the rainy night air, and the lights inside seemed to warmly invite him to enter. The congregation was just beginning a new song as Baldridge moved up on the steps and under the portico where he stood for a moment listening.

> Sowing in the sunshine, sowing in the shadows
> Fearing neither clouds nor winter's chilling
>   breeze.
> By and by the harvest and the labor ended
> We shall come rejoicing, bringing in the sheaves.
> Bringing in the sheaves, bringing in the sheaves
> We shall come rejoicing, bringing in the sheaves
> Bringing in the sheaves, bringing in the sheaves
> We shall come rejoicing, bringing in the sheaves.

That was Rachael's favorite song. He had heard her sing it dozens of times during the two years they were married. And they had played it at her funeral. Baldridge relived the horror of those days anew as the strains of the hymn flowed from the building. A loving wife and a much anticipated child, then the miscarriage and his family gone in an instant—making it so easy to join up when the war came a year later.

Baldridge slipped into the back of the half-empty sanctuary, drawing several curious glances as he took a seat on the rear pew. Water dripped from his coat and made a puddle at his feet as he picked up a hymnal and thumbed through it to find the song they were singing. He rose to his feet and tried to sing, but the words would not come—only tears, tears and pain of his years without Rachel.

> Going forth with weeping, sowing for the Master
> Tho' the loss sustained our spirit often grieves.
> When our weeping's over, He will bid us welcome
> We shall come rejoicing, bringing in the sheaves.

The song mercifully ended and the congregation sat. Several were pointing at Baldridge and whispering, and he realized he was the only one still standing. He wiped away the tears and quickly sat down.

"Brothers and sisters," the preacher began, "God is sending his rain this evening to bless the earth. To renew the harvest." Baldridge pulled his flask from his pocket and took a swig. "And though it's cold and bad outside, we are warm with the spirit within."

"Amen!" a parishioner shouted.

"Amen!" Baldridge echoed, a little too loud. A well-dressed lady two rows in front of him turned and stared. He held up his flask as if to offer her a drink, and she quickly turned back around in embarrassment. He knew what she was thinking. Another tramp. Another worthless bum off the street come in to confess his sins.

From his vantage point, he eyed each pew in search of William Dodd. An older couple was seated at the end of one pew, the wife unable to keep from glancing back at him. Near her was a man in an expensive suit, and beside him another well-dressed lady. But up in the second row, not far from the preacher, he spotted Mrs. Dodd. She looked so much different than the day he had seen her in the garden at the Dodd ranch, yet when she turned slightly, he recalled her dark-blond hair and round face. She had seemed much too decent a woman to be with a man like Dodd. And sitting beside her, his long, reddish sideburns making him stand out, was Dodd himself. Baldridge watched him sitting there all pious and proper, his arm over the back of the pew and around his lovely wife. He was the very essence of virtue. How could he do it? How could he sit here in God's house, knowing what happened to Cassie Pierce? Baldridge would call his bluff. He would show Dodd up for the hypocrite he was. And here was his chance.

The preacher called for testimony, and a church member spoke briefly of some blessing he had received.

"Can anyone else testify?" the minister asked them.

Baldridge, energized by the wine, rose to his feet.

"I can!"

The preacher hesitated as the crowd turned to view this disheveled man in a torn, soaking-wet coat and crumpled hat, with a two-day stubble. Baldridge took joy in the look on Dodd's face as he stepped from the rear pew and limped unsteadily down the aisle.

"Yes, brother?" the preacher said cautiously.

"He's drunk!" a woman whispered as he passed.

"I can smell it on him," her companion said.

Baldridge halted, leaned over, and whispered to the women, "Why, honey, I'm just drunk in the spirit. Ain't that what the Bible says? 'Be ye drunk in the spirit'?"

People murmured among themselves as Baldridge continued toward the pulpit.

"Do you have a testimony, brother?" the wary minister inquired.

"Damned straight," Baldridge declared, stepping up on the platform.

The preacher laughed nervously, then moved closer to him and spoke softly. "I think, my brother, you've got a demon of liquor."

Baldridge neared him and spoke as if confiding a secret. "Oh, I've got a demon, all right." He opened his jacket to let the preacher peek in his pocket. "But I got a *bottle* of liquor."

The minister, sensing the concern spreading throughout his congregation, attempted to intercede. "Brother, won't you let me— "

"Have a seat, Preacher."

"Brother, how about—"

Baldridge pulled his revolver and laid it on the pulpit. "I said have a seat, Preacher. And I ain't your brother."

The frightened preacher backed away till he landed on the front row, all in one motion.

"He's got a gun!" somebody shouted.

"Go get the law!" another man yelled. "He's crazy drunk."

Baldridge raised the revolver and fired it once into the ceiling, the crowd responding with a massive, unified flinch.

"Go get the damned law. I don't care! 'Cause I'm gonna testify just like the preacher here asked." Someone slipped out of the front door but Baldridge ignored him. "I'm supposed to stand up here and tell you about my blessings," he continued, lowering his weapon to his side. "Well, I can't really do that, because I ain't got no blessings!" He leaned on the podium. "Unless you call being a cripple a blessing. I'm supposed to joy in my suffering, the preacher said a while ago, but tell me, preacher: How much suffering is a man supposed to take? How much?"

A small, quiet voice in Baldridge's head—far back in the recesses of his mind not yet seared by the alcohol—was telling him to stop, to put the weapon away and walk out. He knew he should heed that voice, but it was as if someone else were speaking, someone or something that he was powerless to control.

"If God really gives and God really takes away," he said, using the pulpit to steady himself, "then tell me why he gave me this leg and took away my Rachael?" Tears cascaded over his cheeks as he continued, his speech growing more slurred. The hushed crowd sat spellbound by his ranting. "How am I suppose to believe in a God that punishes the innocent and lets the guilty go free? Tell me how!" His eyes scanned the congregation and eventually fell upon Dodd. "We have a man among us tonight . . . who knows all about guilt—a man who stands here with you . . . singing to God . . . while an innocent person suffers for someone else's crime." He pointed his free hand at Dodd. "He is here before you . . . William Jenkins Dodd. Liar and murderer."

"Now, see here!" the preacher said, rising to his feet, but a wild-eyed glare from Baldridge silenced him and returned him to his seat. The congregation was looking at Dodd in expectation of some response. Dodd smiled and tried to appear restrained.

"The man's drunk," Dodd said. "He doesn't know what he's saying."

"I'm testifying!" Baldridge shouted. "Ain't that what you said, Preacher? I'm testifying . . . that Mr. Dodd consorts with whores and murderers." The crowd began to murmur. "God knows this is the only place anybody will ever testify against him."

"That's enough, Baldridge!" Dodd shouted back.

"Oh, no! I'm just gettin' started. And when I'm through with you *you'll* be finished. You and your high 'n' mighty plans . . ."

The man who had left the building earlier now reappeared, and Baldridge, drunk as he was, sensed the police weren't far behind.

"Okay, Preacher," he said, pointing his gun overhead. "I hereby end my testimony . . . in the name of the Father!"

BANG! He fired into the ceiling above the left side of the congregation.

"And the Son!"

BANG! Another shot, into the center of the ceiling.

"And the Holy goddamned Ghost!"

BANG! He fired a third round, over the right side of the room. As plaster dust descended like manna over them, the entire congregation, including the preacher, lay prostrate beneath the pews, humble and silent before the new Trinity of Baldridge, Smith & Wesson.

Leaving through a back door, Baldridge staggered into the street and hurried along Jefferson, ducking into an alley and emerging on Adams. He could hear the police reaching the church, moments behind him. The cold rain in his face started to clear his head, and as he made his way through the darkness he began to realize what he had done. The sorrow, like a fog, gradually surrounded him.

A House of God. He had defiled a House of God.

He began sobbing like the lost soul he was, still weaving and stumbling—partly from the liquor, partly from the tears, and partly from the unrelenting rain. He tripped over a hitching post and fell, catching himself as his good knee landed in the mud. His other leg twinged as he pulled himself to his feet and continued, only to slip again. He thought he heard someone behind him and he turned to look, but no one was there. Farther down Adams Street, he again thought he heard someone following, but he saw no one. Finally, at a corner, he leaned against a brick wall, the damp smell of sweat permeating his clothes. His eyes were half-closed as he steadied himself against the wall.

How could he have done that? How could God ever forgive him? If there was a hell that folks really went to, he figured to be driving the wagon; and what gnawed at his soul was knowing that his beloved Rachael would be somewhere else. Eternity without her . . . he couldn't bear the thought. He had to turn himself around. He had to straighten out. Again the tears came and he slumped to a sitting position, his face in his hands, bawling like a baby.

Someone was sloshing through the darkness and mud toward him, so he pulled himself to his feet and fled around the corner, limping as fast as his leg would allow. The stranger followed and was closing upon him when Baldridge stopped, turned, and drew his weapon.

"Don't come no closer," he said, his blurred vision obscuring the face that looked back at him through the rain and the darkness. "Why are you following me?" He received no reply. "Stay the hell away from me!"

But before he could turn to flee, Baldridge was dropped to the muddy street by a sharp blow from behind.

15

Monday, April 7, 8:40 A.M.

"I'M HERE TO see Crawford," Luke Williamson said as he entered the Memphis jail. Marshal Pittman was with him.

"He's down the hall there," the officer at the desk replied, pointing somewhat apprehensively to his right.

Williamson opened the door and, seeing Crawford facing away from him as he talked with another officer, rushed the man. Grabbing his sleeve just above the elbow, he spun Crawford around and delivered a right cross to his chin, sending him to the floor. Before his stunned companion could move, Williamson was kneeling over Crawford and punching him repeatedly in the face.

"I'll teach you to beat one of my men!" Williamson shouted. Crawford struggled to parry his blows.

The officer who had been talking with Crawford moments before attempted to pull Williamson off, but ended up being driven against a nearby cell.

"Whip his ass!" a prisoner yelled from an adjacent cell.

The commotion brought the officer from the front desk racing down the hall, and he, together with the other officer and Pittman, finally got Williamson off Crawford.

Crawford, his nose bleeding and his lip swelling, got to his feet.

"What the hell do you think you're doing?"

Williamson was still wrestling to get at him.

"You're gonna pay for what you did to Jacob," he said. "I'll see to it."

Crawford wiped his lip. He noticed Pittman's badge.

"Sometimes prisoners don't cooperate. The marshal here can tell you that. Right, Marshal?"

Pittman did not answer, but spoke to Williamson instead. "Now, calm down, Captain. This will get us nowhere."

"He's right," Crawford said. "I could arrest you for this."

"Why don't you try it?" Williamson snapped.

Crawford motioned for his men to release the captain.

"What kind of a half-assed operation are you people running here?" Pittman asked. "Beating prisoners—"

"Well, offhand I'd have to say it's an operation that's none of your damned business, *Marshal*. You see, what the captain's boat nigger did ain't no federal crime." He dabbed his bleeding nostril gently. "It's a local matter. Ain't got nothin' to do with the U.S. Marshal's Office."

"Maybe it does."

Crawford managed a pained laugh. "Yeah, in a pig's eye. I halfway figured to see you two down here today. That drunk Baldridge told me you were in town."

"Baldridge? Where did you see Baldridge?" Williamson demanded.

"Where does anybody ever see Baldridge? I talked to him last night at Pete Flanagan's."

"When?"

"Oh, I guess it was five-thirty, maybe six o'clock."

"He was supposed to meet us last night here at the jail," Pittman said.

Having stopped the bleeding, Crawford folded his bandana. "Well, now, I guess your investigator had a more important appointment. With a bottle of Kentucky bourbon."

Williamson looked at Pittman in disgust. "Damn!"

"Oh, now don't take it so hard, Captain. He's been trying real hard to earn that money you paid him. All week long he's been making a nuisance of himself, wandering around town spreading crazy stories about lost gold and all manner of other foolishness." Crawford chuckled. "And all the while I've got the killer of Cassie Pierce right down that other hall."

"But you couldn't beat a confession out of him, could you, Crawford?"

"Don't need one. Baldridge has nothing but theories, and your whore friend—hell, she up and took off to New Orleans. You really ought to hire better help, Captain."

Williamson bolted for him again, but Crawford stepped back and placed his hand on his sidearm, ready to draw. The captain halted. "You better get him bridled," he told the marshal, "before I lose my patience."

"Where's Baldridge now?" Williamson asked.

"Who knows? But there ain't much doubt about where he was last night."

"And where's that?"

"How about crazy drunk? How about shootin' up a house of God?"

"What are you talking about?"

"Last night after I left him at Flanagan's, the drunken fool went crazy. Showed up plastered at a little church over on Jefferson. Pulled a gun on the minister, threatened the congregation, cussed and accused one of the parishioners, and shot up the place. He's lucky no one was killed."

"I can hardly believe that," Williamson said.

"Bullet holes in the ceiling don't lie."

"What happened after that?"

"He took off before me and the boys could get there. Shook up them churchgoing people real bad."

Williamson headed for the office.

"By the way," Crawford said, "Lusk's trial has been moved up to tomorrow."

The captain stopped. "It's supposed to be Thursday."

"This is a serious matter. The judge agrees. He'll hear the case tomorrow. So, if I was you, I'd pick me out a real nice suit of clothes for the funeral, 'cause your boy in there is gonna hang like a side of beef."

16

Monday, April 7, nine A.M.

A STEADY RAIN falling on the tin roof gradually brought Masey Baldridge to consciousness. He lay on his right side, his hands behind his back; a window high on the wall illuminated a dusty floor littered with dry cotton hulls, pigeon droppings, and a few water puddles. When Baldridge started to get up, he realized his hands were tied. His feet also. He lay back and looked up at the roof, spitting several times to clear a strand of cotton from his mouth. Where was he? How had he gotten here?

His right arm was tingling from lying on it, so he rolled over to his left side. He could see across a large open room, empty except for four or five cotton bales lined against the far wall, and a table and three chairs near a doorway. He suspected he was above the ground floor. Somewhere. But where? How? Why?

A pigeon ducked into the corner of the building to escape the rain. It walked along a rafter until it was directly above him; then it ruffled its wings and stopped suddenly, as if it had just noticed Baldridge. The bird peered down curiously at him, rocking back and forth.

If that thing shits on me . . .

Baldridge worked his way into a sitting position and scooted across the floor so he could lean against the wall. The room was damp and chilly. He shivered, and realized his coat was missing. So were his knife and revolver. He closed his eyes and tried to remember. Going into Pete Flanagan's for a quick drink, Sunday afternoon. He remembered meeting the *Paragon* when it arrived from St. Louis—arguing with Luke Williamson—there was some marshal—Crawford had been at Flanagan's. He had done it this time. He had drunk too much, stayed too long. But how long? And how did he get here? Outside he could hear an occasional wagon clopping and squeaking along a cobblestone street. He must be near the river, somewhere near the wharf. With his hands and ankles bound and his bad leg unable to fully bend, Baldridge had to struggle for almost five minutes to get to his feet. The windows were too high to see out of, so he began shuffling across the floor in tiny steps and short hops toward the doorway. The pigeon startled him as it flew across the room and landed on another rafter not far from the doorway, where it sat impassively watching his struggle.

When he reached the doorway, he leaned against it to catch his breath, and heard the unmistakable sound of a round being chambered into a rifle. Slowly he peered around the door jamb and down the stairwell.

"I thought I heard you," said a man standing in the shadows.

Baldridge pushed himself away from the wall, nearly losing his balance, as the man came up the stairs, rifle shouldered. He backed up awkwardly as Grady, Dodd's ranch hand, emerged on the second floor, his cheek pressed against the stock of a Winchester.

"Go on over to that table," Grady said, motioning with the weapon. "Go on, now. I ain't playin' with you."

Baldridge pulled a chair out with his foot and plopped into it. Everything was starting to come back now. He had been drinking Kentucky bourbon and plenty of it, and talking to Crawford in Pete Flanagan's. Then Crawford had left. He himself had started along Front Street to meet Williamson at the jail. Something hit him from behind. He blacked out.

The room echoed each step as Grady approached.

"Where in the hell am I?"

"Out of the way, where you belong," Grady said. "You been out all night."

"How did I get here?" His mouth tasted chalky.

"I found you wandering the streets last night. Thought you might need a place to sleep it off."

"You jumped me from behind, didn't you?"

"You ask too many damned questions." Grady smiled. "But in a way, I guess I ought to thank you."

"What for?"

"I'm gonna be a rich man thanks to all those questions."

"What are you talking about?"

"Five years I worked like a dog for Dodd. Did all his dirty work for him, saw after his hired help—"

"What's that got to do with me?"

"Hadn't been for you, I would never have found out what I've been hauling around all these years."

"And what's that?"

"Gold, Baldridge. More gold than a man could spend in two lifetimes. But I got me a cut coming now. Mr. Dodd said so. All I got to do is see to it you don't get in the way." Baldridge saw Grady draw his rifle to the side. He tried to dodge what was coming, but he moved too slowly.

"Thank you," Grady said, as his rifle butt caught Baldridge on his right temple and sent him to the floor, the chair tumbling from beneath him. From the pocket of his own coat, Grady took Baldridge's flask. He removed the lid and took a drink.

"That's some damned good wine you got there." He wiped his mouth with his sleeve, returned the flask to his jacket pocket, and promptly kicked Baldridge in the ribs. Baldridge groaned and tried to roll away. Grady kicked him again, this time catching him in the left thigh.

"You ain't gonna cause no more problems for nobody." Baldridge tugged futilely at the rope binding his hands. As Grady stepped toward him again, Baldridge curled into a ball and tightened every muscle in anticipation of the next blow. "I ain't about to let you come between me and a fortune. I done killed me a whore for Mr. Dodd, I might as well kill me a drunk, too." That was the last thing Baldridge heard before something struck him in the back of the head.

PERHAPS IT WAS the cold that brought him to, or maybe the pain, but when Baldridge awoke his head was throbbing fit to burst. It was dark outside, and only a solitary lantern shone in the room, but he noticed immediately that his shirt was wet. For a terrifying moment, in the poor light, he thought the liquid was blood. But it was only water from the leaky roof finding its mark. He lay within a few feet of the table, in the same spot he had fallen. Lifting his head, he expected to find Grady standing over him, but instead he saw William Jenkins Dodd sitting at the table.

"I want to tell you how disappointed I am in you, Mr. Baldridge." Dodd spoke softly, matter-of-factly, as if he were discussing a business deal. "After I made the gesture of providing your Negro with my own attorney, you rewarded my kindness by accusing me."

Baldridge struggled to clear his head.

"You're guilty as hell, Dodd."

Dodd shook his head sadly. "Oh yes, words of wisdom from our newly ordained minister."

Dodd's words called up a blurry memory. "Bringing in the Sheaves." A church.

"You made quite a fool of yourself last night, Baldridge." His face grew stern. "But what's worse, you embarrassed and insulted me in front of my wife, my friends, and my congregation. You've been running around Memphis for the last week trying to tie me to that trash that got herself killed on your friend's boat."

"You shouldn't have lied to me about knowing Dillard Quick," Baldridge said, working himself up into a sitting position.

"And you should have minded your own business."

"Did you help Grady kill Cassie Pierce?"

"Please, Mr. Baldridge. Do not insult me. I do not consort with women of no virtue."

"But Dillard Quick does."

"Yes, that is an unfortunate character flaw in Mr. Quick. Very unfortunate, as it turned out."

"What does Quick do for you?"

"He's a business associate of mine."

"And your business?"

"I have many business interests, Mr. Baldridge: my ranch, the railroad I'm building . . ."

"Confederate coins . . ."

"See? See, Mr. Baldridge? That is precisely the kind of meddling I'm talking about."

"How did you and Quick get your hands on gold from the Confederate treasury? And don't bother lying to me, because I know that's where the coin came from. I checked."

"Yes, I'm aware of your little visit to Jefferson Davis."

"How did you know—"

"I've had you watched, Mr. Baldridge. Ever since you came to my farm on Thursday, my man Grady's been keeping an eye on you."

"I hear you cut him in too."

"Yes. Though I must attribute that unexpected development to you. Oh, he was perfectly willing to get rid of that prostitute; after all, I do pay him well. But when you came around asking questions, Grady demanded to know more. I had to bring him into my confidence."

"To keep him quiet."

"Exactly."

"That's how you finance it all, isn't it, Dodd? Your big fancy ranch, and this railroad."

"Bond issue, Mr. Baldridge. I'm raising a bond issue for the railroad. Of course, it helped to have the initial start-up capital."

"And your bid for governor," Baldridge added. "It wouldn't hurt to have a little extra to bankroll that."

"You've complicated my work!" Dodd shouted, coming to his feet.

"I'm sure I have. If people ever found out how you were financing your little empire—"

"But they won't find out! What happened to that Pierce woman was an unfortunate accident. My business associate, Mr. Quick, inadvertently paid for his carnal desire with a piece of my gold."

"*Your* gold?"

"That's correct, Mr. Baldridge. *My* gold."

"So you had Cassie Pierce killed to get it back."

"Yes, but that's not important."

"It's important to Jacob Lusk."

"It's unfortunate about your Mr. Lusk. But sometimes we have to sacrifice—"

"We? *We* ain't sacrificing. Jacob Lusk is."

"Don't you understand? Mr. Lusk must sacrifice himself for the good of his kind. I am in the business of helping the Negro people. Do you have any idea how many freedmen I've assisted since the war?"

"Doesn't matter. It doesn't give you a license to kill."

Dodd walked around the table and stood near Baldridge. "Oh, but it does, Mr. Baldridge. I am finally going to be in a position to really accomplish something—something more than just a few dollars here and there for these people. With the railroad, I'll be able to hire hundreds of Negroes. With the governorship next year, I can return Tennessee to the policies of Governor Brownlow and get you ex-Johnnies under control again. I'll be able to see to it that land and wealth are properly distributed."

"You mean steal people's property," Baldridge said.

"Stealing? No more than the white man stole the Negro's very life when he condemned him to slavery. It's simply a matter of fair play."

"Returning to Brownlow's policies will only bring the Ku Klux out again in force. It will mean blood in the streets. And how can you talk about helping the coloreds, and let a man hang for a crime he didn't commit?"

"You just don't understand. Men like you never will. That one little coin in the wrong hands could destroy everything I've worked for. It could expose my financing and tie me to that whore."

"Mr. Dodd! Mr. Dodd! We got a problem," Grady shouted as he bounded up the stairs.

"What is it?"

"I went down to the wharf like I was supposed to," he said, trying to catch his breath. "I got me a real good spot on the roof where I could get off a shot, but it got dark before that boat came in."

"Did you find her?"

"Yes, sir. But I had to end up waitin' at the landing. Mr. Dodd, Dillard Quick wasn't with her. But there weren't no lawmen around, neither. It was strange. She just come right off the boat and got herself a dray and went on to the Overton Hotel. Hell, even if Quick had been there I couldn't have gotten no shot off with all them passengers around."

Sally Tyner. They had to be talking about Sally.

"All right. If she doesn't have Quick, that's one less problem. But the telegram said she had proof."

Telegram? Baldridge had seen no telegram. Where did they get it?

"I'm afraid she does," Grady said. "She has Quick's chest with her. The one he uses to carry the money back to New Orleans. As many times as I've hauled it around, I'd know it anywhere."

Dodd looked worried. "If she's found the coins I sent back with Quick, then what happened to him?"

"I don't know, Mr. Dodd, but he wasn't on the boat," Grady said.

"And she went to the Overton?"

"Yes, sir."

"I must get that chest back." Dodd pointed to Baldridge. "The one coin he's got won't matter if she's got Quick's chest."

"You want me to go get it? She's by herself. I could take it—"

"No, that's too risky. I have a better idea, but we'll have to move fast before she meets Williamson and that marshal." Dodd looked at Baldridge. "We'll make us a little trade." He studied him a moment. "Don't look so surprised, Mr. Baldridge. You think I don't know about that marshal your captain friend brought down from St. Louis? Very little escapes my attention. Very little."

From a drawer beneath the table, Dodd took some paper,

an inkwell, and a pen. He picked up the pen, then reconsidered and called to Grady. "Come over here and write what I tell you." He dictated a message offering to exchange Baldridge for the "merchandise" tomorrow morning, and Grady departed with the note. Dodd returned to his seat.

"I figure your whore will trade that trunk of coins for your life. And that's only fair considering the trouble you've already caused me." Dodd laughed. "Take Grady Teeter, for instance. Because of you, he's been running around here all week. The poor man's exhausted. But he thinks he's going to get rich for his efforts. Under other circumstances, it might be quite comic. All these years of picking up and delivering thousands of dollars in gold . . . and not even knowing it. But then, not even my dear wife knows. Only now, thanks to your meddling, have I had to bring Grady into my confidence. And, of course, now he expects a share. Now there's someone else involved. Another loose end. Another hand in my pocket. Someone else to distract—to take money away from my important work."

"Where did you get the gold, Dodd?"

Dodd smiled and looked away. "Those were exciting days as the war ended, Mr. Baldridge. A whole mass of people, starved for freedom, were finally going to have it. I saw a chance to be a part of all that."

"Most of the Yankees I met didn't give a damn about the plight of the coloreds. They were in this war for the Union."

"Well, Mr. Baldridge, I wasn't 'most Yankees.' I held a higher principle. Thus, when the opportunity came along to get my hands on enough gold to actually make a difference, I could not turn my back."

"From the looks of your ranch, I'd say you took care of yourself first."

"There is no sin in that, Mr. Baldridge. No sin at all. A penniless man has little influence in matters of state. Few men heed the counsel of a pauper. So, after the war, I determined to make myself heard."

"You mean 'rich,' don't you?"

"As you wish."

"I know that gold came from the Confederate treasury. What happened to James Semple?" Dodd looked at him strangely. "Come on, Dodd, you know who I'm talking about. How did you get the money from him?"

Dodd seemed momentarily surprised, but walked over to Baldridge and stood before him, arms folded. "Your Mr. Semple and one of his colleagues were captured near Tunica, Mississippi, in late May of 1865. Most regular forces had surrendered or were being paroled, so we suspected them to be guerrillas. They were rendered to my command in the stockade at Fort Pickering."

"And the gold?"

"I might never have known about it had Semple's compatriot not been, shall we say, less than firm in his loyalty to the South. Not being a man of virtue, Mr. Baldridge, he came to my office at the fort with this outrageous story about thousands of dollars in gold coins. He sought to strike a bargain for his release. Naturally, I didn't believe him at first, but he spoke so convincingly that I eventually allowed him, under my personal guard of course, to take me to a place about twenty miles south of Memphis. Imagine my surprise when I discovered he was telling the truth. Apparently he and Semple had secreted the money just before their capture by one of our patrols. It was in a cave some half a mile from the river. They had this ridiculous notion of crossing the Mississippi and linking up with Rebel forces in the Trans-Mississippi. Can you imagine that? Prolonging this terrible war! I, of course, took charge of the money, moved it to a safer place where I could keep an eye on it, and I rewarded the man appropriately."

"And how's that?"

"Let's just say he's been taken care of."

"And Semple?"

"It's unfortunate about Semple. He disappeared from the stockade. Strangely enough, my guards found him missing during roll call one evening. Our search never turned him up. We presume he tried to escape by swimming the river. Most likely he drowned."

"Most likely he had help."

"Mr. Baldridge, must you always think the worst of people?"

"Just comes natural when I'm around them."

Half an hour later, Grady Teeter came rushing up. "I left the message, Mr. Dodd."

"Did anyone see you?"

"Just the desk clerk. He don't know me from Adam."

"Good. Very good, Grady." Dodd stood up. "Mr. Baldridge and I have had an enlightening conversation, but I'm afraid it's growing late. Would you be so kind as to tie Mr. Baldridge to that pillar in the center of the room. And put something in his mouth. I don't want him shouting and drawing attention."

The back of Baldridge's head met with the wooden pillar hard as Grady strung a piece of rope across his mouth and pulled it tight behind the pillar. The hemp fibers in the quarter-inch rope dug into the corners of his mouth and Baldridge bit down on it to try and relieve the pressure. The rope tasted bitter and smelled of horsehair. His hands were still tied behind him; Grady put another rope around his waist and wound it down to his feet, then secured it behind the pole.

Grady stepped back, dusted his hands off, and with a look of satisfaction on his face, said, "That should do it, Mr. Dodd."

Baldridge cut his eyes to the left; his head was immobile and he dared not move it for fear the rope would tear deeper into the edges of his mouth. The table and the lamp were to his extreme left and slightly behind the pillar. Grady stood to his left front, not more than five feet away, a sickening grin on his face. Dodd walked over and stood directly in front of Baldridge.

"Do you think that whore will show up tomorrow with the gold?" Grady asked Dodd.

"Mr. Baldridge had best hope she does." Dodd checked the tightness of the rope. "Grady will stay with you tonight so you don't get lonely. And tomorrow morning about nine o'clock, if all goes well, you may be a free man."

Dodd crossed the room and started down the stairwell with Grady close behind.

"I'll sit right down here at the bottom of these stairs where I can keep an eye on the front door, Mr. Dodd."

"You do that, Grady. And if you handle tomorrow correctly, you'll be a wealthy man."

Baldridge listened as they tramped down the stairs. He heard the front door close; then Grady moved back across the lower floor to take a seat.

"Don't you get no ideas up there," Grady called, "because I'll be checkin' on you."

Why they hadn't finished him off Baldridge could only guess. He allowed himself a glimmer of hope that maybe Dodd would make the trade after all. More likely he would just keep him alive long enough to get the money back. Baldridge took a deep breath and let it out slowly. After about five minutes, the lamp, low on oil, flickered and the light began to fade. Within a couple more minutes, the room was dark. His shirt, wet from sweat, now chilled him in the damp air. His bad leg ached. His cheeks, made raw by the rope, burned. He could hear an occasional boat whistle from the river, but otherwise all was quiet. God, he needed a drink! In the stillness it occurred to him that Grady was probably finishing off the last of Eli's blackberry wine. So close, and yet . . .

17

Monday, April 7, 5:20 P.M.

SALINA TYNER WAS standing on the foredeck of the *Susie Silver* as the vessel nudged the wharfboat at the Memphis landing. The air was still heavy and damp from the daylong rain yesterday, and her curls, which a chambermaid had spent two hours putting into her hair, were threatening to collapse at any moment. She tugged impatiently at the light-green mitts that matched her dress and glanced behind her at the two trunks sitting on the deck. A tall, lean roustabout who had been watching her looked away quickly.

"Now you be ready as soon as that landing stage comes down," she said to him. "And you might as well get some help. You'll need it with that other trunk."

"Yes, ma'am," the roustabout said, retreating down the deck for reinforcements.

Watching the other deckhands prepare the boat for arrival, Tyner wondered whether Masey Baldridge had received her telegram and gotten the law on William Dodd. She halfway hoped he hadn't. Nothing would give her greater pleasure, she thought—gently rubbing her right foot against the derringer strapped to her left ankle—than to shoot the bastard herself.

"Passengers may go ashore now," the mud clerk called from the bow of the *Susie Silver*, so Tyner motioned for the four roustabouts now waiting behind her to follow her ashore. Retaining the services of a young German man minding a dray, she had the roustabouts load her trunks on the cart.

"If ze missus vould care for a carriage to ze hotel, I vill follow with your trunks," the dray operator said.

"No, thank you," Tyner replied, gently patting one of the trunks. "I'll just come along with you."

"As ze missus pleases."

Tyner peered up and down the busy landing at the row of steamboats, which stretched for nearly a quarter of a mile. Several men standing near a load of flour barrels were staring at her and talking among themselves. One of them, in particular, seemed to leer more than the others.

"Is the *Paragon* here?"

"Ze *Paragon* left yesterday, missus."

"All right. Then I'd like to go to the Overton Hotel."

"As ze missus pleases."

Tyner thought she heard a sound from somewhere near the dray. "And quickly, please. It's getting dark."

Thomas was already on duty. Seeing Tyner, he rushed out from behind the registration desk. "You're back!" He took her hand and smiled. "How do you always look so refreshed after such a trip?"

"Save the bullshit, Thomas. I'm not refreshed, I'm worn out," she said, noticing that his eyes were searching the doorway behind her. "What is it?"

"Oh, nothing," he said. "I was just seeing if that horrible Baldridge man was with you." He patted her hand. "You're so much better off without him."

Tyner appeared puzzled. "You mean he's not *here?*"

"Oh, no, thank goodness." Thomas seemed frustrated. "Can you believe he checked out of here and still expected me and the day clerk to keep messages for him? He's just the rudest thing I've ever—"

"You haven't seen Baldridge?"

"No," Thomas replied, "and you're certainly not the only one who's been asking about him." He leaned close to her and lowered his voice. "What kind of trouble is he in, anyway?"

"What do you mean?"

"Well, a U.S. marshal and that big, tall riverboat captain—Williamson—came in here yesterday looking for him." He shook his finger at her. "I told you he was trouble."

"A U.S. marshal, huh?"

"They left word that if Mr. Baldridge showed up they would be at the courthouse today."

"But the *Paragon* left Memphis yesterday."

"Maybe so, but the captain didn't go with her."

"*What?*"

"That Captain Williamson," Thomas said, "he made it real clear he was going to be here in town should Mr. Baldridge come back."

"I've never known Luke Williamson to let the *Paragon* go anywhere without him."

"Well, all I know is what I heard," Thomas said. "Now, won't you go on upstairs and I'll help your man with your trunk . . . uh, trunks. You've got two now? Oh, well," he offered with a wave of his hand, "we'll take care of them. And I'll get someone to draw you a hot bath—"

"I don't want a bath, Thomas. Just get my things up to my room. I need to find Baldridge."

"Well, good luck! Though I can't imagine why anyone would want to." Tyner started up the stairs, but paused at the landing. "Two-oh-one," Thomas called to her. "We'll be right along."

"I'll just wait for you."

Tyner sat in her room for about fifteen minutes, trying to figure out what to do next. The courthouse was long since closed for the day. No use going there. Maybe Williamson had gotten lucky. Maybe Jacob Lusk was already free. Probably not. The jail. That was where she would go. If Williamson was still in town, he would be there. But Baldridge . . . he was another matter.

The knock at her door startled her. Baldridge, she thought. It was about damned time. She opened the door and was about to set Masey straight when she realized she had two callers, Luke Williamson and Marshal Pittman, instead.

"Desk clerk said you were back," Williamson said, immediately entering the room. The marshal remained in the hall. "Have you heard from Baldridge?"

"No, haven't you?"

"Hell, no! Not since we first got here. Saw him maybe all of ten minutes until he got mad and left. The son of a bitch is probably drunk somewhere. What was I thinking when I hired him?" Williamson looked hard at Tyner. "And what were *you* doing in New Orleans? I thought I asked you to help—"

"Now, just a minute, Captain." Tyner's face reddened. "I ain't working for you, and I damned sure don't answer to you. I'll tell you about New Orleans, but not until you change your tune."

They stared at each other for several seconds, then Williamson noticed that Pittman was still in the hallway. He motioned for him. "Come on in, Marshal. This is Miss Salina Tyner. The lady I told you about. Miss Tyner, this is Marshal Rolf Pittman of St. Louis."

"Marshal," Tyner said with a nod.

"Good evening, ma'am." He closed the door.

Williamson began pacing the room like a caged animal. "Jacob's in trouble," he told Tyner. "They're gonna hang him—hang him for sure if I don't come up with something."

"But he was just arraigned the other day," Tyner said.

"Guess again. Crawford got the trial moved up to tomorrow. We've spent all day trying to see a judge, when we weren't hunting Baldridge."

"How did it go?"

"Bad. I tried to get the judge to listen. Tried to tell him about the Confederate money and this Quick fella who Jacob said you and Baldridge were looking for. But he ruled me out of order."

"What about Dodd?"

"William Dodd? The fella who gave Jacob his lawyer?"

"Yes."

"It was damned nice of him to let his lawyer represent Jacob, but it didn't do any good."

"Well, of course it didn't!"

"What do you mean?"

"Dodd. Baldridge didn't tell you about Dodd?"

"I told you. We barely spoke to Baldridge before he stormed off, all upset about the marshal here."

"And my telegram?"

"Somebody else picked it up."

"Who?"

"I don't know. The desk clerk didn't recognize him."

Tyner paled. "Thomas didn't say anything about giving my telegram to a stranger. Come to think of it, he didn't even mention that he *got* the telegram. I was so tired, I didn't think to ask."

"Well, he sure as hell gave it to somebody," Williamson said, "and it wasn't Masey Baldridge."

"Something's wrong."

"You're damned straight something's wrong."

"No, I mean with Baldridge."

"Right again."

"No, will you *listen* to me?" Tyner described the results of her trip to New Orleans.

Williamson sat down on the end of the bed and looked at Tyner. "You mean to tell me that all this time I've been talking to this lawyer, everything I said was getting back to William Dodd?"

"Probably."

He glanced out the window and back at Tyner. "And one of Dodd's men killed Cassie Pierce?" Tyner nodded. "And set Jacob up for the murder?"

"I'm sure of it."

Marshal Pittman spoke up. "But why? It sounds as if this Dodd is a successful businessman. Why would he have anything to do with killing that prostitute?"

"Because of the coin," Tyner said. "It's like I told you, Quick said Dodd sent a man to the *Paragon* that night to get back the coin he accidentally gave Cassie Pierce. Baldridge told me before I left for New Orleans that William Dodd is planning to run for governor."

Williamson stood up. "If he's financing his business and his run for governor with coins he had Quick recast, he's finished if word ever gets out. That's why he wanted that coin back so bad."

"Bad enough to have Cassie Pierce killed," Tyner said.

"Even if all this is true," Marshal Pittman said to Williamson, "we're still stuck. Without evidence—and I mean more than just someone guessing—that judge is going to find your man Lusk guilty tomorrow. And without this Quick fella, we've got nothing."

Tyner strolled over to one of the trunks, a smile breaking across her face. "Oh, Marshal . . . I wouldn't worry about that." Releasing the straps, she lifted the lid of one trunk and stood aside. "As a good friend of mine in New Orleans would say, *voilà!*"

Both men peered into the trunk.

"Jesus Christ, Salina!" Williamson exclaimed, jumping back from the trunk.

"Marshal Pittman, you look a little pale," Tyner remarked.

Filling virtually every inch of the trunk, curled into the fetal position, bound and gagged, lay Dillard Quick.

Williamson leaned in for a closer look. "That's not—"

"Oh, yes it is!"

The marshal looked at her suspiciously.

"Oh, relax, Marshal," Tyner said, slapping him on the shoulder. "He ain't dead. But I bet he wishes he was."

"Looks like somebody beat the shit out of him," Williamson observed.

"He tried to bed me," Tyner said. "Just couldn't handle it." Pittman cleared his throat, and she shot him an amused look. "But he told me what I needed to know."

Williamson examined Quick more closely. "How'd you keep him in this trunk for two days? How'd you keep him quiet on the boat?"

From her other trunk Tyner produced a bottle. "Courtesy of a friend of mine in New Orleans."

Williamson sniffed it and jerked back, then handed it to the marshal. "Chloroform?"

Tyner motioned at Quick with her head. "*He* didn't complain. In fact, he didn't say a word the whole trip."

Williamson lifted Quick's groggy head. "Hell, Salina, you could've killed him!"

"I wanted to kill him. I may do it yet. But I figure he's got some explaining to do to the law."

Williamson saw Pittman's look of disapproval. "Now don't go quoting the law to me, Marshal. I don't give a good goddamn right now. If I can bring him to, I'm taking him to a judge tonight. You don't have to come along if you don't want to."

"Captain, it's like I said: I'm investigating those Confederate coins, and without them, I've got no—"

"You'd be lookin' for these, then, wouldn't you, Marshal?" Tyner opened her other trunk and pulled back a cloth cover to reveal over a hundred Confederate twenty-dollar gold pieces stacked neatly in the bottom.

Pittman picked one up. "Well, I'll be damned. They *do* exist."

"I want both of you to realize the sacrifice I made to get these here," Tyner said. "I had to leave two dresses and a pair of shoes in New Orleans just to make room."

It took almost two hours of alternately bathing his face with a cool cloth and pricking him with one of Salina Tyner's hatpins, to bring Quick, now stretched on his back across the bed, to something like consciousness. The whole time an uneasy Marshal Pittman sat on the far side of the room making occasional observations about kidnapping—observations that were largely ignored by Tyner and Williamson. Once or twice, when she glanced over at him, Tyner was sure the good marshal was on the verge of leaving, his legal sensibilities were so besieged by their treatment of Quick. But she also suspected that the sight of those Confederate coins, and the feel of them in his hands, and the vision of arresting Quick and William Jenkins Dodd on what was sure to be a high-profile treasury case were enough to keep his feelings about unlawful imprisonment in check. If he had known Cassie, she thought, he would probably have offered to help them.

Quick was showing some signs of coming around when there was a knock on the door. Pittman opened it a few inches.

"Excuse me," Thomas said, "but I have something for Captain Williamson." He held up a leather satchel. "A rider brought it in just a few moments ago." Thomas tried to look inside. "Is the captain still here?"

Pittman nearly closed the door on Thomas's nose; when the startled desk clerk drew back, he reached out and grabbed the bag.

"Well, you needn't be so rude!"

"I'll see he gets it," Pittman said.

"Was that Thomas?" Tyner asked, but before Pittman could answer, she was slipping out the door. "I want to talk to him!" Thomas was scurrying down the hall toward the stairs as Tyner closed the door behind her. "And where do you think you're going?"

He halted and turned around slowly.

"Sally, I've got to get back downstairs. There's no one to watch the desk." He wouldn't look at her directly.

"Thomas, why didn't you tell me about the telegram?" The clerk continued to stare at the carpet. "You knew I was worried about Masey."

"I'm sorry," he said, eventually looking up at her with puppy-dog eyes. "After the captain and that lawman started asking questions, I thought I'd get in trouble. I—I was afraid."

"And why did you give my telegram to somebody else?"

"Mr. Baldridge hasn't been very nice to me."

"You'd better hope he turns up in one piece," Tyner informed him, "or some other people aren't going to be very nice to you."

Thomas nodded, looking away again. "I do. I do hope he shows up safe, 'cause you seem to like him."

"Well, I wouldn't go that far—"

But just then Pittman called her, so she left Thomas to return to his post.

After taking the satchel from Pittman, Williamson carried it to table, where a lantern was now burning. Inside the bag were a note and a knife. "It's Baldridge's." He laid the weapon on the table and began to read the note.

Tyner moved beside him. "What is it?"

"Somebody's got Baldridge," Williamson said. "This says we've got something they want, and they'll trade Baldridge for it. If we don't go along, they'll kill him."

"It has to be from Dodd," Tyner said.

Williamson looked at Quick, who was trying to sit up on the bed. "How did he know we have Dillard Quick?"

"He doesn't know. It can't be Quick he's after. Nobody knows I've got him. Nobody. As far as Dodd knows, Quick is in New Orleans."

"But the telegram you sent?" Pittman asked. "If somebody got hold of it and knew you were returning—"

"There was nothing in that telegram about Dillard Quick. I made sure of it. I just said I was coming back with proof."

"Then they know you've got something."

"Wait a minute," Tyner said. "Tonight at the wharf there was a man—I didn't recognize him, but now that I think back on it, I'm sure he was watching me. But all he saw was me and the two trunks."

"But one of them was Quick's. So it's got to be the coins," Williamson mused. "Dodd wants the coins. He must think that's all you've got—all that will hurt him, or connect him with Quick. He's got to figure, if we can't find Quick, and he gets the coins back, then—"

Pittman spoke up. "Then he's clear."

"But what about the coin Masey's got? That's what started this whole thing."

"It won't prove a thing without Quick or the rest of the money," Williamson said somberly. "Jacob hangs for the murder—"

"And Dodd, or whoever killed Pierce, goes free," Tyner said.

The room was almost silent for several moments; the only

sounds were low moans and groans as Quick came out of the chloroform. Eventually Pittman spoke.

"Where do they want to meet?"

"Doesn't say," Williamson told him. "Says someone will contact us tomorrow morning at eight o'clock. If we've got the merchandise, they'll take us to Baldridge."

"You can't believe them, you know," Pittman said. "I've seen these things before. If Dodd's behind this, then once he's got the coins, your man Baldridge is dead."

"Can't we show this to the judge tomorrow? Maybe get the trial delayed?" Tyner asked.

"I doubt it will work," Pittman said, taking the note from Williamson and examining it. "There's nothing here that will tie Dodd or anyone else to the murder. No mention of Pierce or the coins specifically, or even of Baldridge by name. He just talks about merchandise. There's nothing a judge could draw from this that would justify stopping the trial." He handed the note to Tyner. "But that's the way somebody wants it."

"What'll we do?" Tyner said.

"You'd damned well better find your man Baldridge before they kill him," Pittman said. "Otherwise, you've got absolutely nothing on Dodd except what we can get out of *him*." He pointed at Quick. "And frankly, he ain't looking too good."

"Any chance they'll make the switch clean?" Williamson asked Pittman.

"What do you think? Do you really believe a man with his eyes on the governorship is going to leave any loose ends? If Dodd finds out we've got Quick, he'll come after him next. If you wait until eight tomorrow and hand the coins to whoever shows up, you'll get Baldridge back all right . . . but stretched across a saddle."

"We've got to find him first," Tyner said. "What about Dodd's ranch? Masey said he had a big spread south of town."

"Could be Baldridge is there," Williamson said. "But it's the first place anybody would look. I figure they've got to be holding him somewhere right here in Memphis."

"It's a big town," Pittman noted.

"Maybe." Williamson glanced at the increasingly restless Quick. "But I know somebody who's going to make it smaller for us.

"Marshal, we're going to talk to Mr. Quick when he comes around in just a minute."

"Captain, I can't condone—"

"I ain't asking you to *condone* jackshit," Williamson said. "I guess I'm asking you to help me save two innocent men's lives. You can condone that, can't you?" Pittman was silent. "It might be a real good time for you to go down to the lobby. I understand they have good coffee here at the Overton."

Pittman looked worried as he left; only moments later, Quick came to enough to recognize Salina Tyner. He began to struggle.

"Get her away from me!" he shouted. "Get her away!" Still weak from the chloroform, he grasped at Luke Williamson's shirt. "You—you've got to help me! She's crazy. Crazy, I tell you!"

"Sorry, Mr. Quick," Williamson said, pushing him away.

"Not until you help me."

"No!" he said, his eyes desperate. "You don't understand." He pointed at Tyner, who now stood at the foot of the bed, her arms folded across her chest. She blew him a kiss. "That woman's crazy. She'll hurt you."

"No," Williamson calmly observed, "she won't hurt me. But she sure would like to hurt *you*. And she may. I may not be able to stop her." Quick tucked his feet underneath him and hugged the headboard. "That is, unless you cooperate with me."

Quick began to cry. "What do you want? What do you want with me?"

"Now don't start crying," Williamson warned him, "because

it makes her angry to see men cry. She figures they're cowards."

"I ain't no coward," Quick said with a sob.

"Then I want some answers," Williamson said. "What do you know about Dodd's property in Memphis?"

IT WAS ALMOST two A.M. when Salina Tyner walked into the Overton's restaurant and pulled up a chair next to Rolf Pittman.

"How's your friend?"

"He's talking," Tyner said, "but I swear, I don't think he knows anything. From what he told us, Dodd never got any of the coins himself. He was always careful to have Grady Teeter make the exchange, and do it in a different place each trip. Dodd owns a lot of property around Memphis. They could have Masey in any one of a dozen spots."

"That's too bad."

It was growing late, and Tyner had begun to feel desperate, when someone stepped up to the table.

"Uh . . . excuse me, ma'am." A gray-haired Negro stood before them hat in hand, his brow crumpled with concern. "Would you be Miss Tyner?"

She turned to face him directly. "Yes, I am."

"You're a friend of Masey Baldridge, right?"

"Yes, I am. Who are you?"

"My name's Eli Rawls. Masey's been stayin' with me the last few days."

"You're the man from the livery across the street?"

"Yes, ma'am, that's right." He stepped closer to her, and the smell of damp horseflesh permeated the air. "Something's happened to Masey. I'm right sure of it. He didn't come back to stay with me last night, and when he hadn't showed up by supper tonight, I got to wonderin'."

"Mr. Rawls, Masey *is* in trouble." She introduced Marshal

Pittman and continued. "Somebody's holding him, and there's a good chance they'll kill him if we don't find him first. But we don't have any idea where they've taken him."

"I might be able to help you with that."

"How?" Pittman asked.

"Well, sir, like I said, I got to wonderin' 'bout Masey this evenin'. That's when I seen that fella he was so interested in."

"What fella?" Tyner asked.

"The one picked up that Mr. Quick here last Tuesday. One of William Dodd's men."

"Where did you see him?"

"He come by here a couple of hours ago. I recognized his horse. He run inside the hotel and wasn't here hardly a minute, till he come back out and rode off."

"That would've been when we got the message about Baldridge," Pittman said.

A broad smile crossed Rawls's face. "But I know where he went. A customer had just turned in a horse he rented for the evenin', so when I seen that fella, I just mounted up and rode a spell."

"You followed him?" Marshal Pittman asked.

"Yes, sir, I did. He went down to a warehouse near the wharf. The place looked dark, except for maybe one light up on the second floor. I come right on back, seein' as how I didn't want to make Mr. Terrell mad. But when Masey still didn't show up, I thought I'd best tell you what I knew." Eli looked at Tyner. "I seen you when you come in tonight."

"Can you tell us how to get to this warehouse?"

"That ain't no problem, Miss Tyner. It's right at the foot of Union Street, just across Chickasaw."

LUKE WILLIAMSON WAS ready to shoot his way in that night.

But Pittman shook his head. "Bad idea. In the darkness, in a building you've never been in, chances are you'd kill Baldridge in the process. Besides, there's no telling how many men Dodd has working for him."

"Then what?"

"Wait till daylight," Pittman said. "Dodd needs Baldridge alive to trade for the coins. He won't do anything to him until he's got that money in hand. You need daylight and plenty of help to go into that warehouse."

"I don't like the idea of waiting," Williamson said. "What if they move him during the night? Somebody's got to watch that building."

"Luke's right," Tyner said.

"All right, Captain." Pittman rubbed his beard. "How about this? You go keep an eye on the warehouse. Miss Tyner and I will go right now and see that judge. It may take all night, but with Dillard Quick in hand and talking, and with these Confederate coins you brought back from New Orleans, I think I can convince him to set Mr. Lusk free. I'll ask him to issue a warrant for Dodd's arrest for counterfeiting—that's really all we can prove right now. I'll get Crawford and the Memphis police and meet you at that warehouse first thing in the morning."

Williamson grabbed his Henry rifle. "Where's Eli Rawls?"

"At the livery across the street," Tyner said.

"Captain," Pittman called to him as he left the room, "wait for us. Don't try to go in there by yourself."

18

Tuesday, April 8, daybreak

A RUSTLING NOISE roused Baldridge out of a restless sleep. When he tried to incline his ear toward the stairwell, a pain shot through his neck, stiff as it was from the awkward way his head had hung during the night. The rope gag was damp and bitter; his lips were chapped and his throat sore from breathing through an open mouth all night. The noise was probably Grady coming to get him. But no—the sound wasn't coming from downstairs. Baldridge took a deep breath and struggled to see around the post to which he was tied. Over the cotton bales in the corner, where there was a row of windows high on the wall, was someone climbing down.

In the early-morning light, Baldridge failed to recognize the man until he was upon him.

"Looks like you got yourself in a hell of a mess," Crawford whispered. All Baldridge could do was nod and moan. Crawford removed the rope from his mouth and began untying him.

"One of Dodd's men is downstairs," Baldridge whispered, pointing below. He licked his chapped lips and slowly rotated his stiff neck. "How did you find me?"

"Oh, I just did some checkin' on William Dodd." Crawford smiled. "Turns out he ain't what he seems."

"No kidding." Baldridge worked on loosening his shoulder joint. Crawford pointed to a bag he had placed in one of the chairs.

"You'll find a revolver in there."

"There's one man downstairs," Baldridge explained softly, checking the cylinder on the revolver.

"We'll get to him," Crawford assured him.

Empty.

"Crawford, this damned weapon's unloaded. Grady's liable to be up here any minute. You'd better get over there—"

"Hold it right there!" Grady shouted from the top of the steps. "Back away from that man."

Crawford took a couple of steps back and held his hands in the air. Baldridge was furious. How stupid could one man be? Crawford should have taken care of Grady immediately instead of standing around. And why had he given Baldridge an unloaded gun? Grady moved closer, then lowered his rifle.

"What the hell are you doin'? You scared the shit out of me!" Grady said.

"Calm down," Crawford told him.

"Calm down, nothin'! How did you get in here?"

"Window."

Grady looked at Crawford in disbelief. "You ain't supposed to be here, anyway. Mr. Dodd is planning to—"

"I changed the plan," Crawford said.

"No, no. Oh, no," Grady protested. "Mr. Dodd said we was gonna swap Baldridge for the gold that whore brought back from New Orleans. I'm gettin' a share of that gold, and you ain't doin' nothing to get in the way."

"Now listen, Grady—"

"No, no. I'm serious. I did your dirty work and Dodd's on that boat, and I damned well deserve what's coming to me." He motioned to Baldridge. "You get over there next to that wall." To Crawford: "Mr. Dodd didn't say nothin' about—"

Crawford looked at Grady. "Does that Smith & Wesson you're carrying belong to Baldridge?"

"Yeah. What of it?"

"Give it to me."

"Why?"

Crawford reached over and took it from Grady's belt. "You gonna shoot him *now*?" Grady said.

Baldridge swallowed hard.

"If you shoot him, how are we gonna swap him for the money?"

Crawford cocked the weapon; Baldridge focused on the barrel first, then looked into Crawford's eyes. He should have known. He should have suspected Crawford was more than just a fool. But he had never made the connection between him and Dodd. They were too different. They had nothing in common. Nothing—except, perhaps, money. In those agonizing seconds Baldridge realized why Dodd had known so much about his investigation. His thoughts were racing now, and it was as if he weren't even present, as if he were watching the whole thing unfold while someone else was standing in front of that loaded revolver.

Crawford extended his arm and pointed the weapon at Baldridge's chest. "This thing has gotten out of hand, Grady."

"You just gonna shoot him? Just like that?"

"Too many loose ends. Too many people involved."

Sweat rolled from Baldridge's forehead into his eyes, and in that instant he determined not to die without a struggle. He was about to rush Crawford when he sensed a sudden movement and then the earsplitting report of the revolver. Warm blood splattered the side of his head and ran down his cheek, and though he lunged toward Crawford, it was Grady Teeter who fell to the floor in front of him. Crawford stepped back and cocked the revolver again.

"Don't come any closer!" Crawford ordered.

Baldridge stopped. In the brisk air, he caught the sharp smell of gunpowder and heard the low moan of Teeter writhing on the floor, a bullet in his brain. In a few moments all was quiet. A shiver crawled down Baldridge's spine.

Crawford shook his head. "Everything's gone to hell, thanks to you. You and that whore and that riverboat captain." Baldridge glanced down at Teeter, whose dying hand grasped at the floor. "They all showed up at the courthouse early this morning, draggin' that stupid little Dillard Quick. I told Dodd we should have sent somebody down to New Orleans to kill Quick. But oh, no. The fool thought we were safe because he always dealt with Quick through ol' Grady here. But Grady was a fool, too." Crawford managed a laugh.

"How long has Dodd owned you?"

Crawford laughed. "No, no. You got it backwards. Without me, William J. Dodd wouldn't be nothin'. And now it's up to me to save his ass."

"So you're gonna trade me for the money?"

"That was Dodd's idea, but he's full of shit. I changed the plan. Last night, when Dodd set this up, he didn't know your whore had Quick. Neither did I, until early this morning. I still don't know how she got him here, but I guess it really don't matter. That bigmouthed coward will get 'em a warrant for sure."

"It's over," Baldridge said.

Crawford smiled. "Not quite. In a couple of days I'll see to it they find ol' Quick dead in his cell—long before he can testify."

"The molasses is out of the bottle, Crawford, and you're gonna play hell putting it back."

"That's where you're wrong. With ol' Grady here being tits-up, and you and Quick dead, there's nothing to tie Dodd to either the dead whore or the money." Crawford grinned. "And there sure ain't nothin' to connect me."

"But Luke Williamson and the marshal—"

"With Quick dead, it's all just hearsay. And do you really think anybody's gonna take the word of a riverboat whore against the next governor of Tennessee?"

With his back to the doorway, Baldridge could only guess how close he was to the stairwell. If he made a break, if he dove for it, could he make it? He needed to buy time. To keep Crawford talking.

"I don't get it. How would a man like you and a man like Dodd ever get together?"

"The war brought a lot of strange people together."

"But you told me last week you were in the Orphan Brigade."

"At the start of the war, yes. But after that I was part of General Breckinridge's escort. Right up until the end. That's when I ran into Dodd."

"The escort!" Baldridge said. "Semple's escort."

Crawford smiled. "Got that from ol' Jeff Davis, did you?"

"It was *you* with Paymaster Semple."

"We got all the way to the river before the Yankees captured us."

"And you sold out. Dodd told me about it."

"Sittin' in a prison—maybe even facing hangin' for being a guerrilla—gives a man time to think, Baldridge. Over four long years of fighting . . . for nothing. You'd have done the same thing to save your own ass."

"I don't think so."

"Hell, yeah, you would!"

"You sold out. You whored yourself to a Yankee commandant, didn't you?"

"I've heard about all I want to hear out of you," Crawford said.

Baldridge eased back another step. "Ain't killin' me right here in Dodd's warehouse gonna look a little funny?"

"To who?" Crawford grinned. "This is *my* case. Besides, it's real simple. You were already dead when I got here. You and Grady must have shot each other. Mr. Dodd knew nothing about it. It was Grady passing the gold all along." Again Crawford took aim. "Hell, Baldridge, you're a drunk. Ain't nobody gonna care about one more drunk."

Baldridge thought it rather strange, but he wasn't frightened. He was past being scared. He was mad—sick and tired of people pointing guns in his face and beating the hell out of him. Sooner or later, one of them was going to get him, and he didn't think he could stand looking down another barrel. A tiny movement in the rafters on the far side of the building gave him an idea. The chance was a slim one, but he figured it was all he had. Curling his sore tongue behind his teeth, he whistled as loudly as he could, simultaneously clapping his hands. The earsplitting sound bounced off the far wall of the warehouse and echoed through the building, and it was followed by the loud rustle and flutter of two pigeons flushing from their quiet roost along the center rafter. The noise startled Crawford and he spun around. Baldridge leapt for the stairwell, hitting his chest hard on the first step. The breath nearly knocked out of him, he began crawling down the steps toward the first landing. The report of Crawford's weapon echoed through the second floor of the warehouse. The round passed just over Baldridge's ass. His diaphragm cramped and he struggled to breathe as he crawled headfirst down the stairs. Crawford rushed toward him just as he made it to the first landing. He got to his feet, saw Crawford take aim from the top of the stairwell, and ducked against the solid inside rail as another bullet splintered wood from the railing just above his head. A large chunk of plaster fell from the wall behind him.

"Ain't no use in runnin'," Crawford said patiently as Baldridge stumbled down to the first floor. "Ain't no place to hide." He followed Baldridge down the steps and deliberately took aim as he fled toward the door. The sound of the weapon stung Baldridge's ears—but something was amiss. The sound had come from in front of him, not from the stairwell. A shadow now appeared in the main door to the warehouse, and from the front came another rifle shot. Baldridge ducked behind a support pillar in the center of the huge room. The figure moved inside.

Luke Williamson, shouldering a smoking Henry rifle, made his way to the cover of another support pole some thirty feet away.

Pointing over his shoulder with his thumb, Baldridge called to him. "It's Crawford." He continued to try and catch the breath the top step had taken out of him. "He's in it with Dodd."

"Son of a bitch," Williamson said. "No wonder the marshal hasn't gotten here with help." At the noise of footsteps crossing the floor above them, Williamson fired three shots into the ceiling, tracking the sound. But Baldridge figured they didn't penetrate the heavy floor. Williamson pointed at the revolver in Baldridge's belt. "Why didn't you return fire?"

"It's not loaded."

Williamson gave him a patronizing look and slid a Navy Colt across the floor to him. Baldridge checked the cylinder.

"Don't worry. *That* one's loaded. Anybody with him?" Williamson said, pointing up with his rifle barrel.

"No." Baldridge limped to support a column nearer the stairwell. "And this is the only way upstairs."

"How do you know?"

"Believe me, I had plenty of time to study the floor plan."

From the first landing, Baldridge could see a spattering of blood on the upper flight of stairs: Williamson must have wounded Crawford. Cautiously, Baldridge peeked into the upper room. All was quiet, but a few drops of blood led across the floor in the direction of the two cotton bales in the northwest corner.

"Cover me," he told Williamson as the captain lay next to him in the stairwell. He rushed forward and took cover behind the overturned table, but to his surprise drew no fire. When he spotted the open window on the wall above the cotton bales, he knew why. Williamson climbed the bales; the captain immediately found the blood smeared on the glass. Crawford had slipped onto the roof of the adjacent building and disappeared.

ROLF PITTMAN AND Salina Tyner were still in the judge's chambers. Under the threat of hanging for conspiracy to commit murder, Dillard Quick had spent the past hour telling the judge everything he knew about William Jenkins Dodd and Grady Teeter. His statement, coupled with the coins Tyner produced, was enough for the judge to order Jacob Lusk's release. With Quick on the way to jail under police escort, and Tyner along to pickup Lusk, Pittman had gotten a federal warrant for counterfeiting and a state warrant for conspiracy to commit murder against William Jenkins Dodd. Still, he was furious when Baldridge and Williamson met him in the courthouse hall.

"I can't believe this!" He banged his fist on a table near the front door. "I can't find a law officer around here anywhere. Who's watching the warehouse?" Pittman asked.

"Nobody."

Baldridge limped through the door.

Pittman looked puzzled. "Where did *he* come from?"

"I couldn't wait for you, Marshal," Williamson said. "I heard firing inside the warehouse and—"

"Are you all right?" Pittman asked Baldridge.

"I reckon so, but not by much."

"Crawford's in this with Dodd," Williamson said, and Baldridge explained what had happened at the warehouse.

"Well, that's it, then," Pittman declared. "About five o'clock this morning, somebody sent every available man up north of here."

"Crawford," Baldridge said.

"More than likely," Pittman agreed.

"Now that we know about him," Baldridge said, "I figure he'll warn Dodd and they'll go for the money. That's why he sent his police buddies north. To buy time."

Marshal Pittman spoke up. "So he's headed—"

"South," Baldridge confirmed.

"Dodd's place?"

"Two or three miles south of town," Baldridge confirmed.

Luke Williamson reloaded his Henry. "Guess we'd better get started. I'll borrow some horses. Ain't no use waiting on a posse, and after what he did to Jacob, I'll be damned if I'm letting that son of a bitch get away."

"Which one?" Pittman asked.

"*Both* of 'em," Baldridge said, leading Williamson and the marshal out the courthouse door.

19

Later Tuesday morning

DODD'S RANCH APPEARED deserted as the three men approached, but they were taking no chances. With weapons drawn, the three men rode the fence line that led to the house, watching both sides of the road and keeping a close eye on the outbuildings. The front door of the house stood open; Baldridge and Williamson ran up the steps and across the porch. Marshal Pittman kept watch outside.

"Watch my back," Baldridge said as he ran through the doorway and took cover by the stairs. Peering through the banisters, he could see no movement down the hall, so with his back against the wall, he leaned around the edge of the doorway to look into the room behind him. Nothing.

"Do you hear that?" he called to Williamson.

"Hear what?"

"I'm not sure. It sounds like—like somebody crying."

Williamson leaned forward. "Yeah, I hear it. Up-stairs," he said, pointing with his rifle. The two men crept up to the second floor; in the master bedroom they found

Mrs. Dodd, on her knees before the window, hands on the sill, weeping.

"He's not here," she sobbed, without looking at them. "William's gone."

The two men advanced no closer. "Gone where, Mrs. Dodd?"

She shook her head, throwing her hands up in frustration as she turned to look at them. "I—I don't know." Before her on the windowsill was a picture of Dodd. She picked it up and stood slowly. "I didn't know about any of this," she began, turning to face Baldridge. "Not until last night. I thought . . . I just thought he . . . we always had plenty of money for whatever we needed. I just thought William was a good businessman." She let her arm fall so the picture hung loosely by her side. Her expression was dazed. "He owned the farm before I met him, you know. My father certainly thought he was—"

"Mrs. Dodd, do you have any idea where your husband might have gone?"

"I've come to discover that there is a great deal about my husband I do not know, Mr. Baldridge." Mrs. Dodd tried to compose herself, then looked up at Baldridge, her reddening eyes both angry and sad. "I hated you for what you did at our church Sunday night. The terrible things you said about William, the blasphemous behavior. If I'd had a gun I would have killed you myself." She wiped away her tears. "And yet, deep in my heart I knew something was wrong. So last night I confronted William. He'd been acting very strange, even before you called here last week. And then that Memphis policeman he knows came by last night."

"Crawford?"

"Yes. William was angry—more angry than I've ever seen him. I listened to their conversation through the door. Perhaps I shouldn't have, but . . . I was worried about my husband. That's when I heard him mention that woman on the boat." Tears rolled down her face. "After Crawford left, I spoke with him." Mrs. Dodd looked at the two men in dismay. "He *lied* to me, Mr. Baldridge. At first he swore he knew nothing about that woman's death, just as he had done the day you came here. But there were too many things he could not explain. The night that woman died, William left the house. He told me that morning at breakfast that there had been some trouble with the livestock." Again she looked at his picture. "But there was no trouble with the livestock that night. I know. I checked. Not with Grady Teeter, but with men I trust." She again turned to look out the window. "And the next day, when he hurried off to town with Grady, I could never get him to tell me what he was doing. I wanted so to believe him, Mr. Baldridge. Not just for my sake, but"—she touched her abdomen—"but for the sake of our child." She looked up at him in despair. "Whatever shall I do, Mr. Baldridge? Whatever shall I do?"

"Mrs. Dodd, my name's Luke Williamson. I'm captain of the river packet *Paragon*. It was my first mate, Mr. Jacob Lusk, who almost hanged for the murder your husband ordered."

The woman turned away, her hands beginning to tremble. "Last night he talked of that young woman as though . . . as though she were an animal that could be killed for its own good. I don't know William Dodd anymore."

From his post on the porch, Pittman had made his way upstairs and had been standing in the hallway listening to the conversation.

"Mrs. Dodd, I'm Marshal Rolf Pittman, from St. Louis. Your husband is wanted for ordering the murder of Miss Cassie Pierce and for counterfeiting government specie."

"I never knew about any of this gold. Not until last night. You must believe me, Marshal."

Baldridge walked across the room and stood near her. He spoke softly. "Ma'am, I don't believe your husband will go far without the gold. Can you think of anyplace he might have hidden it? Someplace he went alone, that maybe he mentioned to you in passing?"

"Mr. Baldridge, my husband went many places. We have a large ranch here, and there are the lands involved in his railroad dealings. He might have secreted money in any of a hundred places."

"Then maybe not the ranch. Maybe someplace else. Someplace nearby, but still away from where most people would go."

"I don't know, Mr. Baldridge. I can't really think very clearly. So much has happened." Mrs. Dodd wavered momentarily. "I think I need to sit down." Baldridge helped her into a rocking chair.

"Which way did he go when he left here?" Pittman asked.

"Toward the river, I think. I'm just not sure of anything anymore."

Luke Williamson knelt beside her. "Mrs. Dodd, was there anyplace near the river that your husband would go? Did he own any land there?"

"All William's land is right here. As far as I know. His horses, our home, everything is right here—or so I thought." The tears came again. "Except for that old fort, I can't think of any place William might have—"

"What old fort?" Williamson asked.

"The one the Yankees built. I heard William mention it when he was talking to that man last night."

"Fort Pickering?" Baldridge asked. The woman nodded.

"You know it?" Pittman said to Baldridge.

"Yeah, but ain't nobody been up there in three or four years. Most of the buildings have burned, and all that's left is some breastworks and a handful of bunkers. . . ." Baldridge looked up at him. "But Dodd was commandant there. That's where Crawford and Semple were in prison."

"Who's Semple?" Pittman asked.

"Never mind. I'll tell you later."

"So Dodd would know the lay of the land," Pittman said.

"He sent the police in the opposite direction this morning," Baldridge pointed out. "I say the fort's where he's headed." He put his hand lightly against Mrs. Dodd's shoulder. "Ma'am, some other Memphis policemen—good men—will be here before long. When they come, just tell them what you told us and they'll treat you right. They'll take care of you." Williamson and Marshal Pittman had already started down the stairs. "We're gonna go now. You just wait right here until somebody comes." Mrs. Dodd was crying harder now, and Baldridge wasn't sure she even heard him, but there was no time to waste. He followed the other two outside, and they rode for the river.

Almost seven years had passed since Baldridge had been to Fort Pickering. He and some other ex-Confederates had gone to give a deposition regarding the treatment of Memphis citizens by the occupation Federal forces after the war. The post was closing down even then, and the young commander, a captain of the Engineer Corps, had seemed bothered by the entire business—a bunch of ex-Johnnies causing a troublesome interruption in his more important tasks. Given that attitude and the three subsequent weeks of failure to bridle the unruly Federal troops, Baldridge had decided the visit was a waste of time. He only hoped this one would be more profitable, but being in the company of two more Yankees didn't make him very comfortable.

Fort Pickering lay along more than a mile of the Chickasaw Bluffs, high above the river, some two miles south of Memphis. It stretched a quarter-mile inland in places. During the war the fort had mounted a series of thirty-two-pound Parrott guns to guard against land assault, and, from its commanding heights above the Mississippi, formidable eight-

inch seacoast howitzers had overlooked traffic on the river.
The batteries had been dismantled now, the occupying army
was long gone, but the breastworks stood as a grim reminder
to Baldridge of what had been.

Fresh wagon tracks in the mud told them that somebody
had come down the main road and into the confines of the old
fort. Baldridge sensed that someone was Dodd. He wasn't
sure why. Certainly, someone else could have had a wagon
down there, but he doubted it. The tracks led past the burned-
out barracks, past the old corral, and stretched toward the
south. On the day of the deposition, he recalled, he'd seen a
well-stocked woodyard; it had long since been picked clean
by the many Negro refugees who had insisted on making
camp at the fort until two or three years back. An outbreak of
yellow fever had cleared them out and left the place deserted,
except for an occasional scavenger and the ever-present wild
dogs that plagued that end of town. No, the wagon had to be
Dodd's.

A sound off to Williamson's left sent him reaching for his
Henry, but he stopped short when he realized the noise was
only the wind making a reinforced wooden window squeak
on its hinge.

"Take it easy, Captain," Baldridge said. "You can start
getting jumpy when we run out of tracks to follow."

"It sure looks different from up here," Williamson said.

"How's that?"

"I've passed this fort hundreds of times over the years,
but down there, on the river. And back during the war, I used
to look up at the howitzers and they made me feel safe. I knew
I was covered."

Baldridge laughed. "And me and my boys were thinkin'
up ways to send them over the bluff."

"Guess you got your way."

"What do you mean?"

"They're gone, aren't they?"

"Yeah, but the damned Yankees are still around." Baldridge glared at Pittman.

The tracks led back east and around the keep, the spot where the highest earthworks had protected the fort; then they continued south. This end of the old fort was more heavily overgrown with scrub oaks and thickets; in summer, the old trail would probably be impassable. But the new growth of spring was everywhere, and the scent of dogwood blossoms was heavy. The wagon tracks turned west now, leading back toward the river. Baldridge figured they had to be getting close: Standing water was still oozing back into the wheel ruts.

Pittman dismounted and examined the tracks closely. "What do you make of that?" he said, pointing toward the river. Some 100 yards away, on a gently rising slope, the wagon tracks seemed to leave the trail, and the switch willows and undergrowth had been trampled off to the left and south.

Williamson shrugged. "Don't ask me. I watch for snags and sandbars—never could track worth a damn."

Baldridge leaned over, his saddle slipping slightly. He shifted it back into position. "Well, I'd say there's been a rider along here after the wagon. See that print in the middle of the wheel rut? Looks like—"

A rifle cracked in the distance, sending Baldridge and Williamson riding for cover in the tangled brush nearby. Another shot. This time Williamson dismounted.

"I guess its time to get jumpy," he said. "You'd better get down before he puts a bullet in your head."

"Where's the marshal?" Baldridge asked.

Out in the roadbed, Pittman's horse was trotting away from the gunfire, but the marshal lay in the ooze, grasping his side and trying to crawl to cover. Another round spattered the mud nearby. Baldridge spurred his horse and rode up beside

Pittman, shielding him with the animal. Shoving the Navy Colt under his belt, he grasped his saddlehorn with his left hand, then leaned over his good right leg and clutched Pittman's outstretched arm. Kicking the animal firmly, he rode for the undergrowth on the opposite side of the roadbed, dragging Pittman with him. But under the weight of the marshal, the loose girth slipped and the saddle dropped to the horse's side. Baldridge squeezed his legs together, desperately holding on; he barely reached cover before the saddle slid completely under the horse and deposited him rudely on the ground next to Pittman.

Baldridge got up cussing. "If I ever find the fool that put that saddle on . . ." He knelt beside Pittman and examined the wound.

"Bullet went clear through," Pittman said, trying to hide the pain. Baldridge took the scarf from Pittman's neck, folded it, and placed it over the entry and exit wounds, only three or four inches apart and just above the hip.

Williamson worked his way across the roadbed and joined them. "How bad is it?"

"I'll be all right," Pittman said, rolling onto his good side. "Looks like you're gonna have to finish this by yourselves, though." He laid his revolver on the ground beside him and lifted his right hand.

"What the hell are you doing, checkin' the wind?" Baldridge asked.

"I got to swear you in," Pittman grunted. "Didn't have a chance before."

"Bullshit!" Baldridge said, starting off toward the sound of the firing.

"Wait!" Pittman called. Baldridge hesitated. "We've got to do this right. Got to deputize you two as federal marshals."

"The hell you say!" Baldridge replied. "I ain't swearin' to no *federal* nothin'!"

Williamson lifted his hand. "Come on, Baldridge."

"Hell, no!"

"What's it going to hurt?" Williamson asked.

Another rifle shot hummed through the switch willows. Baldridge reluctantly raised his left hand.

"Your right hand," Pittman said.

"Oh, hell, just do it!"

"Do you solemnly swear to uphold the Constitution and the laws of the United States of America?"

"I do," Williamson responded.

Baldridge said nothing. He'd never thought he would see the day— deputized by a U.S. marshal, along with an ex-Yankee gunboat pilot. He lowered his hand. "Hell, yes, I suppose so. Now, let's go before he kills us right here." Baldridge motioned to his left. "You go around that way. I'll work my way straight up."

"Why can't a man have a good gunboat howitzer when he needs on?" Williamson mumbled as he headed off into the brush.

This wasn't going to be easy. The Winchester seemed to have eyes; wherever Baldridge moved, the rounds struck uncomfortably close. He found a mound of earth and cozied up behind it. Maybe he could talk the man out.

"Listen to me, Dodd! Nobody has to get killed here today. Give yourself up." For the first time, he caught a glimpse of someone rising above the earthworks near the river to fire at him. Crawford. Baldridge was just about to take a shot at him when he heard Williamson's Henry rifle. Three rounds kicked up dirt beside Crawford and sent him for cover.

"Damn, he shoots pretty good for a Yankee," Baldridge muttered. Taking advantage of the lull, he worked his way closer, crossing the compressed brush where the wagon had passed, until he found an old footpath leading up to what used to be an artillery emplacement. In the next few moments there was no more shooting; horses nickered close by, and Baldridge figured he was within a hundred feet of Crawford. But where was Dodd? And why had the shooting stopped?

Suddenly, Crawford popped up from behind the earthworks, firing once where Baldridge had been lying moments before. Working the rifle's lever feverishly, Crawford began to fire his Winchester wild—once or twice in Baldridge's direction and once or twice in Williamson's. Baldridge took aim with his revolver and squeezed off a shot. He saw Crawford flinch and roll over on his side, then disappear behind the gun emplacement. Sensing the kill, Baldridge rushed from his position, checking the horizon for some sign of Williamson. As he moved up the foot trail he heard horses stirring, the sound of a whip, and the slopping of hoofs in the mud. Up from the gun emplacement and into Baldridge's face raced a team pulling a wagon. So close was he that he could smell the horses as he dove to his left, firing in the direction of where the driver should be. Surprised by Baldridge's presence, and spooked by a shot so near, the horses shied to their left. When the right-hand animal balked and reared in the harness, Baldridge saw William Dodd struggling to bring the team under control. But the horses, slipping in the mud, pulled the wagon ever closer to the edge of the bluff. Dodd, determined to escape, stood up and reapplied the whip, sending the animals into even greater frenzy.

"Heeeyaaah!" he shouted, jerking the reins to his right and laying on the whip with his left hand. Baldridge noticed motion off to his left. Instantly he turned toward it.

"Wait up!" shouted Crawford, limping toward the wagon. "Wait for me, Dodd!" With his mind totally upon catching up with the wagon, Crawford did not see Baldridge. Baldridge watched him approach and when he was only five or six yards away, he stepped out of the brush and confronted him.

"Drop the rifle!"

Crawford stopped and their eyes met. Baldridge could tell he had been hit twice—an older wound in the leg just above the knee, and a fresh wound in the shoulder. Crawford's eyes flashed toward Dodd some fifty feet up the road and still feverishly whipping the team. He looked back at Baldridge, and there was no doubt what he was thinking.

"I said, 'Drop the rifle,' " Baldridge repeated, but uselessly; he could see it in Crawford's eyes. He was powerless to stop what was about to happen, even if he had wanted to. But he didn't. The barrel of the Winchester swept toward him, but only made it a few inches before Baldridge fired. The round entered Crawford's chest and staggered him. A second time Baldridge pulled the trigger, and he saw Crawford offer one last hopeless glance at Dodd before dropping face first into the mud.

Dodd screamed as the wagon crept out of the dense mud and on to slightly firmer ground. Baldridge had picked up the Winchester and was working to get a shot through the undergrowth, when he again heard Williamson's rifle. Dodd stood up straight and twisted slightly to the left. Baldridge could see blood near his right shoulder blade, yet still, like a man possessed, he attempted to drive the team. He had progressed some thirty or forty feet, the frightened animals still slipping in the mud, still fleeing the gunfire and the sting of the whip, when Baldridge saw the right front wheel of the wagon strike a rock. It rose slowly from the ground, along with the right rear wheel, and the wagon briefly balanced on two wheels, the horses still struggling forward, until it tipped over on its left side, sending Dodd crashing to the ground, tumbling toward the edge of the bluff. Baldridge rushed toward Dodd as the captain hurried to catch the wagon team.

As he reached the precipice, some hundred and fifty feet above the rushing river, Baldridge saw William Jenkins Dodd, flat on his belly, his hands on the leather grip of a large wooden chest that was teetering on the edge of the cliff. Kneeling down, he grabbed Dodd by the leg, but the trouser leg was soaked, and Baldridge's hands were slippery with mud, and the weight of the chest was pulling both men toward the edge.

"I can't hold you!" Baldridge shouted. "Let it go!" Dodd offered no answer, but Baldridge could hear him sobbing. "Damn it, Dodd, let go! You're gonna kill us both." He looked behind him. "Captain, get over here quick!"

Williamson, having released the team, was already on his way, but the trunk was half over the edge of the bluff now, dragging Dodd and Baldridge with it. Baldridge stuck his foot behind a root and prayed it would hold. There was just no traction in that mud.

"Let go, man. Let go!" he shouted, feeling the root tear. Any second the two of them would plunge down the bank and into the river.

"It's mine!" Dodd cried through his sobs. "It's mine! I can do so much good!"

"Let go, you fool!" Baldridge shouted. Williamson was only a few feet from them when, at the same instant, Dodd slipped from Baldridge's grip and the root gave way. The chest plunged toward the river; Dodd, his death grip in place, followed it down like a streamer. Baldridge thought for an instant he would surely follow from the sheer momentum, but Williamson caught him by the shoulder and steadied him. Fifty feet down, the chest struck an outcropping; it spun into the air and out over the water, separating itself from Dodd. Dodd's body snagged on the jagged end of a broken river birch. He hung there limp, his neck snapped and pinned in the crotch of two thick branches.

The chest struck the river with tremendous force and sank momentarily, then popped back to the surface. But the unrelenting current caught it and swept it out, and the water began to seep in, and the river dragged it slowly but certainly to the muddy bottom.

20

WHEN THE *PARAGON* steamed up to the Memphis landing on Sunday, April 13th, Luke Williamson and Jacob Lusk were anxiously waiting.

"Cap'n, I'm mighty glad to see that ol' boat," Lusk declared.

"She does look pretty good, doesn't she?"

The roustabouts were lined up on deck; when they recognized Lusk and the captain, a general cheer broke out among them, followed closely by a rousing song.

> Rouster, rouster you know the rule,
> Eat yo' breakfast an' tote like a fool
> Tote yo' bales and stack 'em right,
> Let's git on the big boat Sad-day night.
> Ah-ha-ha, Ding-a-ling Doey
> Women and chilun all is goin' to ruin.

"Looks like ol' Davis has got 'em singin'," Lusk said. "But I don't believe I recognize the ditty." The rouster began the second verse as they secured the lines and lowered the landing stage.

Look a-yonder boys, a-standin' on the shore
They's Memphis rich and river poor.
Lower the stage an' welcome 'em aboard,
For the Cap'n and the mate, we a-thankin' the Lord.
Ah-ha-ha, Ding-a-ling Doey
We're leavin' here tonight boun' for Saint Louie.

Williamson and Lusk strolled across the landing stage to the applause of twenty or thirty passengers standing on the boiler deck, and the crew met them with handshakes all around. Steven Tibedeau saluted Williamson awkwardly, and the day pilot, Martin, who had been Acting Captain, rolled his eyes.

"Welcome back, Captain, Jacob," Tibedeau said.

"Glad to be back. How did the run to New Orleans go?"

"Everything was—" Martin began.

"—smooth, Captain," Tibedeau interrupted. "Smoother than a baby's butt."

When Tibedeau turned to shake hands with Lusk, Martin stepped closer to the captain and whispered: "I'm sure glad you're back. Tib's been strutting and clucking around here like he thought *he* was the captain. We mostly just ignored him, but his head's really starting to swell."

Williamson smiled. "I'm grateful for what all of you have done—keeping us on schedule and making the run without me."

"Wasn't the same without you, Captain. But we kinda halfway enjoyed it." Several of the crewmen laughed.

"Well, don't get ideas, because I don't plan to miss any more," Williamson assured them.

Standing at the rear of the welcoming crewmen was Anabel McBree. Williamson motioned her forward. She shook the captain's hand, and when she got to Lusk, she gave him a big hug—a hug that did not go unnoticed by the crew.

"Oooooooh," several of them moaned. When a couple began to whistle, Anabel pulled away quickly and took Lusk's hand in a more formal grip. "How's our first mate?" she asked.

"Just glad to be back on the water," Lusk said.

Anabel smiled. "We missed you around here." Williamson thought Lusk was about to say something to Anabel, but it seemed the crowd pressing around him changed his mind. Instead he just smiled at her, looked about him, and shouted to the crew.

"What are all you yardbirds standin' around for? Ain't you ever made a landing before? Let's go! There's cargo to be unloaded. Davis, get these men movin'. They're burnin' daylight!"

AT THREE O'CLOCK the captain was in his cabin shaving when Steven Tibedeau knocked.

"What is it?"

"Everything's coming along on schedule, Captain Luke. We should head out for St. Louis about five."

"Good," he said, wiping away the remaining lather with a damp cloth. Williamson gazed momentarily in the long polished-tin shaving mirror. He had been impressed with Rolf Pittman's appearance. Williamson had left him at the hospital last night—he was expected to recover fully from his wound—and even then, he thought the marshal's beard gave him a dignified countenance, something rather unusual, Williamson thought, for a man lying in a hospital bed. He turned to Tibedeau. "How do you think I'd look with a full beard?"

"Well . . ." He studied Williamson's face. "Captain, I'd have to say I think you should just stay with your mustache. A beard takes a lot of keeping up. As busy as you are . . ."

"Maybe you're right."

"Captain, I also wanted to tell you that Baldridge fella is on board. He wanted to see you. He's waiting down—"

"—at the bar," Williamson said.

Tibedeau looked surprised. "Well, that's right, Captain. What should I tell him?"

"Tell him I'll be down in about ten minutes."

"Very good, Captain."

"Steven, I heard you really had the crew hopping while I was gone."

Tibedeau adjusted his jacket and fairly beamed. "I kept an eye on everybody, Captain. I certainly did."

The captain stifled a laugh. "Well, I really appreciate that."

"My pleasure, Captain."

"Good, good. But, Steven . . ."

"Yes, sir?"

"You can relax now. Everything's back to normal."

"Yes, sir. Will there be anything else, Captain?"

"No. I'll be down to see Baldridge in a few minutes."

"Very good, sir."

Once Tibedeau left, Williamson broke out laughing. He was a fine mud clerk, the best on the river. But he acted like a man in constant need of a good bowel movement.

Baldridge was nursing a brandy—the ones he had complained about during the Natchez affair—when Williamson joined him.

"You took my advice," Baldridge said, lifting his glass. "The brandy is much better."

"I'm glad you approve."

"Captain—"

"Don't you think it's time you called me Luke? It's not like you're a crew member."

Baldridge took another drink. "Okay. Luke, if you'll call me Masey. I just want to thank you for hiring me."

"I should be thanking *you*. I don't know what would have happened to Jacob if I hadn't hired you. He'd probably be swinging at the end of a rope. Why, between you and Salina Tyner . . ."

"Maybe. But you saved my life back at that warehouse."

"Look, I figure that makes us even, considering what you did at Natchez." Baldridge nodded and Williamson watched his eyes. He had never sat and talked with him long enough to notice it before, but Baldridge looked like a man who'd seen more than his share of hard times. It wasn't a matter of the bruises Dodd's men had left on his face; those would be gone in a few days. But his eyes seemed to suggest a man in perpetual pain. And Williamson figured he might be hitting the bottle a little hard himself if he was saddled with a leg like this man's. "So, is everything wrapped up with the police?"

"Seems to be," Baldridge said. "Quick's in jail under extra guard, but with Crawford and Dodd dead, I figure he's safe enough until he goes to trial."

Williamson placed his feet in an empty chair. "There's something I don't get about Crawford."

"What's that?"

"How come he didn't have more of the money? And what happened to his share?"

"You've got to understand where Crawford was when he approached Dodd in the first place. He was a prisoner at Fort Pickering. If they could have proved he was a guerrilla—hell, even if they couldn't prove it—they could have hung him. He traded the location of the gold for his freedom . . . and I doubt he was in a position to bargain hard. Still, he did all right for himself."

"How's that?"

"His job with the police. How many ex-Rebs do you figure have been hired by the Memphis police?"

"I don't know."

"One. With Dodd's influence, I'm sure."

"And Crawford's share of the money? The recast coins?"

"Who knows? The police say they can't find a bank account. Knowing Crawford, he probably buried 'em."

"Wonder where?"

Baldridge shrugged. "They may turn up one of these days. As soon as he's able to travel, Marshal Pittman will take the money Tyner found back to St. Louis and turn it over to the treasury." Baldridge folded his arms and looked up at the ceiling. "But there is one thing I've been thinking about."

"What's that?"

"Dodd's money chest, the one that fell in the river."

"What about it?"

"You don't reckon a man could get him a johnboat and maybe drag— "

Williamson laughed. "No way in hell!"

"Why not?"

"Masey, that stretch of river is not only deep, but the currents below the bluff are some of the strongest around."

"Yeah, but—"

"If that chest stayed in one piece, which I seriously doubt, there's no telling where the current carried it. It could tumble along that bottom for miles. And if it broke apart, that money's liable to be strewn from here to New Orleans."

Baldridge nodded. "Well, it just seems like a waste." They sat silently for a moment.

"So, what now?" Williamson said.

"What do you mean?"

"What will you do? Keep working for Mid-South?"

"I really don't know."

"Your name has been in the Memphis paper for the last two days," Williamson said. "Why, with the way you trailed

Dodd and Crawford, you're liable to be quite a hero around these parts."

Baldridge laughed. "Yeah, for a week or two. Then nobody knows your name. Besides, everybody knows I had lots of help."

"True, but if you want to keep doing what you're doing—I mean, investigating and the like—I figure people will hire you again."

Baldridge put his glass on the table and stared at Williamson. "And you? Would you hire me again?"

Williamson had to admit that if he had been asked that question four days ago, the answer would have been a firm no. Yet this strange man had a way of coming out on top. So the captain nodded. "If I really needed help. Yeah, I'd hire you."

Baldridge's eyes brightened. "You know, I'll have to admit that since Wednesday I've thought about that."

"What?"

"About doing this for a living. Hell, sometimes I actually enjoyed it." He lifted his hands. "No, not the getting shot at, or beaten up. But the hunt. I liked the hunt in it all. Do you know what I mean?"

Williamson knew. He had sensed that, too. And as much as Baldridge frustrated him, he liked having the guy around. Still, there was no sense in admitting it. "I'd just as soon keep my crewmen out of jail," he said, "if it's all the same to you."

"I know. I know. I'm just talking about myself. Sometimes, I think I could make a go of this business . . . you know, on my own. I really think I could."

"Could what?" Salina Tyner appeared beside their table. Williamson stood and Baldridge, taking his cue, awkwardly rose to his feet. "Could what?" she repeated.

"Masey, here, thinks he might want to be a detective."

She took a seat and the men followed. "Is that right?"

Baldridge looked down at the table. "I don't know. It's just talk, really."

Tyner reached into her purse and took out a telegram. "Well, that's too bad. 'Cause I suppose you won't be answering this."

Baldridge took the telegram. "It's unsealed."

"So?"

"But it's addressed to *me*."

"So?"

"You *read* it!"

"Of course I read it. I tipped the boy who brought it for you at the Overton. God knows *you* wouldn't have. I figure that gives me the right to read it."

Baldridge read the telegram, then sat quietly holding it for several moments. Salina Tyner's grin broadened by the second.

"Well?" Williamson said, glancing at each of them. "Isn't somebody going to tell me what's going on?"

Baldridge started to speak but Tyner interrupted him.

"It's from the Pinkerton Agency in Chicago," she said.

"The detectives?" Williamson asked.

"Yes," Baldridge said, "it seems they want—"

Tyner cut him off. "They want him to come to Chicago. Say they read all about him in the papers and they want him to work for them."

Baldridge folded his arms. "Well, why don't you just go on and tell it *all*?"

"Okay," she said with a nod, "I will." She turned to Williamson. "Seems they've got some case down here they want help with. They need somebody that knows Tennessee, Kentucky, and Missouri. And someone that knows the river. He's supposed to wire them if he'll come to Chicago and talk to them."

"Are you going?" Williamson asked.

"I don't know. Chicago's—"

"He's going," Tyner said.

"How do *you* know?" Baldridge snapped.

"Because I've already wired them and told them so."

"Sally, you had no right—"

"In fact," she said, looking at the captain, "we're both going." Baldridge looked aghast. "Don't think I'm going to let you have all the fun!" Baldridge began to sulk. "Oh, come on, Masey. You might as well. Where else you gonna go? You've got no place to live. You've got no job. You've got no horse. Hell, I'll bet you're broke right now."

"I've got a few dollars."

"All you've got is that toad-sticker you carry and a pistol."

Baldridge smiled like a child with a new toy. "I got ol' Grady's Winchester."

Tyner smiled. "He's going."

Williamson eyed him. "Masey?"

"Maybe."

"Good! I'll get a cabin ready for you as my guests, at least as far as St. Louis."

"Uh, Captain . . . make it *two* cabins." Tyner adjusted her dress to reveal more cleavage. "I ain't workin' for the Pinkertons yet."

"Very well, two it is. I've got some duties to attend to. Sounds like you need to talk this over anyway."

SHORTLY BEFORE THE five o'clock departure, Luke Williamson was walking along the rear deck near the paddle wheel, smoking his pipe and thinking back on the past two weeks. He wanted a few minutes to himself before they left—a chance to relish being back on the *Paragon* and having Jacob Lusk with him. The bills were going to be paid, because his crew had hung together. He was proud of that.

Proud they loved the *Paragon* enough to keep her going without him. Sure, they got paid for it. But their dedication took more than just pay. They had to love the river the way he did, and because of that, he felt a kinship to them he had never felt before.

Tyner approached wearing a bright blue evening dress.

"Getting started a little early, aren't you?" he asked.

"Well, there are just so many courteous gentlemen on board, it seems a shame to deny any of them my company."

He pointed his pipe at her. "You know, you and Masey can be dangerous."

She feigned surprise. "Oh, do you really think so?" Then her expression grew solemn as she gazed past the paddle wheel at the busy Memphis landing. Walking over to the edge of the deck, she stared at the water for a moment. "I still miss Cassie so much. I can't get it out of my mind, Luke. I close my eyes at night and I see this deck and I see those rousters lifting her from the water." She noticed something near her feet. "What's this?"

Williamson stepped up beside her and took a scrap of cloth off a metal shard near the wheel housing.

"Is that . . . ?"

"Yes," Williamson said softly. "It came from Cassie's dress. I saw it tear the morning they brought her aboard."

Tyner took the scrap from him and held it close. She began to cry and Williamson took her in his arms. In a moment she stepped back from him.

"Will you keep it?" he asked.

She seemed to deliberate for a moment, then she walked to the edge of the deck and tossed the cloth into the brown water. She fought back the tears and forced a smile.

"Life goes on. That's what Cassie would say."

Williamson put his arm around her shoulder and the two of them began walking toward the stairway. Just then he heard a *thump* from near the paddle wheel. He started to walk on, then hesitated.

Thump, thump, thump . . .

"Just a moment," he said, and walked back to the paddle wheel. "I've got to check on this." The noise grew louder as he leaned over the stern near the wheel sprocket. *Not again.* From the water he retrieved a two-foot piece of driftwood snagged in the wheel driver and tossed it away from the boat, just as Martin sounded the whistle signaling the *Paragon's* departure for St. Louis. Returning to Tyner, he motioned for her to precede him up the stairs.

"Will you join me at the captain's table this evening?" he asked.

"Oh, I'd just love to, but I've already promised to have dinner with four other gentlemen. I just don't know how I'll manage it."

"Oh, you'll figure out something."